The Stone Garden

Michael L. Thompson

PublishAmerica

Baltimore

First printing

ISBN: 1-4137-6436-3
PUBLISHED BY PUBLISHAMERICA, LLLP
www.publishamerica.com
Baltimore

Printed in the United States of America

Prologue

The sky lay like a demon's claw. It was waiting to strike with anger, ready to break a city engulfed in lights. It was watching…moving with the wind. The cold and moist texture of a thirst pulling toward the ground was lightly touching the flesh of each person. Perhaps it was a faint breeze, but the wind's fingers left a vulnerable impression, one that was palpable to the beast waiting in the sky.

He sat next to the window inside the café. True, it was chic, but he was just mesmerized by the masses of people that would flock to places such as this and wondered what would bring them here.

However, the storm outside had a stronger beckoning. He saw the face hiding in the clouds, a monster laughing loudly enough to shake the earth. His skin felt as if it were screaming to be touched by the reflection of this force.

He looked to his right and saw a young woman standing in front of the entrance. She was dressed seductively in plain clothes, and the light shone in her eyes. She was at ease and walked toward him as if she were on a cloud.

She sat in front of him, on the other side of the booth. She arched an eyebrow and then spoke. "It's been a while."

He smiled, slightly. "That it has. How's life been treating you?"

"It's been treating me with incredible irony."

He laughed at her biting humor.

"You know, it's odd that you would ask me to meet you in a café," she said.

"Maybe I didn't want to be the only one here this time."

"You were always the only one, Blake. You made very sure of that in everything you did."

He exhaled, lightly. "Let's try to avoid that subject, shall we?"

"Whatever you like, but I really want to know. Why did you ask me to meet you, here, in a café? Of all places, it's so—"

He smiled, once more. "Unlike me?"

"Well…yes."

"I, uh, just wanted to escape myself for a little while."

"That statement would make more sense if this meeting weren't about your work."

"I never said I wanted to escape that part of me," he said with a hint of loathing.

"Blake, why do you always try to be such a mystery?"

He stared at her for a few moments, and then scratched his bleached blond hair, which was short and cropped. "Let's get on the subject of why we came here in the first place."

She sat back in the seat. "Finally."

"David asked you if you would, and you said yes—"

"Only if I know what it is, exactly, I'll be doing."

"Yes, and now you're here."

"So I am."

"You know, we haven't seen each other in I don't know how long. I'm surprised you haven't been trying to initiate some sort of nostalgic conversation."

She sucked in her lips to push them forward and formed a curved smile, creating a condescending and sarcastic look. "Yeah, well, we stopped being big on conversation ever since you slept with my ex-husband."

"I've told you that story many times."

She put her hand up. "Save it," she said as she put it back down and then looked at him very nonchalantly, as if she had already forgotten the conversation, all together. "Let's just talk about what we're going to do, now."

He exhaled, once again. There was a pang of guilt building inside him. Pushing it down with quick rationalizations, he said, "Okay, fine." He looked down at the table and back up at her. His body was moving periodically, nervously, like some sort of machine with impatient gears. He began to tap his index finger on the table and flashed a quick smile with an equally quick glance, trying to avoid the piercing sense of telepathy in her mahogany eyes. "Okay." He slid back in his seat and laid his head against the hard surface of it. "Okay."

"Are you going to talk or are you just going to play timid again?"

She spoke with such confidence that it was almost infuriating to him. There was even an ominous reflection of assertion painting itself on her face.

That took him back into his original state of thinking. He inhaled one deep breath as his chest strained against his black buttoned-down shirt that wrapped tightly around his trim physique.

"So, you want to know what we'll be doing, exactly?"

"That would be nice, yes."

The first drops of rain began to fall as they made only a small impression against the glass. It would have to be very close to silence in order to hear it.

He looked at her for a few moments and studied her face. "You still have a beautiful body."

"I'm glad you remembered something good about me. Will this body be shackled, again?"

"I don't know. I guess whatever comes to mind will happen."

"I never liked it when you said that, and I still don't. 'Whatever comes to mind.'"

He smiled, slightly. "It's not as if you never enjoyed it."

She blinked her eyes a few times, as if she did not expect him to say that. She quickly regained a face of confidence, and said, "Well, that's true, but you still haven't answered my question."

He leaned forward while folding his arms. "Why do you always have to know so much? You never put up any kind of protest before." He lifted up his left arm halfway, with his fingers pointed up and shook his head a little, to emphasize his last words.

"Maybe that was before things happened," she said with a voice full of conviction.

"You mean before things got so fucked up."

"You always had a way of being blunt," she said while bowing her head slightly.

"We still can't agree on which one was the first to fuck up."

She stared at him for a few moments. Her eyes were now even more piercing. He knew that her irritation was showing from how she pursed her lips, tensely. There was no smile, no frown, not even a slight grimace, just a menacing simplicity shadowing her face into another mask, one of indifference. "Let's not get into that, shall we? I really don't feel like arguing again."

He held his lips inward for a moment while widening his eyes. "Fine," he said, rapidly, as with forced emotion and a genuine attempt to get past this emptying emotion of redundancy. "Let's not get into it. Let's just ignore everything…again."

"Blake, don't be a dick about this. If you start your shit again, I'm just going to leave."

He closed his eyes just enough to form a slit as a look of suspicion began to take possession of his face. "Why haven't you left already?" The voice sounded smug, as though he knew something that she did not.

She folded her arms and said, "You always loved to play that familiar power game, as if there was some secret that I was left out on. That game is getting really old, Blake."

He exhaled with a laugh of surprise; he then regained his seeming look of cool by attempting to smirk. "What power trip? What power did I have? The way I remember it, my power was very limited."

She looked down. She was growing tired of this subject. When she looked back up at him, she did so with eyes of authenticity. "Look, we both agreed to come here today. We both agreed to do this one thing. I think that we should try to make it as painless as possible. Do you think you can do that?"

He weakly smiled as his lips folded inward and there became a line at the bottom of his face resembling a frail crescent. "Sure. I'm sorry."

"All right then."

For a moment there was complete silence between them and only the tapping of the rain against the window was heard. It was faint——like fingertips teasing one's skin. The water hitting the window held itself within tiny circles, denying the release into seemingly forgiving streams.

"I notice, though," she said, "that there's no coffee or even a cappuccino here on the table."

He looked at her with confusion. "So?"

"So, you always used to have something whenever you went to these places."

His face displaying even more confusion as he asked, "How exactly did you know that I ever went to these places to begin with?"

"I come to these places, too, sometimes, Blake. I know that's hard to believe, but I do. I've seen you around here."

"I never saw you. I don't ever remember us talking."

"What makes you think that I'd want to talk to you?"

He was about to say something else and then she put her hand up again. So he let the unspoken words burn on his tongue. She must have known how torturously they stayed trapped inside his mouth, his trembling lips begging to unleash words ingenious only to him.

"Look, let's just order some damn coffee, or cappuccino, or an iced cappuccino, or something. I don't care. Just as long as it's something to drink and can at least keep us from creating useless conversation."

"Fine." They waited for a moment more. "So who's going to...?"

"I'll do it," she said through a sigh as she got up and rapidly walked away.

His stomach felt laden, again, with the fraught emotion of guilt, like he had felt so many times before. His eyes were becoming sorrowful, the blue in them slowly transforming into a saddening color. Maybe he should have gone up there himself. Maybe he should have never asked. Perhaps this entire situation could have been avoided by him just saying nothing.

Then, it came, the deeply shameful feeling biting inside him like wolves coming to feed. He could feel it tearing through him, now, a desperate crying that was lifting to a scream just beneath his flesh. He had to release this nervousness and embarrassment.

She was coming back, but it was as if she were walking in slow motion, taunting him with a slight annoyance weighing into her footsteps. The gentle and overpowering persuasion of her body was made complete with the dangerous sarcasm trapped inside her eyes. She had two cups of hot cappuccino and placed them on either side of the table before sitting back down.

He wanted to say he was sorry again, but what was that going to do? He knew how she'd respond, with an annoyed expectancy. He apologized too many times before and began to see that apologies, to her, were nothing more than a gateway toward accusation and manipulation.

She could see it on his lips. "Okay," she said as she exhaled. "So say it."

He looked down with now an obvious regret that such thoughts had ever crossed his mind. "What?"

"Don't give me that. Just say it, say it so you can get it out of you."

His eyes became incredibly menacing. "Say what?"

She formed a smug look on her face. "You know exactly what. Just say it. I deserve it, anyway, don't I?"

"I'm beginning to not think so."

She leaned forward. He could see it in her eyes. She was pulling the apology out of him, aching for those words. He could read her intentions well, but was too intimidated and knowingly became illiterate to her obvious body language.

"I'm sorry," he said with a quick and dismissive voice as he tilted his head away.

She leaned back and said, "You always are."

He suddenly felt burned and foolish for knowing, fully well, the kind of trap he was falling into. He couldn't say anything else for fear that she would take his words and make them into something else. So, they sat in another silence with their cups sitting on the table. The steam appeared as thin trails curving upward from the searing heat inside, the foam tipping over the edges of their cups as if tempting them. He took the handle of his cup and she did the same. They cooled the hot liquid by blowing on it for a very long while. They sipped on the liquid and let it slide down as they were enjoying and elongating every passing second of it and then put the cups back in their places.

"When are we leaving?" she asked, rapidly.

He looked at her, surprised and frustrated. "First, you want to know exactly what you're doing, and now, you're all gung ho to leave."

"I trust you."

"Do you?"

"Yes, I do," she said with a definite tone. "I trust you to the only extent I am able to."

"And how far does that trust reach? Or are you just saying this?"

She exhaled as if from exasperation. "I'm tired of playing this game, Blake. Can't I ever say anything and let it mean just that? There you go again, looking into something more than it should be. Sometimes, things just are."

He looked down for a moment and away from her knowing eyes, attempting, just for a second, to escape her all-too-confident presence. "Yes, I-I suppose you're right. Maybe it's just as simple as that."

"Whatever happened to your introspection?"

He lifted his left eyebrow, minimizing a look of superior authority. "Remind me again of whose playing games?"

"Aw-w-w-w," she said in a playfully taunting pose. "I thought you liked playing games, Blake. I remember you specifically saying that you desired a person of mystery. Someone that could make you feel so many emotions instead of just playing with them."

He leaned forward and said, "Okay, first of all, you're acting as if we're still friends. Second of all, when did I ever say that?"

She looked at him as if he already knew the answer.

He laughed out loud with an intimidated sound as he scratched his right eyebrow, digging his nail into the dark brown hairs. "You're going to count that one time?"

She kept looking at him for a moment longer. After that, she said, "When are we leaving...Blake?"

His anger was building just enough to cause a prickly exasperation. "Are you teasing me?"

"I want to go, Blake. I want to go wherever you're taking me."

"Whatever happened to you wanting to know so much?"

"Fuck it. Besides, knowing too much can spoil everything."

He exhaled and could feel himself slipping away into a dream-like discomfort. He didn't trust this feeling, and he wanted to say no—just to leave her behind. But he knew it couldn't be that way, not with his submissive nature.

Even with defiance beating against his skull, he knew that she obviously had the power. "Fine," he said like a child proven wrong. "Let's go."

She smiled, slightly, as he took his coat. She then got up and said, "I hope that you can do my figure justice."

He stood for a moment with the coat in his hand and replied, "Have I ever let you down?"

Body Image

The sky was dark, but the rain captured glimpses of light from the moisture, teasing them with a delicate touch. They followed the climate as if they were nothing more than shadows.

They walked to either side of his midnight-blue car that was intriguing to the sight, an intrigue that could only be shown. There was no mystery with him. His words, his movements, everything he did spoke perfectly of his character. He was vulnerable in definition, and the midnight blue was his only defense.

They got in the car as they both put on their safety belts. "You almost seem to be anxious by doing this."

She turned to him with aggressive comfort in her eyes. "I never feel anxiety. I'm the 'bitch of ice queens.'"

He stopped, thinking about those words for only moments, and then started the car. "I said that a long time ago. And besides, it was out of anger. People rarely mean what they say when they're angry."

"Maybe they speak the unbearable truth with severe emotions."

He turned to her and said, "You're fucking with my head, and I don't like it. Just remain silent for the rest of the ride, all right?"

"Are you going to speak?"

"Just shut up." He put the emergency break down and backed out.

He pressed his hands firmly against the wheel as he drove forward. His heart was losing pace in a rapid beat. Once they reached their destination, would discussion continue?

He wasn't sure of anything at the moment. All he knew was that the friendship they once shared was gone, and he had to accept that.

"You still look good, though," she said. "That's all I want to say for the moment. You haven't lost your looks. Your body is still in shape, and your face still looks good...real good." Her voice was soft and questionably thoughtful.

Her words immediately started to play into his head and he couldn't handle such suspect compliments from her. "Thank you," he said, expecting her to stop talking.

"Obviously, you still think I have a good body."

"Will you please stop talking!" he blurted out. "It's not like that, and you know it."

"How do you know what I'm implying?"

He arched his left eyebrow. "I don't, and that's the fun for you, isn't it?"

"You're no innocent yourself there, Blake."

"God!" he screamed as he abruptly lifted his head upward. "Shut up!"

She sat back in her seat. It was obvious she felt scorned. He could tell that she did not like the fact that the last word was not hers.

So, they began to ride in genuine silence. No games. No conflicting words, nothing.

The wind was showing little sympathy by continuously pushing the darkening skies with a heartless force. However, the rain's serenity persisted through the dense fog that resembled a collection of fists bleeding water.

He set his thoughts free to run everywhere, as they usually did. He wanted to allow the festering inside so that he could let go. All he needed was a few minutes of self-loathing and internal tears. This emotional need was shaped like an addicting drug running cold in his veins.

Her complimentary words of his physical characteristics were in the back of his head, creating an imbalance of tearful truths and vain realities. Were his blue eyes still as deep as they always were? Was it a good idea to bleach his hair blond? Did it compliment the rest of his face? Was his body still attractive? He then tried to push those thoughts away. He did not need this at a time when he was knowingly using introspection as an excuse for self pity. He wanted the sadness, because this stone-cold thinking was a dramatic attempt for him to play the victim. It was the only way he could feel like he wasn't responsible.

He turned onto an alleyway named "Willfire." He was halfway toward the destination. It couldn't come soon enough, but at the same time, it was something to dread.

He wondered what she was thinking. He would ask if her words wouldn't destroy the belligerence he chose to unleash upon himself.

Though, someone had to speak. There couldn't be just silence. Silence was like a slow murder.

The alley was narrow and desolate. The bricks on either side were of a vibrant red closing in. A strong sound was coming off the tires as they pressed against the gravel. It was an uncomfortable sound, a grit that got in-between one's thoughts. All the noises echoed, since there was nothing to restrain them. You could even picture every thought inside your head. Depending on your outlook, this deafening silence could either be a walking dream or a living nightmare.

For them, it was neither. This silence was a discomfort for him. He wasn't sure what it was like for her. If the tears he felt were real, they would bleed from a broken mind.

He slowed the car as he saw the building coming near, the building where his apartment was located. He looked around for a place to park, hoping to see a space, because he couldn't stand sitting in this car for a moment longer. It was beginning to feel confined. A space appeared in between two cars. He went for it, rapidly. He hoped to God that a mistake didn't occur. He didn't need to make yet another apology for banging into someone else's car.

He calmed himself with one long breath… he was perfectly parked.

"Well, let's go."

Before he got out of the car she asked, "So…what are we doing?"

He sat back down with a sudden movement. He turned his head as he looked at her with a nonchalant irritation. "I thought you said you didn't care."

"Maybe I changed my mind."

He curved his mouth as a rage began to scream inside him. "We're already here. It doesn't mean SHIT now." His voice was of a dead calm, except for that one obscenity, of which was exclaimed in a shrill vengeance.

"You're certainly in a mood," she said. "All I want to know is what's going to happen. Is that so much to ask for?" She had her arms folded as she stared at him.

"What the fuck does it matter now!?" he asked with great irritation. "You said you didn't care. You said that knowing too much could spoil everything."

"That wasn't all I said." Her voice was calm and far from intimidated.

"Oh, wait, that's right. You also said you wanted to know, then you said you wanted to go, then … YOU SAID YOU WANTED TO KNOW AGAIN!" He unleashed his words from an internal fire as his face contorted into an intense emotion.

"Blake," she laughed. "Blake, Blake, Blake. You just take things too seriously. Now will you please stop being so dramatic and let's just get going."

He exhaled. "I hope you're not going to be like this all day."

"You're the one that wanted me to come over."

He exhaled, once more. "Let's just go, okay? Let's just get out of the car and get this over with."

They both got out and began to walk toward the building. His apartment was at the very top. He took the key from his pocket as they walked up to the door. The building itself was of a black so thick that it appeared charred. The structure was very resilient. Yet, from the surface, it looked inherently weak.

He opened the door and they went inside. The interior was different. It was attractive with a tremendous structure, and the sight of it was massive enough to imitate the spacious grounds of a castle.

They took the elevator to floor "46."

"It's ironic that someone who suffers from acrophobia lives in a place so high."

He only acknowledged her words mentally.

"I can see you've made good," she said. "Your work must be getting well known by now."

He smiled, only slightly. The real answer was written right on his face.

"It's not from your work, is it? This obvious sum of money you're earning."

This was another truth he couldn't hide from. He looked to her. "No, it's not." His eyes begged for sympathy. "I had to become something else to support my work."

"You mean to support your*self*."

"Yes." His eyes met with hers and remained completely exposed.

"So what did you have to become?"

He turned his head. "Let's not get into that, shall we?"

"No, tell me, Blake, what did you have to become?"

"Why do you want to know?" he asked without looking at her.

"I just want to know, Blake." Her voice was taunting. "Tell me. Tell me what you had to do since everyone was right about the survival of your work."

"I had to become an accountant, all right!" he yelled, his voice shuddering off the compacted walls of the elevator.

"So, I see, an accountant."

"Yes."

"So...you had to become the one thing you disliked."

"Yes."

She cracked a small laugh. "How humorously ironic, to become a part of the world you rejected for so long, just to be able to survive in your *own* little world."

"YES! YES! YES! We get the fucking point! I had to do it to survive!" He rapidly turned his head toward her. "I'm not ashamed," he said as he quickly brought his voice down. "It's what I had to do."

"Then why would you have let me go on thinking that your work provided this exquisite place, if you're so unashamed?"

"I said I wasn't ashamed. I never said I would be upfront about it."

"You've just contradicted yourself."

"Do *you* always make sense?"

She just looked at him and then turned away from him as he did the same. Floor "46" was now reached. The elevator doors opened into a hallway.

"Very nice," she said as she walked out into it. "Nice."

He followed her in as the doors closed.

The apartment had a small number of poles reaching from the ceiling to the floor randomly placed in an organized format. The wooden floor was a shiny brown, making the reflections perfectly familiar. In fact, all of the walls were a mirrored brown.

Configurations stood all over the apartment on steel easels, each one different from the other. Some were an orgasm of masculine bodies, while others were neutral portrayals of feminine ones. One commonality was that each body lay in a twisted garden of sadistic mentalities. There was no glimmer or sparkle dancing on the papers, only a cry for wanting and desperate needing. It was painful to look, but even more painful not to. Every stroke was energetic and still seemed to pulsate with the stilled movement.

"Nora?"

She turned to him after he called her name, her eyes lifted in attentive curiosity, her stance seemingly unoffending.

"Are you going to get ready?"

"To pose?" she asked, rhetorically.

"Um, uh, yes."

She lightly caressed her brown hair with her fingertips.

"Of course," she said as she began to undress.

He immediately turned his head the other way.

"You were never so shy before," she said, arching her eyebrow and speaking with a patronizing tone.

"Yes, well, I would just think of it as a betrayal to my art if I looked before I painted."

"I'm sure you looked at all those male models before you started painting."

He didn't respond.

She smiled, slightly, reveling in the fact that she was right. "Hypocritical, don't you think? To look at men with such intrigue and wanting, and feel only neutrality for the women?" She was slowly unbuttoning her shirt, hoping that he would turn his head.

"Life is full of hypocrisy."

She laughed. "So, it is." She stopped undressing. "Blake, Blake, look at me," she said softly.

"I don't really want to at the moment."

She could hear the fluctuation in his voice. He was feeling defiance against her and she knew it.

"Damn it, Blake. Just because you're gay doesn't mean that you can't at least look at women."

He didn't respond.

"Blake," she said, becoming completely still. "I'm not going to follow through with this if you don't look at me."

"Why do I have to look at you?"

She turned her head somewhat forward. She needed an audience for this, even if it was just one person.

"I don't want you to be ashamed of me," she said.

"This has nothing to do with shame."

"Blake, don't make me feel alone." She tried to make her voice sound as if it were pleading, and manipulated the tone into a delicate sound. It was like silk softly crashing into his ears.

Slowly, he began to turn his body. She smiled, slightly. She had pulled the right string and she could feel him coming one step closer to her seduction.

When he was completely turned around, he saw that her shirt was open, revealing a vibrant brazier, the cups pushing her breasts up into perfectly shaped circles. "There," she said, trying to hide the victory in her voice. "Now, was that so bad?" Her eyes did not leave his as she continued, slowly releasing her shapely body from her clothes.

To her, being naked was not feeling exposed. It was just another way to feel powerful. Even if that power lay inside the mind of no temptations. However, she knew that that was just for the moment as she moved her hands over her body. They were lightly touching her flesh as she reached into the material of her tightly clinging pants.

It was obvious that this was a show. But she didn't care. This was how to play the game, where mere appearances meant everything and definition had no place.

She was standing in her undergarments and proceeded to remove her bra while still looking at him. The two perfect orbs of flesh were beginning to fall into their natural shape as the brazier was letting go. She allowed the slow release of her full bosom as the brazier fell to the floor. Removing the final layer, she was sure that he was enthralled.

"What are you doing?" he asked with an irritated curiosity.

"What do you mean?" she asked as she slid the thinly lined underwear down her legs.

"You know exactly what I mean. This is just a pose, not a fucking strip tease. If you're going to be like this, then why don't you just go?"

With her failure realized, she had to think of something to say in order to gain her dignity back. "Do you really want me to leave?"

He stared at her as through pupils that turned to stone. "If you're going to be like this, your games are not wanted here, Nora, not right now. So, yeah, if this is the way it'll be, then I want you to go."

She wanted to scream at him for not giving in. She quickly buried that emotion as she said, "You can be such a spoil sport." She purposely put humor in her voice to distract the sound of anger. "Where do you want me to stand?"

"Right there is just fine."

"Okay, how do you want me to stand?"

"Wait."

He retrieved his brushes and pallet from the floor behind him as he stood in front of one of the easels.

"Okay," he said, "why don't you put your arms up over your head and push the center of your body…outward."

She followed his direction as she said, "I hope this isn't going to take too long."

"Actually, I've painted most of it; I just needed some reinforcement of what you looked like."

"Then why didn't you just get one of my pictures?"

He looked up at her as if to speak the answer, nothing came out of his mouth.

She wanted to smile because the probing question affected him, but she hid it. She didn't need to show that, yet.

18

"Well, I would have them if someone hadn't burned them all."

She looked straight at him, infuriated with his statement. This was her victory and he took it from her. She thought of something to throw back in his face. "I was drunk."

"You think that's an excuse?" He let out one laugh, guided by a knowing tone. "It's funny, though. I thought you said you couldn't remember."

"I never said that."

He laughed again, with relished conviction. "Now you're lying."

She eyed him with a cold stare. This was not the way things should be going. The game was hers, and she was the one that set the rules. "People say many things, Blake. How am I supposed to remember them all?"

"Look up," he commanded.

She looked up with quick movement and knew that she needed to think of something to calm her down. Her mind began to distinctly picture how he was painting her. She imagined every stroke of the brush creating a perfect reflection. The brush felt like it was caressing her skin, fashioning her form in an elegant portrayal. She could see him swooping downward, circulating the shape of her breasts, creating the shadows hiding beneath the lines. Her body was being painted in an intriguing flesh tone. She could see him separating each hair on her head, letting it fall lightly onto her shoulders.

"You've become silent," he said. "I suppose you've said everything you could say."

"For now," she said while still thinking of his hands at work. In the back of her mind, though, she was planning a new game.

The storm outside was showing through the windows. It entered into the apartment as a shadow of its billowing skies. It maintained the brittle rain as the clouds prepared themselves for a release and the thunder rolled throughout the sky, belligerent in its continuing retention. Only a light shower followed. It had yet to scream with its full impact upon the earth.

She could see the storm out of the corner of her eye. It was even more pleasurable for her because she was standing naked in front of her prey and the storm just outside the window intensified the game. She felt playful as the remembrance of all those times she played in the rain came back to her. She could see herself as a little girl splashing in the puddles, laughing at the destruction of sand castles.

She smiled, slightly, as her thoughts began to illuminate her face.

"I'm surprised you haven't asked about David, yet."

That statement brought her back to the present and she suddenly remembered the very person that brought this meeting to a reality. "I forgot all about him. I'm surprised he's not here, since he's usually sprawled out on the sofa watching television."

"You know, you've always made him sound so simple," he said as he continued to move his brush.

"Why do you say that, Blake? I never tried to make that assumption."

"Bullshit," he said as his words were pushed from surprised laughter.

"I never said David was simple."

"You never had to. It was right in your face, or those little statements you always make around him, or how you always try to act superior to him."

"You make me sound so dominant."

"Don't flatter yourself. I was just saying you try to be dominant."

She exhaled, slowly, as she felt a light blow from his words. She had to retaliate. "Blake, maybe the reason I act like I'm above everyone else is because I have yet to meet any of your friends that meet with my level of intelligence."

"I thank God for that. I would never want to befriend someone who is so conniving and deceitful."

She then met her head with his as she said, "If you continue with statements like that, I *will* leave. I didn't deserve that and you know it."

He pressed his lips together as he continued painting. She could see the apologetic look on his face. Once again, his sorrow was brought out and she could see that his vulnerability was as naked as she was. Yet, she couldn't help but to find it ironic that she was the one who had more power and she wasn't even clothed.

She was about to say the words that would bring out his regret, once more. "Okay, say it."

"I'm sorry," he said, rapidly, as if to get it out and over with.

"That one was fast. You're getting much better at this, Blake."

She moved her head back up while mentally holding onto the look of his face. He was obviously biting his tongue. He needed to say something but didn't because of her presence, which made her feel rapturous.

"I thought we were talking about David," she said, bringing him further into his own despair.

"Why do you want to talk about him if that will just engage us in another argument?"

"Blake, I never mean to argue. It just happens. Arguments are never really intentional, people just fall into them."

"That's not always true. Sometimes the conflict is intentional. It could be because two people are trying to find a way to separate from one another, or one person is trying to manipulate the other, or—"

"Are you trying to be introspective, again?"

"You should talk, Nora. You are the queen of introspection."

"Thank you."

"That is, when you want to gain control over someone."

"Oh, Blake, look who's trying to play the game, now. Does it hurt to lose so many times?"

He nodded his head slowly in a back and forth motion, commenting on her attitude.

"How are you painting me?"

"The only way that you deserve."

"Should I trust that statement?"

"I would never demean a person, Nora…even if one were asking for it. I use my art to express—"

"Your own emotions; yes, I know. I have never seen so many conflicting emotions in my life."

She felt appreciated when she heard him exhale from what seemed like longing. All she had to do was speak and he would feel indebted. This was definitely her game.

He was brushing with a passion. However, this passion was not complimentary towards her. It was a celebration of her, but at the same time, mourning her nature. He tried painting the picture he had always envisioned her in.

He liked the fact that she couldn't see what he was creating. It gave him a small sense of power over her. He knew that somewhere, she was deeply curious about what this would turn out to be. All those years of having her in his life must have had some kind of outcome and he knew that she needed to see what that exactly was. It wasn't like Nora to not want to know something that was about her. However, he also knew that she would gladly sacrifice this unknown knowledge to keep hold of the continuing game she had to play for her life.

"So…you wanted to talk about Dave?" he asked.

"I thought you wanted to avoid that subject."

He pressed the brush harder for a moment. He was beginning to feel left behind. This couldn't be. He could feel alone, but feeling left was more than he could bear. "Did you ever hear me say that?"

"What makes you think I want to continue talking about him?"

"Damn it, Nora! Let's just talk about him, okay? I don't like it when you tease me."

"I never tease."

"Whatever. Anyway, what other negative emotions have you felt toward Dave?"

"Just because I've said a few negative things about Dave doesn't mean I hate him."

"But you don't like him either."

"Well...he's not one of my favorite people."

"What kind of people are? That should be an interesting answer."

"Why do you say that?"

He laughed, once more, with a biting sarcasm. "I can only imagine the kind of people you'd befriend."

He could see she formed an irritated face. Maybe he should stop pushing. Maybe there was such a thing as digging too much. He tried to ignore those passing thoughts. He didn't need a conscience if she wasn't going to use hers, either.

"What exactly are you getting at, Blake?"

He could hear the tone hiding inside her powerful portrayal. He was now beginning to suspect that she was making contradictions only to make her true feelings vague.

"Nothing, really, I'm just saying that you're a person who goes after what she wants, and doesn't care who's in the way."

"You know, I'm wondering. If you think I'm this vile and despicable person, then why did you befriend me in the first place?"

He now knew that she was trying to let him fall on his own words. So, he simply said, "That was before I really knew you. For most of the time that we were friends, you were practically an angel. Then, all of a sudden, you changed one day. You became someone completely," he concentrated for a moment on one of his strokes, "different."

There was silence for a few minutes. Usually, he would've felt some sort of nervousness from this, but now that he was enthralled in his world of creation, he became lost in it. It felt as if nothing could bring him out of it.

"Yes, well..." she said with an incredibly smug tone, "I guess that was before it happened."

He suddenly stopped his painting. The world he had built around him was now starting to de-construct. There was a heavy emotion of exposure within the pit of his toned stomach. He looked up at her as she put her head down to meet his, almost as if she knew what she had done.

"You're not going to bring that up, are you?"

"I just did."

"Oh, my God!" he said just as lightning fluttered throughout the sky. "So, we slept together! Once, only once! It happened one time how many years ago?!"

She looked at the window and could now see that the rain was falling freely in overdue relief from burdened clouds. "Why don't you continue painting?"

"No!"

"Let's just forget about it, Blake. Just paint." She was going to ignore the subject she had just brought up. Inside, she was laughing.

"No!" he yelled as he slammed his pallet and paint brushes on the floor. The sudden clatter echoed throughout the spacious apartment as the paint splattered all over the wooden floor, staining the reflections. "You brought it up! Now...you're going to talk about it! With me!"

She could hear his voice shudder in her skull. However, she tried to ignore this. It was not wise to quit, now, now that she'd come so far. So she continued to stand in the same position he told her to originally be in.

"Nora! Nora, answer me! I will not play this with you! I'm not going to let you hurt me again!" His voice then calmed to a softer tone. "Why are you doing this? Please, let's just talk about it. You've put it in my head and I can't get rid of it until it's spoken." His voice was weak and cracked as he spoke. He looked at her, pleadingly, his face now softly shaped and vulnerable.

She continued to stay silent. There was a light tremor creeping into the center of her firm stomach that she was now pushing down. It wasn't as if she felt it before, it was just a casualty that must be endured to succeed in her chosen path.

He exhaled with a release of breath that burned in her mind. It was long and torturous and it carried itself into her conscience. But she learned a long time ago that a conscience showed weakness.

The storm outside was more forceful. It had yet to release its full power, but the trembling could still be felt. The clouds were crying, now. The faces that contorted in condensed fog were twisting in a gritty discomfort. The midnight blue had become dampening.

"I'll, uh, get another pallet."

She realized that it had worked. Even after his pushed emotions were exposed, he still gave in. In a way though, she wished that it wasn't like this, that trust could really be a truth. But that wasn't how life had played out for her. Her existence relied on cruel trickery, and, sometimes, she hated herself for it. But that feeling never lasted.

He came back with another pallet upon which he proceeded to squeeze different colors of paint. He picked up one of the brushes that was thrown on the floor and dipped it into a concrete gray.

There was silence, now, and no one was going to attempt to break it. All they heard was the light brushing of bristles that screamed while twisting against the canvas.

Shudders of thunder were felt slamming through the walls after strikes of hauntingly white lightning conflicted with the darkness of the skies. Their shadows danced on the floor through the quick flashes of white.

The spacious apartment now seemed to contract as their minds saw the walls closing in, slowly forcing their shattered feelings out from their hiding places. These emotions could almost be seen twisting into one another, desperately attempting to merge inside the heartless exposure surfaced from the lightning.

Still, no words, not even tears could fall from their faces. The storm was the only thing crying. It was fighting amongst rolling clouds, shouting thunder, painfully bright lightning and dense waters, changing the world into a demonically dark blue.

Still, not a word was spoken, just two wounded hearts trying to feel.

Then, Nora spoke. "So…what are you painting?"

"You already asked that," he replied, fast and with little emotion.

She could feel inside herself that she wanted to apologize, but it couldn't be brought out. She was still struggling to hold onto her mystery. "Yes, well, I'm just asking again."

He was beginning to see the obvious attempt she was making. He was thinking of at least trying to respond. However, he couldn't help but to wonder if this was her still at play.

"Even if it isn't too flattering of me, I'm beginning to think I won't mind," she said. Her voice had a hint of fluctuation, but she rapidly swallowed it. "It's your vision." She seemed unaffected, again. It was the perfect disguise. And at the moment, the one thing she really needed was that.

He could hear an apology spoken between her words. Should he take that as it was? Could he go on letting her feel truly naked? He slowly began to see that even she didn't deserve that much exposure.

"Well…thank you. Thank you. I will still try…to do you some, uh, justice." He was slowly finding his words after the crippling silence.

She could almost smile now, but didn't. She wanted to approach him with a tenderness she had never shown before, but that was not Nora. That was not the person she had learned to become. So, once again, she hid her feelings and continued allowing her stance to be entrapping.

"I'm glad you feel that way," was the only thing she could say. It was compassionate enough to show thanks, but vague enough to hold the position of mystery.

He tried to go back to that world of comfort he was in just moments ago. But he found that he couldn't. The only way to bring back some sort of contentment was to try and converse with her on anything else. "By the way," he said, "Dave will probably come over today."

"Oh?" she said. "I figured that since he wasn't here, he wouldn't even show up."

"Well, he might. He's usually here, every day, anyway."

"Are you sure that he's coming over?"

"I'm pretty sure."

"Um, what time?"

He stopped his painting for a moment and looked up. "You seem to be awfully curious about this subject."

"Well, I'm just asking so I can prepare myself."

"What does that mean?"

"Nothing, I mean, you said it yourself. He and I don't really get along." She was trying to find a way to be as sympathetic as possible. She didn't want to have another debate, not now.

"So I see." He wanted to delve into the situation a little further. But he knew that would just lead to another debate, and that wasn't needed now, not again. "Well, I never thought it was about you two getting along, you and he just aren't on the same wave length."

"Probably not." She then silenced herself for a moment and contemplated whether or not to ask the next question. "Do you think that you and I are on the same wave length?"

He could detect the need in her voice to find a commonality. Maybe she was trying to redeem herself. "Well, if we weren't, then we would've never been friends. How…how do you think things, um, uh, fell apart between us?" He was asking this while still painting. He grappled to maintain the balance between these two worlds of thought.

"Well, I don't really know, Blake," she said while the real answer was just below her lips, but she didn't want to speak it. So she began to rationalize, and tried to make herself believe a different response. "I just think that we lost contact over the years. We were going in separate directions. Our lives were bound to move on, distancing us from each other." She said all of this as if she were thinking out loud.

"Yeah, yeah I can see that." His agreement was an obstruction from his real thoughts. But right now was not the time to be completely open. "Perhaps we just didn't feel comfortable around each other anymore."

"Why do you say that?" She regretted asking that right after she spoke the question. But she couldn't take it back now.

"Well…because, things…happened." His voice was trailing off.

"Things did happen, things that didn't put us at very good places."

There was a sudden knock at the door. Blake stopped his current stroke, and put the brush down. As his footsteps faded away from her, suspicions of it being Dave gripped her mind.

He opened the door ajar, just enough to see a portion of a face he did not recognize. However, it was a very attractive face. "Yes," the man said, "is Nora here?"

His voice had such a hypnotic tone that Blake almost forgot what he had asked. "What?"

"Is Nora here?"

Nora heard the voice from behind the door. She did not want that door opened.

Blake had some suspicions about this man. He wondered if telling him she was here would be a good decision. He followed his instincts and said, "Um, no, not at the moment. Do you want me to tell her that you were here?"

"No, that's okay," the man answered rather quickly, almost like he was trying to avert that action. He walked away. Blake slowly closed the door as the figure faded into the distance of the hallway.

After completely closing the door, he turned around to look at Nora. He could obviously see that she was slightly shaken. His suspicions were confirmed.

"Um, so…who was that?"

"I, I don't really know, but he came asking for you. Do you know who it might have been?"

She continued to look up and took an elongated, silent breath. "Um, no, no

I don't."

He believed that she was lying. "If you didn't know who that was, then why was he asking for you?"

"I didn't even hear his voice."

"That couldn't be, because if you really didn't hear his voice, then you wouldn't have said you didn't know."

"Look," she said as she was starting to feel weak, "can we just not talk about this?" The truth was swimming against her nerves.

He went over to the easel and picked his paint brush back up, continuing with his creation. He could see that she was beginning to be comforted by his silence. But that man was running around his head.

She was just beginning to find contentment. She hoped that his next question wouldn't concentrate on wanting to know who this man was. If he had asked once more, the truth would have to come spilling out of her. However, at the same time, she wanted to tell him. But this couldn't be. It wouldn't be the right time, not when they were both at their most vulnerable.

He could sense the vulnerability in the room. Maybe he shouldn't ask, maybe he should try to hold down his curiosity.

The room was silent once more. The only sound was the brush running against the paper and the storm. They let these sounds provide a conversation all their own.

"So, um, ah, what have you been doing with your life?" he asked her.

"Why do you ask?"

"You've found out all this information about me, I have yet to find out anything about you. I at least have to know something, just to make things fair."

"So I see."

"Are you seeing anyone?"

"Not at the moment," she answered, quickly. "I've just been working and going out."

"Where do you work?"

She was silent for a moment. This was one truth she couldn't hide from. She put him through enough of her games for right now. He deserved some sort of shared conversation. "Well...I, ah, work at the bank."

He stopped his brush for a second, and then continued. "So, you work at the bank."

"Yes," she responded, with one fast word.

He smirked a little. "So I see."

Inside Out

"Tell me a story," she said.

He thought of something while he painted. "Why?"

"I don't know. I just want you to tell me a story."

"What kind of story?"

"Any kind of story, anything that happened in your life, I don't care what it is."

"Okay," he responded while still confused by her question. He began to think of an occurrence in his life. Maybe something that would ease the tension completely away from the room. "Well, I can tell you about one of the most memorable nights I've ever had."

She laughed. "Really, this sounds interesting. Tell me, how did this 'memorable night' go?"

"Why should I continue if you're already laughing at me?" His voice sounded mocking.

She exhaled. "I wasn't laughing at you, Blake. I want to hear the story and think it would be interesting, like I said before. So, just tell the story. I promise, I won't laugh at you."

He thought for a moment as he painted. Then, he decided to begin the story.

"Okay, it went like this. Actually, it started like any other night: me at yet another night club, feeling as if I'm wasting away. Usually I would be intrigued by any nice-looking guy that would approach me, but not that night. This night felt different, somehow. It was like I was expecting something else to happen.

"So, I start to leave the club until I hear a voice. It's very faint compared to the deafening music blaring all around, but I can still hear it. I turn around, and I see this bartender motioning me to come over. Well, I still feel bored with the evening, but I think why not, try to find some sort of entertainment tonight.

"So, I'm walking over to the bar and I take a seat. He takes care of another customer before he comes back to me.

"When he comes over he asks me, 'Why are you leaving?'

"I'm a bit surprised by this question, this is true. But, I'm willing to answer it anyway, since this guy was very attractive to say the least."

"What did he look like?"

"Well, let's see if I can remember. He was wearing one of those sleeveless shirts. You know the kind, the ones that completely cover everything except for the neck and arms. His hair was cropped very short and his face was soft. His eyes were what I like to call 'autumn eyes,' because they were like the color of autumn, a very soft brown.

"Anyway, I said to him, 'Why do you ask?'

"Our voices were struggling over the music as we spoke.

"He said to me, 'Because, you shouldn't of left this place without talking to me. Now, tell me, why were going to leave?'

"I said to him, 'I was getting bored. This scene never changes.'

"'Well, maybe it's because you've never experienced anything different,' he told me.

"'What do you mean by different?'

"He then came up to my face really close and said, 'Wait until I get off. I'll show you something very different.'

"So, I said, 'Okay.'

"He went to help some other customers as I began to wonder about my decision, like if this was the kind of guy I should be wandering off somewhere with. I usually never say 'yes' to someone that asks to me to leave with them. After all, you know how cautious I am.

"I decided to go on back to the dance floor and wait for him. My nerves were beginning to shake. With my curiosity peaking, I kept wondering what this guy wanted to do and if this was wise of me. My mind was going everywhere as I could feel myself counting down the time to when he'd approach me to leave.

"A lot of guys asked me to dance that night. And, I decide to say 'yes.' This curiosity breathed new life to the night and I expressed that anticipation through my movements. I let them hold me anyway they liked, not saying no to any of their advances. I began to lose myself in the moment until I noticed that the bartender at the table was gone. I told the current guy I was dancing with that I had to leave for the night. He slipped me his number and I put it in my back pocket as I rushed to the bar. I asked one of the bartenders where he went off to, he told me that he'd left for the night.

"Thinking that maybe he'd been looking for me, I sat in the pool-table room. I looked at some of the other people playing and I was feeling a little impatient. I was looking forward to this, to the excitement and mystery, but now there was the possibility that it wouldn't even happen.

"So, I waited, and I waited, and I waited. Now, I was completely disappointed and decided to leave the club. Right before I walked through the doors, though, guess who showed up?

"He apologized for taking so long; he said that it was just some business he had to take care of.

"He then leaned over to me and said, 'So, you want something different in your life?'

"I looked at him suspiciously and asked, 'It's not drugs, is it?'

"He laughed and said, 'No, it's not drugs. However, I just want to make sure that you feel safe doing this. Do you want to leave with me, tonight? Are you completely sure?'

"'Should I be worried?'

"'No,' he said with a smile, 'I just want to know if you feel safe. Nothing is ever fun if you don't feel completely comfortable.'

"I said, 'Well, I suppose you're right,' through some nervous laughter. I was actually feeling nervous. After all these years of casual sex, I was actually a little apprehensive.

"I then said, 'Yes, I feel completely comfortable with this.'

"'Good,' he said with the very calm voice and an intrigued look. 'So, why don't you follow me in your car and I will lead you.'

"'Where are we going to go?' I asked him.

"'Don't worry about it. Just let things happen.'

"So, he went and left through the doors and I did the same, against my better judgment. I got in my car as he got in his and then I started to follow him. Well, while I was doing this, I was still wondering what was going to happen, and what kind of person this guy was, and just so much shit was swimming through my head.

"Then, I noticed as I followed him, there was this other car behind me. I really didn't take much notice, until he started getting close to my bumper. I passed him off as a tail-gaiter. I assumed that he just had to get somewhere two minutes faster than everyone else.

"Then, all of a sudden there was this sudden bump in the back of my car. This other car that had been behind me has rammed into me. The bartender wasn't doing anything, and I assumed he didn't notice. The car behind me rammed me again and I ended up slamming into the bartender's car. Now, I was really starting to get worried, because the bartender wasn't doing anything, he just continued to drive. The car behind me was now pulling up really close and the bartender was slowing down. I became sandwiched in between them. Now, I realized that I had to do something.

"I saw an exit ramp to my left, and I went for it. Just as I did, a gunshot went right through my window and I started flying out of there. Both the bartender and this other car were chasing me now down the road. By that point I was really trying to find a populated area. However, I didn't know what was populated at this time of night—or should I say morning?

"Anyway, I started to sweat and my heart was pumping really fast. I didn't know where I was going and I wasn't sure if I was going to live to see the sun rise again.

"I saw a gas station and pulled into it. There were a couple of trucks and some customers in the convenient store. I pulled into one of the parking spots. The other car left and the bartender pulled into the gas station.

"The next thing he did was get out of his car and walk up to mine. I started my engine and I was about to get out of there. He stepped right up to my car. I was dying of panic. He then put his face right to my window, and I could hear his voice through the glass. He said, 'I told you it would be something different.'

"He then walked off, got back into his car and left.

"And that was my most memorable night to date."

"That didn't happen to you," she said with incredible skepticism.

"Of course it did."

"No, it didn't."

"Okay, then, tell me, why do you believe this didn't happen?"

"I saw the same thing on television last week."

"Why would I pick something out of a movie?"

"To fuck with me."

He arched his right eyebrow. "I would never fuck with you."

"Of course you do, it's just that you never succeed."

He stopped painting for a moment and looked at her with grave seriousness buried in his pupils. "Are we going to get into another argument?"

"No, no, we're not."

31

He resumed his work. "So, why don't you tell me a story?"

"Why?"

"Oh, come on, humor me."

She exhaled through a sigh and said, "Sure. However, this one will be true."

"Just tell the damn story."

She smiled a bit and began to speak.

"Well, I remember something that happened back when I was about six years old. I was in my father's house at the time. Both he and my mother were separated at that time because of a nasty occurrence, but that's a different story. Anyway, I can remember being so attracted to these curtains that my father had. They were very long and practically translucent. To me, they looked like limber paper.

"They were connected to this long hallway of windows and I can remember every time those windows were open and the curtains would practically float away.

"Don't ask me why I was so fascinated with these curtains, I really don't know. There seemed to be some kind of purity about them, kind of a stained purity. Almost as if they were hauntingly white.

"I can remember one day I was playing in that room and no one was around. I decided to go up to the curtains and I began trailing my fingers back and forth through them, letting their soft touch caress my hands. It matched the day as well. I was becoming lost in the cloudless skies that were made complete with that vibrant purity.

"The wind played with my hair which made me content. The wind then started to pick up. I felt the curtains begin to contract against my skin and I invited the sensation. I endured it with the most vulnerable feeling I could find. To me, it was becoming a very delicate dance.

"The curtains began to distort my surrounding. Their flapping rhythms were becoming stronger. I must admit, I *was* getting a little frightened, but I couldn't stop. I had started this, now I had to go finish it. They began wrapping around me as I continued to run. Then, they slipped under my feet, making me fall forward. Everything started to spin around me, but I continued to dance with them. I began breathing through them as they were slowly mummifying me. I could have called for help, I could have said something. But I didn't. I couldn't end this, it had become my addiction.

"I could feel myself coming closer to the ledge, but I still wouldn't stop myself. I started to look back on my short little life as my eyes focused on this hauntingly white draping over everything.

32

"Right before I fell, my father caught me. He released the curtains around me and pulled me close, he didn't even look to see if I was crying. He said he was sorry for leaving me alone, that he promised he would look after me better from now on.

"Funny thing was, though, I wasn't even traumatized, not even in the least. I was actually kind of intrigued by it all.

"Well, needless to say, I've never really looked at life the same way again."

He painted for a few short moments as his eyes moved up to her. In the back of his mind, there was an obvious question pressing forward.

"So you're saying that death intrigues you?"

"No," she said, "that's not what I'm saying at all. I just think that if you know you're life is going to end in the next few seconds, then you should try to make it as powerful as possible."

"Of course," he said. "It's all about power with you, isn't it?"

"Power has nothing to do with it, Blake. It just has everything to do with living, and how you live. Besides, at least I told you a real story."

"What if I said I saw that exact same thing on television?"

"You didn't."

"How would you know?"

"Because, Blake, I know you. In addition to the fact that I know what's happened in my own life. You can't play along in this, you don't have the wits."

"Why do you still believe that the story I told you is fake?"

"Because, Blake, I saw it…on television. I think you told it because you felt threatened."

"Threatened!? Threatened by what?"

"By exposing yourself."

"You said it yourself, Nora, you know me, why would I have to lie if you do?"

"I only knew you from the time I befriended you. We both have pasts that we have never shared."

He exhaled. "Fine, you want to hear a real story?"

"So, you're admitting its fake?"

"Fuck that. I'm just asking if you want to hear a real story."

"In your life, I would."

He exhaled. As the strokes began to echo in his mind, he said, "It all happened, actually, within the course of one weekend.

"It started out like a bad day from hell. I woke up late for work because my alarm clock had finally broken. I hurriedly got in the shower and got dressed.

I knew that my position in this job was hanging on by a string, anyway.
"This was before I became an accountant. At this point in my life, I was working for a gas station. They were looking for the slightest excuse to get rid of me, mainly because I really didn't fit the image of their little store. I had bleached blond hair, like I do now, and earrings. Apparently, this was a bad image. I think they hired me anyway because they thought I'd change and they were in desperate need for help.

"So, as I was getting ready for work, I heard the phone ring. I ran over to it and answered. It was, of course, the gas station.

"'Yeah, hey Blake, it's Winston.' Yes, his name was 'Winston.' I always found that humorous.

"Well, I asked him what he wanted.

"'It is ten o'clock. You were supposed to be here an hour ago.'

"I tried telling him I was sorry and that it would never happen again.

"'Yeah, I know, Blake, because you know what? You're fired!'

"He then actually hung the phone up in my face. I slammed it down and now I was out of a job. Right after that, I heard a knock at the door. I opened it, and there was this guy standing before me dressed very, very casually and holding a piece of paper.

"'You're being evicted.' He handed me the piece of paper. 'You have thirty days to move.'

"I asked him why this was happening.

"'You haven't paid the rent for two months in a row. Sorry.'

"He then walked off. Yeah, he was real sorry, all right. I closed the door and took a deep breath. I thought that nothing else could possibly go wrong. I then heard another knock at the door.

"I opened it and guess who I saw?

"'Hello, Blake.'

"It was Charley. I'm sure you remember Charley.

"'We have to stop seeing each other.'

"I asked him why, as if that would solve anything.

"'Things just aren't working out. Sorry.'

"Yeah, he was real sorry, all right, he walked away just as carelessly as the guy with the eviction notice.

"Now I felt like blowing my brains out. I closed the door and walked up to my little coffee table in my little shit apartment. I then saw an envelope with another name on it with the rest of my mail. Now, usually, I would never go peeking around in other people's mail, but this time I thought I'd make an exception. I mean, since the day had practically gone to hell anyway, I figured why not, getting thrown in jail for some minor offense would be the perfect topper.

"I saw that it was from a 'Glenn Warren' from Nevada, and it was addressed to a 'Jack Warren.'

"I opened the envelope and saw that there was a plane ticket in there. I began to read the letter with it.

"It described the death of a loved one, a family member that everyone had been close to. They were going to have a funeral for her. Apparently she was young, because the writer of the letter described the death as being such a shame and how she had so much going for her.

"The letter never described how she died. It *did* describe, however, that this family had never met this 'Jack Warren.' They didn't even know what he looked like.

"I continued to read the letter as I could feel myself being pulled into this real story.

"I put the letter down and thought, *I wonder what the real Jack would do if he got this letter. Would he even go?* I wasn't entirely sure, and I'm still not. But, out of a sporadic decision, I wanted to be the one to go to this funeral. I needed to get away from here, and I needed to feel as if I were someone else for a few days. Don't ask me why I felt the need to do this, I don't really know. I just felt as if I needed an escape.

"So, I took the plane ticket and I went to the airport. On the way there, I was wondering what I was doing, and why I was doing it. Perhaps this Jack really wanted to go to this funeral, and I would be ruining it for my own selfish reasons. However, I couldn't go on with this day like myself. It had a bad start and I only knew it would get worse. The only way to escape such inevitability was to step into someone else's shoes.

"I stepped out of the car and walked right into the airport. I didn't even bring anything with me, nothing except for a few more clothes. I then boarded the plane to Nevada. The writer stated in the letter that there would be people there waiting for me, family members of this person.

"On the way over there, I really didn't feel apprehensive about any of it. In fact, I had felt quite relieved. I put on the headphones the airliner supplied and listened to some soothing music. It seemed to match the environment.

"After I got off the plain, I saw them standing there. They were all so joyously happy to see me. I guess they should have been suspicious since I really didn't look like them, but it's weird how the human condition can fool you into thinking something else.

"They embraced me, and I felt their acceptance. I felt happy to see them, too, in a way. They escorted me to a limo. I got in after them and we continued to converse.

"'Jack, it's good to see you after so long. We've heard much about you. I hope you've heard good things about us.'

"They all laughed as I did with them. They were mostly women, except for a few men. Each of them was dressed in coordination with one another. All the colors matched, even with each other. It was like a solid block of color sitting in every direction. As people, they were like any other, nothing really unique about any one of them, whatsoever—-actually, boring in a sort of way. However, their clothes spoke very differently. So did their jewelry and basically every material thing in their current possession. They introduced another side to me, a side that I believed they kept as hidden as my real identity to them. They didn't even really ask anything specific about me. It was almost as if they knew I wasn't the real person, but they didn't want to bring that truth out. Like it would destroy their world they had so endearingly built to contribute to the image of this Jack.

"'So, Jack, what do you do, now?'

"I told them that I was a painter. They wanted to know where they could see my work. I told them that it wasn't very popular at the moment. That I was just a struggling artist, which was, of course, true. However, I didn't tell them that I worked for a gas station, or that I had recently been fired. I just told them that I had a job of which paid well. It supplied me with enough to support what I really wanted to do.

"'Well, I would love to see some of your work. Maybe you can show me some time. I would really like to see what your mind can create.'

"I didn't tell them what kind of things I had really painted when they asked me. I thought that I shouldn't reveal that around this crowd. They didn't seem like the kind of people that would open their minds to a deeper sense of thought. Such an embrace would have to endure some sort of negative emotion. These were the kind of people that didn't like to show negativity. They just wanted to wear masks of optimism and pretend everything was in its place.

"We didn't even talk about the young girl. I wouldn't avoid that subject, but I wasn't going to talk about it if it wasn't addressed.

"'So, do you have a special girl in your life, Jack?'

"I didn't tell them the truth with this, either. I just told them that I hadn't met the right person, yet. I didn't describe a gender or even a sexual orientation.

I just left it completely open, thinking that maybe they would get the point. Obviously, they didn't. Or they did, and just weren't showing it.

"The drive over to the house wasn't that long. It wasn't even a house; it was much more of a mansion. It was incredibly oversized and painted in this awfully bright yellow with windows drooping from it like gaudy jewelry. The front door was exaggerated in its design with huge rectangular stained-glass windows on either side. Each window had the exact same design of a collage of colors that did not go together at all. It was as if someone had pushed these colors together and forced them to make sense. The entire construction was a kingdom they had built. It was just to show how much money they could throw around. It was at times like this that I was glad I wasn't incredibly rich.

"As I walked into the house, and saw that the interior was just as much of an eyesore as the exterior, I began to wonder what would happen if I really did get rich from my work. Would my dreams really come true? Or would I just become a victim of my own greed like these people?

"I met the rest of them, or just about the rest of them. They were just the same as the others, colors matching perfectly and over-ecstatic faces. They would extend themselves in a great acceptance, just like the others. They spoke to me just like the others.

"Then, I met the grandmother. I first saw her standing at the top of the staircase, which appeared different from the rest of the house. It was a wooden staircase and stained a dark luscious brown. The color was vibrant and life-like. It was simplistic, not over-designed or gaudy. And the stairs themselves were long and narrow. They almost seemed too weak to walk on.

"The grandmother wasn't dressed in just one color. She displayed an array of them, and they matched. They were colors that were meant to be together, and she looked beautiful. Her hair was not gray-white, or even a pure white. It was a very mysterious and intriguing black, jet black. Her eyes were of a soft hazel brown. Her skin was almost like porcelain. It seemed like I couldn't even touch her without breaking her. She seemed so fragile, but so well put together at the same time. Her fragility and boldness of spirit were collected within her as she walked down the stairs.

"Now, this woman, I knew she would want to know. She would want to know beyond the generalities. Simple answers would not do for her. I could tell by looking at her eyes that she would find me out the second she would talk to me. The thing that I was wondering is if she would care or not. She didn't say a word as she walked down the stairs, she just looked at me. There was no skepticism in her face, only a smile.

"After she got off the last step, she walked over to me. 'Hello, Jack, I'm Glenn.'

"I acknowledged her and shook her hand. She smiled, lightly.

"'I'm glad to see you.'

"She hugged me. This was an embrace different from the others. It wasn't done in a casual way. I could feel real emotion emanating from her. She didn't say much to me in front of the others. It was as if she was on a different level, completely."

"Stop," she said.

"Why?"

"So, you really did this?"

"Yes, I did do it. And don't tell me that you saw it on television, either." She laughed, slightly. "No, I didn't."

"Do you want me to go on?"

"Sure."

"Why did you tell me to stop?"

"Well, I'm just wondering what happened when you actually got to the funeral."

"Well, by then, the story had changed. Glenn found me out by then. We both conversed about the subject, and it turns out that she didn't like the real Jack. The real Jack was actually pretty much a Jack-*ass*. She told me that he did some awful things in the past. She was the only one to ever really see him. She didn't consider it a privilege. I don't know why she didn't say anything when she first saw me. I guess it's because she liked this new person standing before her.

"Well, when we got there, I was wearing some clothes the others bought for 'Jack' at their insistence. It was almost like a business suit, all the same color, midnight blue. The shoes were the only change of color, black.

"The funeral was somewhat of a sad event. However, the only people that were truly saddened were Glenn and, surprisingly enough, me. We had all looked at the girl in the casket one by one. Everyone else said they wish they knew her better, that she was so young, and that it was such a shame. Each of their phrases was cliché. It seemed that they were saying these things just because they had to. They made crying sounds, but I looked and saw no real tears.

"When Glenn got up there, she looked at the girl. She looked for quite a long time. She then whispered, 'I'll try to think of this as a release for you. I hope you're living out every dream you ever thought of up there.'

"She then walked away. I believe I was the only one that heard her. Either that or everyone else was just pretending not to hear it.

"I was the last person to see her. She *did* look very young. It was awful to see her lifeless body lying in the casket. I began to speak: 'I guess you're the only one, besides Glenn, who knows the truth, here. I should at least thank you for letting me step into this life for a few days. I hope you lived *your* life as fully as you could. So, I guess, now, you're free from whatever chains that bound you to this earth. I just wonder if you'll be coming back this way to fulfill whatever destinies you didn't complete. Well, you looked to have been a good person. I hope that continues, no matter where you're headed.'

"So after that, I said goodbye to everyone and I left."

"What happened with the eviction?"

"Oh, I found another shit hole, end of story."

"How did you feel when you returned?"

"I felt a little depressed. I had to live again as Blake Underlord. And I had to find another job, and just continue with the daily grind."

"Well, at least you got to escape for a few days."

"Yeah, a few days out of a lifetime."

"That shouldn't matter, now. Since you're doing exactly what you love and should be doing…painting. Doesn't this make you happy, at all? I mean, true, you have to do this in your spare time, but at least you're doing it."

"Well, I've never looked at it that way."

"What do you mean you've never looked at it that way? You've never gotten lost in any of your paintings?"

"Of course I have. I do every time. Well, anyway, do you think you can tell me another story?"

"You want another story?" she asked.

"Yeah, sure."

She hesitated for a few moments, and then said, "Well, I can tell you about a traumatic experience."

"Why would you want to tell me that?"

"I just do."

"Won't that depress you? And what if it depresses *me*?"

"Look, please, just let me tell you this story." Her voice was almost pleading.

He exhaled while put off by her attitude for a moment. "Okay, tell me about your traumatic event."

"Are you sure you want to hear it?"

He stopped painting and looked directly to her. "Look, either tell me the story or don't! I don't know why you're being so indecisive, it's not like you."

She exhaled and didn't speak for a moment as he continued with his painting. She then said, "Okay, it started during this one night, at a party. One of my friends invited me, and I really didn't want to go. Against my better judgment, I went anyway.

"The main reason I had such defiance about going to this gathering was because I had strong suspicions that it would be full of sex-crazed assholes who only thought of getting laid more than anything else. And, besides, the friend that invited me was a person that had no morals when it came to sex. My suspicions were confirmed when I got there. All I could see were these guys trying to grind against anything in a skirt. They weren't even dancing to the music. The only sound they heard was their dicks growing inside their pants.

"I chose to dress down, and tried not to show too much. Usually, whenever I go out, I would want to look seductive. Not here. I decided to wear something as conservative as possible. The last thing I needed was for these guys to start drooling all over me, looking me over with dilated pupils because they were high on something or just plain drunk, then having to hear their one-liners put together by half-assed words because their minds were drowned from too much crap.

"Anyway, while I was there, I was of course, approached by someone. It was exactly what I expected. Just some guy who was plastered and couldn't even walk straight. When he got up to me, he didn't speak his words...he breathed them.

"He then said, 'Hi, what's your name?' His voice was incredibly weak, obviously, though, not as weak as his adrenalin.

"I didn't tell him my name, thinking that he couldn't even comprehend it, anyway. I'm sure he would have thought that I was talking to him, since his train of thought was superficially delusional.

"'Don't you want to talk to me?'

"Well, he was obviously coherent enough to realize that I had no interest.

"I then said, 'Look, you're drunk as all hell. I don't even know why you're wasting your time talking to me. Why don't you just go off and faint or vomit, or do whatever you have to do.'

"I was about to walk away from him when he grabbed my arm. He turned me toward him and said, 'I think you're being very rude.' He pointed his finger at me. His motion was as slurred as his speech. 'Don't you at least have the decency to tell me your name?'

"I looked at him for a moment and tried to catch a glimpse of an actual person. But all I saw was a walking existence of liquor. I could even smell it on his breath. I then just shook my head and walked away.

"I walked over to my friend and told her that I wanted to go.

"'But, Nora, the party hasn't even gotten started.'

"'Brittany,' I told her, 'this party is full of drunks that just want to get laid. This isn't fun; this is an excuse for an orgy.'

"'But that's the fun.' There was a mischievous smile on her face.

"I told her, 'Look, I really want to go. Please, forgive me for doing this, but I'm just not having fun here.'

"She looked at me for a moment then said that she'd forgive me. She gave me a hug goodbye and I left.

"After I left the party, I looked to see if anyone, especially that pathetic guy who approached me, was following me. When my worries were subsided, I got into the car and drove home...or at least I thought I drove home.

"When the next morning came, I had a massive headache. For a moment, all I could see was a blur of images fading in and out, just the surroundings of my apartment. But as my focus became clearer, I could feel the presence of someone near. In fact, I could see someone in front of me dressing. From what I could see through my clouded vision, a man was zipping his pants up——still, I felt warmth next to me, the kind of warmth that could only be provided by another body. I looked to my left and saw a face. My still-focusing eyes could only see a darkening shadow.

"All of a sudden, my security was shattered, but I had a drive to know what was going on. So, I didn't say a thing until things became clearer. Then, clarity came at a sudden pace. The blurriness quickly came together, and the darkening shadow was leaving this face. I could see. It was the man that had approached me last night. He was in my bed and he was naked. I realized that so was I. I covered myself as the man next to me, said, 'You're up.'

"I looked at the man putting on his coat. 'Come on,' he said, 'let's go.'

"As the other got out of my bed and began to dress, images of last night were slamming into my mind. They were only glimpses, but they were enough to push my sensitivity. They were heartless images, pictures of sexual deviance, and screams, and hurtful laughter, and an overpowering sense of a body's greed. There were two voices merging, two sets of laughter bearing down on me.

"'What happened?' I had asked through my awakening.

"They wouldn't answer; they just continued to dress.

"'What happened?' My voice was getting higher, but they were ignoring me. As they left, I screamed, 'WHAT HAPPENED!?'

"They left through the door, and left me with only unanswered questions. All I could do was hold my body as it shivered under my own deepening misery.

"I began to cry as the images still ripped into my head with no conscience." She stopped, then. She didn't say a word for a few moments.

His painting slowed, and it kept trailing off until it completely stopped. He slowly looked up and saw that she was beginning to shiver.

"I'm sorry," he said.

"Yes, well, it happened, it's over. It's in the past and it should be forgotten." He was confused for a moment. "Then why did you decide to tell me?"

"I don't know," was all she could say right now. She just continued to stand in her imprisoned stance.

He exhaled, slowly. The sound echoed through both their ears. "Please," he said just below a whisper, "get dressed."

She looked down at him. "Don't you want to continue?"

He put the brush down. "No," he said. "I just want you to get dressed. You can leave if you want."

"No, I don't want to leave. Please, just keep on painting." She looked back up.

"I'm almost done now. I don't need your body anymore. I can do the rest from memory."

"Won't you just continue painting? I promise, I won't tell anymore stories."

He put his hand up to his forehead as he looked down. When he looked back up to her, he said, "Yes, but that's not the point." He didn't say anything for the next few seconds. "But you can stay if you want."

She breathed a few times, breaths that were incredibly deep. "Okay," she said as she began to gather her clothes. He put his head down as she began to dress.

This time, there was no seductive dance, no teasing movements. She just casually put her clothes back on. However, her movements still didn't indicate shame. Afterward, she walked over to the couch and sat. "So, when can I see it?"

"When it's done," he said as he walked over to her. He then sat down next to her and looked at her, sympathetically. "Why?"

She looked at him through misunderstanding eyes. "Why what?" Her voice was high and unsure.

"Why, why did you tell me that story?"

Hiding Beneath Colors

The storm was relentless with its malevolent lightning tormenting the skies, screaming for the thunder to complete them. There was no rhythm to the progressively harsh rain. It was as disorganized as that familiar and indifferent gravity pulling the water droplets to the earth, causing them to slam into one another. Their obliteration was coming to a chaotic order. The windows had to endure the force of pressing liquid. It was an ocean in pieces, clutching for their crevices. And this rectangular shape had to intake the warping of its foundation, diminishing its structure close to the breaking point. However, the storm had only begun, and the worst was yet to be seen.

Confusion remained to mask her face. "What do you mean, 'Why did I tell you that story?'"

He brought his face closer. "Nora, you tell me this dramatic and heart-wrenching story, and you describe it with such detail. I know you. You would never put that much emotion into something unless you had a reason."

She looked away from him. "Maybe I just wanted to tell you the story."

"No," he shook his head, lightly. "I think there's more to it than that. I think that maybe you were trying to tell me something."

"I did tell you something." She looked to him, again. "The story, it's as simple as that."

"That's bullshit. That was no simple story. There is a reason why you told it to me. Someone doesn't suddenly decide to tell another a traumatic story such as that just for the hell of it."

"We were exchanging stories, Blake, and I decided to tell you that one."

"God, I hope you're not fucking with me." He paused for a moment as he folded his hands in his lap. Suspicion was shadowing his perception again. "Yes, we were exchanging stories, the kind that were merely happenings and a little introspective. And then you decide to spring *that* one on me."

"What about my story with the curtains? Don't you think that was just as traumatic as the other one?"

"You said it yourself, Nora: 'I wasn't even traumatized, not even in the least.' The curtain story had only intrigue and some emotional damage. But you're whole confession about those two guys, it went beyond just yourself."

She got up from the couch and said, "Blake, sometimes, things just are, like I've been trying to tell you. Just because I tell you something that had an effect on me doesn't mean I'm telling you more." She rapidly turned around. "Maybe that was beginning to surface in my mind after so long and I had to let it out, did you ever think of that?"

He thought for a moment, and then said, "No."

"Well, maybe you should." She turned toward him, again. The only following movement was the angle in her eyes piercing his silent armor.

"But...."

She rolled her eyes while exhaling, deeply as though it carried like a small trail on her breath. "But *what*?" she asked as she straightened her eyes.

"But I still have a suspicion that wasn't the entire truth."

"And what tells you that?" She arched her left eyebrow while folding her arms.

He was now perfectly still and looking at her with perception engraving upon his face. "My instincts."

"Well, sometimes even that can be wrong."

"Not in this case."

"Oh, my God, Blake!" she yelled, exasperated. She thrust her arms downward with enough force to jolt her head. "Will you please just drop it!? I'm getting tired of talking about this!"

She stopped talking for a moment, and then said, "In fact, if you don't drop this, I will leave."

He gave her a smug look. "You're not going to do that."

She let out a quick burst of air weighed inside her voice. "And why is that?"

"Because if you really wanted to leave, you would have done it by now."

She became still, once more. A transparent contemplation was clutching her face. Her eyes said everything. He struck a nerve inside her.

She heavily exhaled once again in a prolonged sigh before walking over to him and slowly sitting down. She put her hands to her sides and said, "Okay, perhaps you're right."

He smiled, satisfied with his brief insight.

"Maybe I am trying to tell you something. Maybe that is correct." She looked down, but as she looked back up, it was obvious that there were scheming thoughts beneath her eyes. "All right, I'll tell you the truth…on one condition."

He tilted his head to its side. "And what's that?"

"I want you to tell me a traumatic story of your own. And don't make it up this time."

"Are you ever going to let me down of that?"

She smiled, slightly. "Maybe."

His eyes were fixated within a blank stare suggesting thought. "Okay," he said, "this won't be easy to confess, but here it goes."

"Wait a minute," she said. "I'm not through, yet."

"Through with what?"

"With what all I want you to do."

"There's more?"

"Yes."

She silenced herself for a moment, looking at him with an arched eyebrow, and then said, "Before you start, I would like you to just stand in front of your easel," she delicately nodded to it, "and undress."

His eyes became two gaping holes buried inside disbelief as the word, "Why?" fell from his lips.

"Blake, you're not shy."

"No, Norah, you should know that about me. I just want to know why you would request such a thing. Is this just a part of a game? Because if it is, I swear—"

"No, no it's not," she said. "Trust me."

"Well, then, why?"

Her eyes were roaming, suggesting that the answer was something she wanted to avoid.

"Be-because. I just want to find some sort of commonality in this. If, um, ah, if I'm going to tell you something, something that I would have trouble confessing in the first place," she stopped for a moment, "I-I just want to find some sort of, um, common ground between us. Even, even if it is just on the, um, surface."

Telling that to him had made something clear. The way she expressed that want, it was beginning to show that this was something she really needed to be, a connection she needed for her own security. And he knew making such vulnerabilities that transparent was something she did not do easily.

He smiled within a comfortable light and complete understanding. "Okay," he said. Even his voice reached absolute contentment.

He got up and walked toward the easel. When he turned around, he reached for the first button and released it as the air was rapidly attending to his exposed flesh. He followed with each plastic circle, doing so at a slow pace. His shirt was loosening its grip, sliding down against his upper body. He began to pull it out of his jeans to reach the remaining buttons. After the last was undone, he removed it and let it fall to the floor.

He removed his shoes and socks, and then let his bare feet touch the slight cold of the floor. His fingers edged for the buckle of his belt and opened it. Slowly, it slithered beneath the denim latches surrounding the top of his jeans. It made a clattering sound as it landed. He detached the button of his pants from its slit, inevitably followed by the zipper. The jeans were letting go. He slowly pulled them down, his fingers sliding against the hairs of his legs. He stepped out of each leg and dropped them.

He reached for the top of his underwear, wedging his thumbs into the upper band and closed the rest of his fingers on the outside. The knuckles of his thumbs were pushing into the outer edges of his buttocks. And slowly, he let the last of his clothing fall to the floor just as carelessly as the rest.

The air was now caressing an exposed body, trim in its appearance.

He stood erect and looked right at her, signifying that his shame was nonexistent.

"It all happened on a night where I thought I'd be safe. It wasn't that long ago. In fact, it was only about seven months ago. Anyway, I was seeing this guy named Rodger. Rodger was quite different from anyone else I knew. And, actually, this was one of the most intense relationships I've ever had. Our sexual play was almost like an alternate world, where any fantasy could be played out. It was almost like touching fire, and getting close enough just to feel the heat searing against your fingertips. I could barely hold onto myself whenever we were having sex. I can remember that when I was even hugging my body around him, I could still feel myself slipping away.

"Anyway, we decided to go to a club one night. It was a club that I had heard of, but I was never willing to approach it. It had this reputation, things I've heard that I can't even imagine. However, Rodger instilled in me this courageous

46

sense that I could approach anything. My security lay completely in his hands.

"As we got in line, I noticed right away that this was the kind of place that was very alternative. I could hear the music inside. It blasted this hardcore sound that was completely alien to me. It was just a sound that thrashed with a beat digging deeper inside my head until it felt like metallic nails.

"Now, I was getting very apprehensive. My heart was practically beating out of my chest and I just wanted to turn to him and say something. So, I did.

"I turned right around to him and said, 'Look, Rodger, I don't think we should do this right now. I really don't think I'm ready.' However, it didn't come out like that. It was just a rambling of words that I could barely even get out because of my extreme nervousness. Rodger understood and he said to me that it was okay, and that we didn't have to do this right now.

"I left with him as we walked away from the club. I was now feeling completely secure and relieved. Little did I know, I was only trapping myself.

"As I've said before, Rodger was a pretty intense guy. He really pushed the limits with me, but I never figured he'd go too far. This night would prove otherwise.

"I noticed we were walking in a desolate area. I was beginning to see less and less people walk by. And I knew that the car wasn't that far away, all though I didn't say anything. Then, the amount of people around us went from barely existent to completely *non*existent. Now, I had to say something. But I didn't get the chance.

"I felt a slam against my head and fell to the floor. I turned my body around as he picked my legs up. He began dragging me at such a fast pace that I couldn't get to him. When we stopped, I was about to punch him. But he turned me around and put a strong hold around my throat with his arm. He began to punch my face, continuously as I tried to grab his fist. His motions were fast and mine were only falling behind.

"I could feel the blood begin to flow, profusely, from my nose. My mouth had to open, or I would lose breath. As a result, the fluid was falling on my tongue and I could feel it dribble toward the back of my mouth. My vision flew by as I could feel myself being pushed to the wall. My entire body vibrated heavily as it was slammed against the reddening bricks of the alleyway. I fell to the floor as he let me go.

"I then looked up. The person I was staring at was not Rodger. Even through my blurred vision, I could see that it wasn't him. I could mainly tell from the color of his coat. It was the only thing that stood out.

"Everything faded to black, and the next morning, I found myself lying in my bed."

She looked to him with sympathy and said, "Where was Rodger when this happened?"

"I don't know. The strangest thing is, though, Rodger was there with me that morning. He told me that he walked away, thinking that I was still with him."

"What did you say?"

"I told him that I didn't believe him. He tried telling me differently. We argued and then we broke up. I never saw him again."

She looked to the floor, the obvious question in the back of her mind. She looked up, quickly forming the words in her head and spoke. "Why would you date a man so dangerous?"

He laughed, slightly. "I thought I could handle it."

"Oh."

He smiled, again, and then began to gather his clothes.

"Now, why did you tell me that story?" he asked as he was pulling his pants back up.

"I will tell you when you finished getting dressed."

After he was completely dressed, he walked over to her and sat down. There was an intense curiosity drowning inside the blue of his eyes. "Tell me," he said almost in a whisper.

"I want to know one more thing about your story."

He looked at her with an annoyance. "What?" he said with a quick tongue.

"The coat, what color was it?"

He exhaled, deeply, and then said, "Midnight blue."

She nodded her head slightly, in acknowledgement, and said nothing as her eyes wandered the room for a moment. When she looked to him again, she said, "You know them."

His eyes expanded into a seemingly knowing curiosity, "Know who?"

"You know who, Blake."

He tilted his head. "You mean the two men…in your story?"

"Yes."

He then arched his eyebrows and delicately shook his head. "How do you know I know them?"

"I just do."

"I wish that you would tell me more, here."

"You just know them. That is all that I know."

He got up from the couch while continuing to look at her. A deeply concentrated stare shot out of his eyes like daggers. "If you know that I have some sort of connection to the people that did this to you, then you should know what that connection is. I don't think that you're telling me everything."

"What do you mean? This is all I know, honest. There is nothing else that I am hiding from you."

"What is that supposed to mean!? Saying that only implicates you're not telling me other things. I knew I shouldn't have trusted you." He shook his head, slowly, as he said that. He then rapidly walked over to the front door and went for the handle.

"No, please. Look, I'm telling you everything. I don't know what I have to say to convince you of this."

He opened the door while standing beside it, looking at her in that deadly gaze. He then said, "I think you know what to do."

She got up and slowly walked toward him. Her eyebrows painted two pleading lines deepened into the folds of her skin. "Blake, please, don't make me go. I can't leave. I can't leave this place."

A new confusion clouded his mind. "What are you getting at, Nora?"

"Look, right now, I feel safe with you. I'm beginning to believe that you're the only person I can trust right now." Her voice was fluctuating as her face became distressed.

He looked at her for a long moment. The silence was slowly dousing the room in a restless shade. He exhaled, slowly, as he began to close the door. She expressed an obvious relief as he pushed the door closed with his back against it.

He put his arms up to his chest and folded them. "Now what are you getting at?"

She looked at him, a concrete fear broken upon the subtle trembles of her face, which remained nearly motionless inside a transparent desperation. "I can't tell you everything."

He threw his arms up and slapped them to his sides as he quickly walked to the couch. "I knew it," he said as he flopped down. "I knew there was something you were hiding from me."

She turned to him. "All I can say is that you know them."

"And why do you feel safer here than anyplace else?"

"I feel very vulnerable out there, Blake. I fear that they might come back."

"What else has been going on, Nora?"

"What do you mean?" A seeming innocence shadowed her voice.

"I mean if you fear these two guys this much, then something more must have happened than that one night. If these were simply two perverted sickos who wanted to get their rocks off through only one night, then you would have just called the police and forgotten about the whole thing."

"I didn't call the police."

He suddenly became still for one moment while looking directly at her. "What do you mean you didn't call the police? Why didn't you call the police?"

She sat next to him in one quick and desperate movement. "Because I just couldn't, that wouldn't have been a good decision."

"Why wouldn't it have been a good decision?"

"Why do you have to question everything? Look, I'm telling all I can tell you right now! I can't say anymore."

"'Right now?' What do you mean by 'right now'?"

"Please."

"All right then. But I want to know another thing."

"What!?"

"That whole experience, with the two men, is that the main reason *why* you agreed to meet with me, today?"

There was a long silence. "Yes."

"And so you had no one else to turn to, and you just thought of your ol' buddy Blake."

"Yes."

"And you came over here just to confess to me these things in your life."

She turned to him and whispered, "Yes."

"So, I see. Well, things certainly haven't changed, you're still using people."

"I never used you."

"Of course you did, you're doing it right now."

She pushed her back off the couch and looked at him with bewilderment in her eyes. "When have I ever used you?"

"Let's remember back and count the ways. You've used some of my friends as some of your little flings. You've taken some of my things without giving them back."

"I can't belie—"

"Oh, yeah, and let's not forget the time that you even used *me* as one of your little flings."

"I told you I didn't want to talk about that!" she yelled as she got up from the couch and began to quickly pace through the apartment.

He followed her and started speaking so close to her that his breath felt hot on her ears as their flickering shadows were floating amongst the darkened reflections of the storm. "Well, you're the one that brought it up, Nora. And

50

since you're here, anyway, let's talk about it. Don't you remember? 'Oh, Blake, I would never do anything to hurt you!' 'Oh, Blake, you're my only true friend!' 'Oh, Blake, please, it'll only be just this once!'"

She turned around quickly, her hair slashing the air like brown flames. "Why are you bringing this up, now!? After what I've just told you! If you wanna talk about using people, let's talk about you and my ex-husband!"

He stepped right up to her and said, "Well, we all know the story behind that, don't we!?"

"What you're saying is a lie! I loved Quinton! I really did! The best years of my life were with that man!"

He laughed with one brief exhalation. "Ha! Don't you mean *year*!?"

"Well, we both know why that was, don't we!? You seduced him! You fucked him!"

"He didn't do anything he didn't want to do. Besides, you weren't exactly wife of the year."

"So what if I cheated on him!"

"You lied every day you were with this dream man of yours!"

She turned away from him. "I cannot believe you, Blake! You are as heartless as any other man in my life!"

"Then why are you even here if you believe that!"

"Because I *have* to be!"

The storm was still raging, still throwing its symphony of sounds and images toward them.

"You know what!?" He stopped for a moment and put his hands to his sides. He lowered his voice to a grave tone as his eyes became motionless and cold. "You know what? You should talk about being heartless. You say you loved Quinton, yet you ran all around town flaunting your shit to any person that would accept it. You were a major slut and you still are. Your whole life has been spent disguising truths and back-stabbing anyone that got close to you. You're a complete loner and you have no friends and no life. The only friends you *do* have are ones that are there just to make things look pretty to the outside world. I think the only reason you've gotten yourself into half these situations is because you put yourself in them."

She stood for a moment. She was completely still for what seemed like an eternity. She then broke her stunned silence. "You're no better."

"Is that right!?"

"Yeah, that's right. You talk all this time about trying to make your dreams come true, trying to make your mark in society when you're too afraid to even take one step outside your little world. You've sacrificed so much of your life just to hide from everything. The only people you ever get involved with are ones that overpower you."

"Fuck you!"

"I'm not finished yet."

He walked away from her. "Yeah, well, you can stop."

"Why should I?"

He turned around and said, "Because if you don't, I am going to throw you out."

She walked up to him, slowly, while running her fingers through her dark brown hair, her soft brown eyes staring coldly into his. She stopped and said, "You wouldn't do that."

"No?"

"No, you wouldn't."

"What makes you think I won't?"

She sighed as she flopped down onto the couch. "Look, are we going to argue all day? Can't we at least try to make peace?"

He smiled, sarcastically. "Peace?" He nodded his head, quickly, a few times as if to emphasize his disrespect for her using such a word. "You completely obliterated any possibility of that." He sat down next to her. "Right now, peace really isn't an option."

"So, we're just going to continue arguing?" She arched her left eyebrow and moved her head forward to the right.

He laid his back on the couch. "I don't know *what* we're going to do."

She began forming a mischievous grin.

He looked at her with incredible skepticism. "Not that. You have more of a one-track mind than anyone else I know."

"Oh, Blake...Blake, Blake, Blake. You were never one for bravery, were you?"

He got back up. "Why do you keep saying that? I do not hide from things."

"Need I remind you of the Kalgon party?"

He formed a look of disbelief. "You're going to bring that up? I had no choice in that situation."

She smiled, smugly. "You had a chance, there, Blake, and you fucked it up. They were all waiting for you."

"Will you please not talk about this?" He got back up from the couch as he spoke.

"Why, you certainly didn't let me down of anything, did you?"

"Look, let's just drop it, okay?" His desperate need to stop the conversation was heavily imprinted on his face and from the way he crossed his arms together and darted them away from each other.

"No, Blake, I'm not going to drop it. You know why?"

"Why!? Go on and tell me. It's not as if I can stop you anyway."

"Because for someone that talked so much about making their dreams come true, you didn't do jack shit to make any of them a reality! You had a real chance their, Blake. You could have been in the spot light for once in your life instead of running away from it. And why didn't any of this happen for you?"

"Don't!" he said while pointing at her with a shaken hand, his eyes widening as he continued to compulsively walk around the apartment.

"No, Blake, tell me why? Why didn't you go?"

"Just shut up!"

She followed him with her stare while moving around on the couch. "Why didn't any of that shit you've been talking about for so long come true?"

"Nora." His voice was scolding.

"Why, Blake?"

He stopped and rapidly turned around. "BECAUSE I DIDN'T TRUST HIM!"

She laughed, quickly, as she slouched down in the couch and looked straight ahead. "You may think that was the reason why, Blake, but it is not so."

"Oh, it's not?" he said, putting his face next to hers then pulling away.

"You were scared, Blake. You didn't go there because you were scared. It wasn't because you didn't trust anyone; you were just scared as all hell. That man had real connections and he could have gotten you places. But you decided to hide inside yourself, once again."

"I would really like it if you would just shut up about this." He began walking in circles around her.

"And, of course, once you made your decision, the first person you called was me."

"Yeah, that was when I thought I could trust you."

"No, you just wanted someone to clear your conscience. You were even invited as one of the honored guests."

"I didn't know if they were going to plagiarize my work! Or if they were going to use me or what!" He tried to engrave a genuine truth to his voice, but it was contradicted by the uncertainty of his face.

"All of those people were really interested and they weren't going to plagiarize your work. You were invited there because they wanted to see it."

He stopped. He walked up to her and laid his hands on either side of her, pressing against the couch. He stared at her with cornered eyebrows. "And how would you know that?"

Her face formed a knowing look. "Because, Blake, I knew them. I knew a lot of people at that party. You seem to forget, I do have connections, too. They were the genuine deal."

His face went completely blank. "Bitch!" He pushed himself off the couch.

"You were practically in tears when you called me, Blake. You wanted so much to know that you were right."

"Why didn't you tell me, why didn't you just say to me that I was wrong!?"

"Because it was too…late."

He stopped. "What do you mean, 'It was too late?'"

"Someone called me just before you did that night."

His eyes became bigger. "You don't mean…."

"Yes, I do. He called me. He told me that he was incredibly interested in your work. He really wanted to take advantage of it all. But he was also very pissed. He said that he didn't want to see you again. That you stood him up and all of the waiting guests that were there to see your work."

"Why would he call you?"

"Because, Blake, I helped set up the party."

An electric stream flashed into the fisted clouds after she said that, capturing her face in the reflection of a conniving ghost.

"He came to me, Walter Kalgon came to me on the very day he met you. He said that he discovered this amazing new talent. He needed help arranging everything and I was one of the people that assisted him. We had a very long discussion on how everything in that party was going to be and especially on this new talent he raved about. It was only when you called me that night that I could put two and two together and I realized that you were the talent."

"You're fucking with me."

"I wouldn't kid around about anything like this, Blake. I speak nothing but the truth."

"You bitch! You lying cunt!"

She raised her head in a scheming way. When she lowered it back down, she said, "I'm sorry, but the truth hurts. That is what happened and you threw it all away."

He walked back toward the wall as he spoke. "It's funny how you went from being in tears to being so calm." When he reached the wall, he laid his back against it. "Quite a mood swing, don't you think?"

54

She smiled, slightly. "I guess it is." Her smile was then depleted into perfectly-aligned lips. "But what you're making me out to be, it's not true."

"Oh? And what am I 'making you out to be'?" The abstract constructions in the apartment cast a shadow overtop his head. However, the reflection of dim lights could be seen hiding inside his pupils.

"You're painting a picture of me that is not true, Blake. You think I'm playing with your mind. I'm just trying to help you."

"Help me?"

"Yes." She sat perfectly still. Her upper body remained completely erect while her hands lay in her lap, assuming the fashioned position of a lady. "I'm trying to bring you out of yourself."

"If you're trying to do this, Nora, then why didn't you tell me about you knowing these people, having these specific connections?"

"I already told you, it was too late."

"You could have gone to any of your other connections."

"The news had already spread, or would have, eventually. There was nothing that I could do. And you certainly never asked me for help."

"You now, all the time that we were friends, I assumed you would have helped me with anything without me having to ask."

"No, Blake. I didn't know whether you wanted my help. You were just so afraid of rejection that I wasn't sure if you would feel comfortable with it. I wasn't sure if it would have made you feel incompetent."

"Incompetent? What the hell are you talking about? All you had to do was ask me if I needed any help. And I think you know that."

"Blake, you're just being difficult. I'm beginning to think that you want to argue just for the sake of arguing."

"You should talk. You're always arguing about something with somebody."

"I never argue. When was the last time you saw me angry?"

He laughed. The laugh was close to a whisper. "I never said that you got angry, I just said that you debate."

"You said 'argue.'"

"Argue, debate, it's the same difference. The only reason you ever 'argue' is because you are trying to get what you want. Sometimes, you act like a spoiled rich girl who only likes certain kinds of people."

"That's not fair, Blake. I have all kinds of friends."

He laughed again. "Well, yeah, but they're all rich. You never even gave Dave a chance. Ever since day one you've given him the cold shoulder."

55

"Are we going to talk about him again?"

"The only reason I'm bringing him up is because you are a very biased person, Nora. If they don't have money, then they're just pretty much shit. You've surrounded yourself with this circle of wealth just so you can ignore the rest of society."

"I didn't ignore you."

"No, you didn't. But that's only because you wanted something from me." She smiled, sarcastically. "And what was that?"

"Well, if it wasn't my support that always seemed to boost your ego, it would be my body."

She made a slight crack of laughter. "Oh, common, just because that one time happened doesn't mean that I lusted after you. I think you're being vain and egotistical, Blake."

"Don't give me that. I always noticed you giving me those looks, not to mention all of those incredibly awkward things you used to say. 'I wonder what it would be like if we were more than friends.' 'Haven't you ever wondered what it would be like with a woman?' Oh, and how about, 'I think you're just confused. You need to sleep with a woman you know, someone you trust.'"

Her mouth gaped open. "I can't believe you picked out those tiny little phrases from the other trillions of things that I have said to you in conversation. You're looking into this too much."

"That's what you always say when you want to find a way out of a conversation."

"I'm not looking for a way out. I'm stating the truth."

"The truth seems to get awfully twisted when you explain it."

"I have been nothing but completely honest with you."

"Now that is a bold-faced lie. You've lied to get you're way out of certain situations. Not to mention that you've lied just to make others feel like they were below you."

"I have never done that. Sometimes, I think you say things a certain way because it sounds better. You have always overstated yourself, in addition to the fact that you are constantly worried about only yourself. 'How does my hair look?' 'Do you think this shirt looks okay?' You would ask me questions like that, constantly."

"So what if I'm vain. You, however, are the queen of vanity."

She sat back in the chair as she crossed her arms over her chest. "I don't continuously ask about myself. And I don't compliment myself all the time."

"Exactly. You just say things about your hair being too flat, or your eyes not being pretty enough, or your figure not being just right. I think you say those things only so you can hear a compliment in return."

"When I do hear those compliments, Blake, I don't really accept them, do I?"

"No, you don't. You just want to derive sympathy from people. You say and do things only to inspire others around you."

"Inspire them to what?"

"Inspire them to compliment you, to want to think the world of you because you don't think that much of yourself. However, that's how things only appear on the surface."

"What makes you think that you know me so well?"

"We *were* friends for quite a while, and you did confess many things to me."

"So, that doesn't mean that you know everything about me."

"Are you kidding me? You exposed just about every thought in your head to me. Every single time that I'd call, you would tell me all these things that were going on in your life, and then you would turn to me whenever you got in any kind of trouble, because I was such the good friend and you just needed someone to talk to." He began to speak mockingly.

"What are you trying to say, Blake?"

"I'm saying that you used me as a crutch, because you knew that I thought so much of you. You took my image of you and used it for your own benefit. That's the only reason that everyone loved you so much. Because you would play the part that was wanted, you could be anything that anybody wanted you to be."

"I am my own person. I do not subject myself to others. I live just fine on my own. You really need to start finding your *own* life, Blake, and stop accusing everyone else of living theirs."

"You are no longer looked upon as my mentor, Nora, so stop acting like it."

She smirked. "The only reason you wanted me to be your mentor was because I was the only one you felt safe around. So you followed me around like a little puppy that's lost his way."

He walked toward her as the shadows slowly escaped from the light. The darkened reflections from the water straggling down the windows were masking his flesh. He then stopped halfway. "You just think that you have everyone figured out, don't you? You were always full of yourself that way."

She sat with crossed legs, resuming her imitation of a lady's position. "I'm beginning to believe that the only reason you think I'm so egotistical is because you're trying to blame me for how much you praised me, how you put me up on this pedestal that no one could possibly reach. I think you needed someone to be good in your life since you weren't going to be."

"You always have an answer for everything, always trying to make everything sound so philosophical and so well planned out, when in reality, you're nothing but hot air."

"It has nothing to do with philosophy, Blake. It is truth, just simple truth. You know, the stuff that you always tried to fit into your world your own little way?"

"I can't believe that you are being so—"

Suddenly, there was a loud buzzing, disrupting their angered conversation with its tearing sound. It was coming from the small rectangular security system next to his front door.

"Oh, well, that's probably Dave," Blake said as he was about to walk over to buzz him in.

Nora turned her head toward him, rapidly. "No, don't!" Her voice became suddenly pleading.

"What do you mean?" he asked while still walking over to it.

"I mean don't let him in, please! You can't!" She looked at him with a new desperation. Her hand was pressing into the arm of the couch, her face lost in a desolate appearance.

"Nora, just because you don't like him doesn't mean that he should be shunned."

"Blake, please, listen to me, you can't let him in."

He ignored her as he went for the button.

"Blake!" Still, no reaction, "Blake, remember my story!? About the two men!?"

He stopped. He turned around, slowly. The box rang out again. His face was completely blank for a few moments. "What do you mean?"

"Blake, listen to what I'm trying to tell you. Why do you think I never really liked Dave? Why do you think we never got along? Dave and I had a past, you know this, but you never knew what kind."

Another beep sounded off.

"You're fucking with me!" he said as he pointed at her.

"No, I'm not! Please, please listen. I'm not playing with your mind this time." Her voice became breathless and her movements began to lose control. "Listen to what I am trying to say, please!"

He waited for a moment, and there was complete silence. Then, the same buzzing sound broke the silence and made them both shudder. He walked over to her, slowly, his face still unsure. She was beckoning him over with her obvious despair. He then sat down on the couch with her. "It's all right," he whispered. He put his hands around her arms, they were quivering. "It's okay." He brought her toward him and they embraced.

Another ripping scream came from the machine. It was becoming a knife that was cutting into them and was almost taunting them in the form of mechanical laughter, making a possibly menacing existence known just outside.

Then, another sound from the machine, this one was prolonged and carried itself on a cry to be heard. They tried to ignore it, even though it was forcing its way into their ears, and grasping their already fearful thoughts inside their skulls. After that, it began to pulsate, segmenting its screams into short gasps of electronic menace. Then, silence.

They waited for another sound, hoping it wouldn't come. Their insides began to twist within a distressing maze. They were holding onto each other, hoping to find a sense of safety. They continued to wait. The time slowed to what seemed like an eternity as the storm was continuing with its raging conflictions almost synchronizing with theirs.

When there wasn't another sound, they let go.

Blake looked at her and said, "When were you going to tell me this?"

She nodded her head, slightly. "I don't know. I knew I just couldn't yet."

"Why?"

"I didn't feel safe enough. I wasn't sure if you would, if you would tell him."

He exhaled through his nose in one long release. Then, his eyebrows arched in confusion. "Wait, if Dave couldn't get up stairs, then how did that man get up here?"

"What man?"

"The man that knocked at the door, the one asking for you."

She stared at him, blankly, for a moment.

He shook his head, quickly, a few times, appearing to find the right words to ask. "Don't you remember?" His eyes were becoming evident of a thirst to know as he pulled himself closer to her, stopping to leave just enough space between their faces. "Don't you remember the man at the door?"

"Yes," she said, her voice was weakened. "Yes, I remember."

He backed away while he sat himself in another position, placing his left foot next to her leg on the couch as he lay back. "Well." His hands went upward. As they went back down, he said, "Aren't you going to say anything? "

She saw that he was obviously trying to put himself at ease. "Yes, I remember the man at the door, the one that was asking for me."

"Didn't he seem familiar? From what you heard of his voice?"

She arched her left eyebrow. "Didn't he seem familiar to *you*?"

He shot back up. "Why?"

"You don't remember his face from anywhere?" She delicately shook her head.

"No, I don't…should I?" His eyes roamed a bit and looked back at her as he spoke.

"I don't know, Blake. I'm just having a thought here, and I'm wondering if you can confirm it."

"What's your thought?" His voice rose up at the end of the statement. His face was becoming curious.

"It's just a thought."

He exhaled with a push of his voice as his hands went up and diverted into opposite directions. "Well, aren't you going to tell me?"

"You have to remember, Blake. You have to be the one to remember."

He got up and walked away from her, then turned around to look back. "Why do *I* have to be the one to remember? Can't you just tell me?"

"No, you have to do this on your own. Don't you remember, Blake? Was Rodger seeing anyone else while he was with you?"

"You're fucking with me!"

"No, I'm not fucking with you." She put her head forward. "Tell me, was Rodger seeing anyone else while he was with you? Even flirting with anyone else?"

He began to walk around the room, again. "I can't believe this."

The storm was now reaching a higher level of intensity as the lightning continued to cut its way into the dark.

He ran his fingers through his hair and slid them downward. "What are you trying to do to me?!"

"Blake, please remember!"

He didn't look up. He began to reach in the back of his mind. His footsteps were feeling heavier. His eyes roamed the floor, staring into the reflections. "I don't know! I don't know! I DON'T KNOW!"

"Blake, you remember, you just don't want to say it."

Still, he didn't look up. "What are you trying to get at?"

"Blake, think about yourself. Think about your life. Does anything seem off…different?"

Her voice was slowly becoming a character working into his mind. The reflections on the floor were now blurring his vision. "What do you mean? Stay consistent with your questions!"

"There can be no consistency here, Blake. Not in the place that you're at, now. Think."

His thoughts were beginning to pulsate inside his head until it ached. There was a blur of memories building around him. He could hear his footsteps becoming lighter, fading into echoes. He was coming closer to a feeling of solitude. It was an unusual emotion, one that was starting to disconnect him.

He looked up and closed his eyes. The only sounds he could hear were that of the storm. The pulsating lights were reaching inside his now overshadowed eyes. The thunder crackled across the sky like a ghost.

Everything around him was fading. His weight was feeling lighter as he kept coming closer to a thought that had been blocked. He was being pulled toward something he wasn't sure of. Pictures were forming inside his mind. Clutters of images ran together. He began to speak.

"I see a collage, a collage of colors. Wait, they're beginning to move. The colors are dancing now. I can see that there is a shadow covering them. It's fading in and out. It's stopped now, leaving only half of the colors to be seen.

"I'm beginning to see what looks like body parts, mostly hands. The hands are moving back and forth and they're connecting to the colors, almost as if the colors are nothing more than…clothes.

"I'm seeing faces, now. But they're not looking at me. They're looking at each other. The top half that was overshadowed is now beginning to turn into something else. I'm seeing that the shadow is forming a depth. It has a construction. It's shaping itself into a form.

"Now, I see. The top of the shadow is the top half of a room, a very big room. And this room is filled with a pulsating light. The colors have turned into completely formed bodies, now. They're dancing with each other.

"But they're around something. I don't know what, though. All I see are two sets of arms sliding against each other. And I'm hearing music blaring. It's vibrating inside my ears.

"Wait, the crowd of bodies, they're spreading apart. And the two sets of arms, now I see that they're two people, two men dancing, almost grinding against one another. The other people, they have formed a wall around them, and I'm standing where this wall ends. I can see the two men dancing against one another. One has his back toward the other's front.

"One of them is Rodger. He's smiling; he's the one dancing with his back against the other. And the other, I see his face now. He's, he's…he's the man that was at the door, the one that knocked on the door."

He opened his eyes, and he found himself back in the apartment. He turned his head to Nora; she was standing in the room.

He looked around, "Where'd the couch go?"

She walked toward him as he looked to her. "Blake, tell me, tell me now what you know."

He looked into her eyes as he could feel his mind being pulled toward them. His thoughts focused in on her pupils at a rapid pace and he saw lightning inside them. He went for the lightning.

He now found himself mentally surrounded by the storm and became lost in it. His thoughts were beginning to focus on what was outside, behind him. His mind slowly pulled backward as it lowered down toward the buildings engulfed in the midnight blue. Each building was almost the same, each one was black, and each one was designed to a dismal perfection.

He pulled his thoughts back into the apartment. He saw Nora's eyes, now. They were filled with lightning. Streaks of a haunting white were fading in and out of existence within her pupils.

He turned toward the wall on the left and saw a small mirror. It was circular. The outer edge was surrounded in an exquisite golden design. He came closer to his reflection. He saw his eyes. They were engulfed in the image of the buildings outside, compressed into the shape of his eyes and embellished in that one color he always identified with himself. His mind was beginning to shatter. "I *am* Rodger."

Suddenly, the glass from the mirror broke. The shards flew outward, reaching for him like small hands. He did not evade them. Motion was beginning to slow. He could see the shards repel a reflective light. The broken pieces of glass became smaller, until they condensed themselves into one merging light that was pulsating all around him inside a spacious room.

He found himself in the room he described and saw the dancing bodies surrounding him. He could feel himself moving. He looked to the back of him and saw he was moving his body against the man who knocked at the door.

He yelled over the blaring sound of the music toward the man he was dancing with and then yelled, "Blake?!"

Lost Thoughts

Strobe lights were connected to the ceiling, casting a sheet of pulsating luminosity over all the people intimately dancing.

He was in the middle of all of this as he looked to the man that seemed to be seducing him, the man now known as Blake. He had vibrant green eyes embellished in a solid shade. His blond eyebrows were painted delicately atop his soft forehead. In fact, his entire face was soft and seemed to glow within the entrapping reflections of the light. He turned back around and put himself completely against the front of Blake. Right now, it was the only place that he felt some kind of closure. As Blake was holding him, using every body part to evoke an erotic curiosity, he tried to pull his thoughts together.

He wasn't entirely sure what was happening at the moment. But the further he tried to make sense of everything, the more lost he became.

"Having fun, Rodge!?" Blake yelled into his ear.

"Yeah, sure!" he answered. With the sexual intensity and confusion swirling inside him, he somehow found that he had to say, "And don't call me Rodge! You know how I hate that name!"

"Yeah, I know! But Rodger just seems too long!"

Finding that talking in the duration of this was driving his faded sense of reality even further into his maze of thoughts, he yelled, "Let's not talk right now! Let's just dance!"

Nothing was heard but the music and the stomping feet vibrating throughout the floor.

He began to push all of his confusion down further into himself, and let the sensual nature of the experience take over, giving into the dance.

He let Blake use him through the movement. He slid the back of his body against Blake. Blake's hands were roaming his chest, Blake's fingers practically teasing his flesh hiding just beneath his clothes.

He could feel himself slowly being taken away by Blake's hands, by his arms, his legs, everything he was using. The two became intertwined in motion. He was losing his breath as he could feel his heart periodically slam against his ribs.

He wanted to take this to another level, but only dancing could be permitted now. The thought of going further was taunting him. He had to bite his bottom lip just to reach comfort as this pleasurable torture was pulling his fluids toward the center of himself.

He could feel that Blake was reaching the same emotion. He then began to use *his* hands to touch Blake. And now *his* fingers were just barely touching Blake's back. They were both tormenting each other, and deriving an excitement from it.

Blake hugged him from behind, pulling him close and Blake's mouth was now just touching the side of his right ear. "Do you want to take a breather and go up to the bar!?" Blake's lips brushed against his ear as his voice was tickling it.

He turned his head backward to face him, again. "Yeah, sure, why not!?"

They both smiled at each other as they walked up to the bar. Then he gripped Blake's hand tighter, Blake turned to face him. "Maybe we can skip the bar and just go off to fool around!"

Blake smiled, almost sarcastically. He then said, "Good one, Rodger!"

He was somewhat confused by that statement. Blake let go his of his hand and was walking away from him and toward the bar.

He stood there for a moment and looked around this place.

Colored spotlights projecting from mechanical devices began swimming through the strobe lights. He couldn't even understand the music because the volume was loud enough to heavily vibrate his ear drums.

He walked toward the bar as Blake was drinking out of a small martini glass. He sat on a swivel chair right next to Blake.

"What did you mean when you said that!?" he yelled toward him.

Blake formed a confusing look. "What do you mean!?"

"I mean, when you said, 'Good one, *Rodger!*'"

Blake looked at him as if he had just spoken an insult. "Oh, come on, Rodge!

Not that again!" He motioned his hands to agree with his words. He then put his left hand on the bar table as the other went for his hip. "We've talked about this I don't how many times! Look, please, let's not delve into this any further!"

He looked at Blake for a few moments as a light remembrance began to build in his brain. There was some sort of defiance Blake had constructed against him, one that was surrounded in supposedly good intentions. He only smiled as he bowed his head downward. When he looked back up, he yelled, "Okay! I'm sorry! Forget I said anything!"

"Don't worry about it! Listen, why don't you go for someone that's more your style!?"

"Someone like who!?"

Blake nodded his head, slightly. "I don't know. Maybe someone like Dave! You know he's been after you for about three weeks now!"

He pulled back after Blake said that. "Yeah, but, I'm not attracted to Dave!" He put his head forward and turned his eyes into a disagreeing stare. "That's what I've been *telling* you for about three weeks, now!" Rodger then turned toward the bar and rested his arms against the counter.

"Well!" Blake yelled, "Now's you're chance to tell him…for the umpteenth time!"

"What do you mean!?"

"He's headed right this way!"

He turned to his right and saw a man walking toward him. There was some sort of familiar presence about him, but he couldn't quite place it. The way his body moved, it almost seemed menacing. He had dark brown hair combed above his head. His eyes looked to be of a murky brown, his face possessing an unattractive form. It appeared that his face was carved harshly from stone, leaving a disturbing shape.

He stopped right in front of him. "Hey, Rodge!" he said as he smiled, which was almost intriguing.

"Don't call me that!" he yelled. "I keep telling everyone that and no one seems to listen!"

"Sorry! So, funny running into *you* here!" His voice was conniving.

He only arched his eyebrow as the bartender walked up to him. "So what do you want, Rodge?" the bartender asked.

Rodger looked at the bartender and was about to demand that he not use that name. But he only stared at the bartender's face and lost his words. "I guess I'll just have a beer!"

"But you hate beer!" the bartender yelled.

"So what! Just give me a damn beer!"

"Fine!"

He went under the bar and pulled out the beer. He then popped the top off with a bottle opener. Rodger was about to pay him when he put up his hand and yelled, "Don't worry about it! This one's on the house!" The bartender's voice seemed to be callous. His eyes were piercing as he walked away with a coldness imprinted upon his movements.

He put his money back in his pocket and then looked to Dave and asked, "Why did he do that!?'

Dave shook his head in disbelief. "Charley always let you have the first one free! Remember the bet!?"

"No!" he answered as he inserted the tip of the bottle into his mouth. The tainted liquid spilled over onto his tongue. Its bitterness choked his sense of taste and his gag reflex was edging against the back of his mouth. Still, he let the liquid fall down into his throat. He slammed the bottle against the counter and swallowed the beer. His resistance was overbearing as he compressed the inner lining of his throat around the foggy water.

"Why are you drinking that if you hate it so much!?" Dave asked.

"I don't know! I just felt like tasting it!" His voice was struggling to sound normal. "Anyway, what's this bet that you were talking about!?"

"We'd better not talk about that here! You know how Charlie gets whenever he hears anyone talking about it!"

"Charlie?!"

"Yeah, Charlie, you know, the guy that serves the drinks?! And the one that you've had the hots for?!"

"What are you talking about!? I don't have a crush on him!" he said this as he reflected back on Charley's looks. He began reconstructing the bartender's body from memory. His eyes were a soft brown.

His train of thought was broken when Dave asked, "Wanna dance?!"

He blinked his eyes a few times, pulling himself out of his memory. "What?!"

"Do…you…want…to…dance?!" Dave spoke to him as if he were simple and couldn't comprehend words.

"No, that's okay, really!"

Dave then looked at him. His stare was intense.

"Its okay, Dave! I really don't want to dance right now!"

"Fine!" Dave said as he got up from his chair. He was obviously disappointed. "I'll just dance with someone else!" He walked off with the same menacing motion.

He picked up the bottle of beer and looked at the liquid. He swirled it around. He was about to take another sip when Blake tapped him on his left shoulder. He turned to see him.

"You wanna go back out on the dance floor!?" Blake asked as he smiled mischievously.

"Why?!"

"Oh, come on, Rodge! Have some fun in your life and stop being such a dud!"

Rodger shook his head and said, "I think not! Why don't you just go back out there and confuse some other poor guy all to hell?!"

Blake pointed his finger at him. "That is not fair, Rodger! All I wanna do is have a little fun! That's it!" His voice was screaming to a point of anger as his face raged with expression. "Can't you ever put things in a platonic state of mind?!"

Rodger softly put his beer bottle on the counter, and then looked at Blake with a scornful stare. "That depends, Blake, why don't you try defining platonic for me!?"

His eyes became bitter and his nostrils began to flare. "Damn it, Rodger! Fine, you know what, FUCK YOU!" He walked away from Rodger. His legs moved at a fast pace.

Rodger still looked at him as he went out on the floor and randomly chose someone to dance with. His body was moving rapidly and his face was still frozen in anger.

He then turned back around to the bar and looked at his beer. He didn't want to try another taste; the last one practically killed him. But, it was that disgust that began to tease his curiosity. So he pushed the apprehensions aside and went for the bottle. He prepared himself as he put the rounded top to his mouth. His lips enclosed it as he tilted his head back.

This time, though, it was more than just a simple taste. He began to suck the liquid from the bottle. His eyes wanted to squint as it burned his tongue. He put his head back down and slammed the bottle to the counter, once more. He was surprised to find that it was already half empty.

The burning sensation still lingered inside him, making its way toward his stomach as the bartender rapidly walked over and yelled, "You okay, Rodge!?"

He looked to the bartender and yelled, "Yeah, I'm fine, Charley! Why do you ask?"

"Nothing, it's just that I've never seen you guzzle down a beer like that, in addition to the fact that you hate beer!"

"You came all the way over here just to ask me that?! You were paying attention that much?"

Charley's eyes squinted as he curved his head forward to the left. "Are you getting smart with me?"

"No, it's just that I find it kind of odd that you'd ask me that, especially in this kind of environment!"

Charley was about to say something when a voice screamed, "Hey, bartender! How about another drink!?" Charley looked at him for a moment, obviously wanting to say something, but then just walked toward the customer.

He let go of the bottle as he looked down at the counter. He noticed that the counter top glowed of neon pink. He touched the counter and slid his fingers across it. The aura was screaming into the air with its vivid shade. Pink was a color that he had detested, its intensity was always too much.

He looked up at what was *behind* the bar. He saw that a multitude of drinks were held inside of a wooden construction. This construction was segmented into many different rectangular shapes large enough to hold drinks inside them. There was a wall of neon pink behind the entirety of it. The color glowed around each bottle, its loud vibrancy entrapping the shape. He became lost in the color as his eyes focused in on it. Everything around him became silent as the pink began to almost blind him.

He shook his head as he closed his eyes for a moment to gather himself. He opened them again and heard that it was still silent. He turned around and saw that the night club was almost empty. It was completely lit up, now, and only the mechanically colored spot lights remained on. The view had changed, and the surrounding became clearer. It looked like a large, festively designed garage.

He heard someone walking behind him. He turned around and saw the bartender.

"I can't believe you're still here. It's a good thing that Blake and the rest of the gang are still here, too, because you look really buzzed." He then shook his head in disbelief. "I can't believe you drank that whole bottle."

He looked down and saw that the bottle was, indeed, empty.

"You drank that awfully fast for someone that doesn't like beer." That was Blake's voice, and it was behind him.

He turned around to see Blake standing in front of him from afar with three other people, one of them being Nora. Dave was with them, along with another person dressed in a collage of colors. The hair was long and jet black and the eyes were of a soft hazel brown.

"Maybe I just wanted to taste bitterness," he whispered in response as they walked toward him.

"What?" Nora asked.

"No-nothing."

Blake then walked up to him. He whispered, "Listen, I'm sorry I blew up at you."

"It's okay," he said.

"Cool, so do you want to go?"

"Yeah, sure."

Before he left, Blake stopped him by putting his hand on his stomach. "By the way, the woman with the long black hair and the funky clothes."

"Yeah?"

"We just met her tonight, well, actually, him. He's a riot, so we invited him to eat with us."

"Great."

Blake walked over to Charley and they talked for a moment as Rodger focused in on the spotlight headed toward him. It was a cylinder shape that became wider as it reached down to the floor. It went for his face, disguising his vision in a repulsively bright pink.

The pink shade doused the material completely. It covered her body in a style reminiscent of the fifties.

He sat with Dave, Blake, Nora, and the invited guest in a booth seat. The seat was a half-circle shape and embroidered in a deathly yellow. The floor was held within a design of checkers. A jukebox stood against the left wall that was mainly shaded in a ruby red. Around the top half of this machine was a surrounding of at least three neon strings of color. There were bubbles swimming inside each string, almost like the continuing cycle of a lava lamp.

They sat next to a large window. Their reflections were cast against a night with not a cloud in the sky. The scenery was only of a street with a few houses dotted on each side. The street itself lay littered in crumpled papers and random garbage.

"Will that be all, hon?" the waitress asked as she finished writing down the last order.

"Huh? Yeah, sure, that's fine," he responded.

She put the pamphlet in the pocket of her apron and walked to the back kitchen.

"Are you with us?" Blake asked.

He looked to the small crowd staring at him. "What do you mean?"

"You seem kind of spaced out," Nora said. "Maybe you got too drunk off of one bottle of beer."

He smiled, slightly. "I think I *do* have an ability to hold my liquor better than that. No, I'm just…thinking."

"So, anyway, what's your name?" Nora asked the person with the long black hair.

"Well, which one would you like to know, my name as this beautiful woman sitting before you or the name of the guy that I live as going through the daily grind?"

"Whichever," Dave said.

"Well, my stage name is Glenn. My real name is…Quinton. I had no idea what the hell my parents were thinking when they named me that."

He suddenly looked at this person as if recognizing her. The feeling quickly faded as Glenn began to speak, again.

She said, "I think that they just wanted to prove that a person could live in normalcy and have a normal name to match."

"Why do you say that?" Blake asked.

"Because that's the bullshit excuse they gave me when I asked them."

They laughed at Glenn's answer. Glenn then looked at him and saw that he was not laughing. "I'll ask again for clarity's sake," Glenn said. "Are you with us, tonight?"

"Yes, I am. I'm just…a little buzzed."

"Ah, so you admit it," Nora said. "You *were* drunk off that one little beer."

"I didn't say I was drunk. All I said was that I was buzzed."

"Well, you *do* look a little high," Blake said.

"Maybe it will lessen those inhibitions you always seem to have," Dave said in a slightly seductive voice.

The others smiled knowingly at each other as he formed a look of a raging despair.

"They're not inhibitions," he said with an embittered tone. "It's called common sense."

"Oh, believe me, honey, common sense is something that only a chosen few of us have," Glenn said. "And even if we *do*, life will still fuck us up."

If anyone else had said that, he would have only formed a scornful look. But since it was Glenn, he didn't. He laughed. Glenn had some sort of power over the table. It was like the very presence of this person amazed each of them and kept their attention.

Dave eyed him with a hint of intrigue. His eyes only stared coldly at Dave, forming a visual rejection. Dave then just sat back and grinned in a childish way. However, even through the immaturity of that grin, he still had a sense of danger about him.

He looked back to the others.

"So, Nora, what are you going to do after you get out of here?" Blake asked. His voice had an obvious wanting in it.

He rolled his eyes as Nora said, "I'm probably going to soak in a nice, hot bubble bath…by myself."

Glenn smiled and said, "Well, looks like no one is making a guest appearance in *your* tub," obviously knowing the situation at hand.

Blake looked at Glenn with an almost scorned look in his eyes.

"Oh, Blake, honey, I'm sorry." Glenn went for Blake's hand while saying this. "If you want, *I* can be your substitute any time."

Blake then smiled as he pulled his hand away. "Thank you very much, Glenn. I'll have to think about that one."

"Don't think too much, honey, thinking too much is a poor characteristic," Glenn said, laughing.

The waitress came back to their table as she laid the plates of food in front of each person. "Okay, I've got chocolate-chip pancakes, a burger and fries, another burger and fries, a malted milk shake, and…toast." She walked away.

"Rodge, why toast?" Nora asked.

"Because I wanted something simple, is that too much of a crime? And don't call me Rodge."

"Don't be so uptight," Dave said.

"Well, on the other hand, that's not necessarily a bad thing to be," Glenn said before taking a sip of the shake.

After Blake swallowed a piece of his pancakes, he said, "Well, I'm sure we all know that *Rodger* definitely hasn't been tight for a few years now."

They all laughed in unison, except for Rodger. Their laughter was mocking, and it was piercing its way into him.

After it stopped, he said, "You don't know everything about me," to Blake.

"Rodge, I know plenty about you. I'm just not going to put it out on the table right now."

Rodger took a bite of his toast and then a few drinks of his water. Everyone was expecting him to say something, but he was silent.

"Don't be a dick," Nora said to Rodger. "You have to learn how to not take everything so seriously."

Rodger was forming a solid intention to command that she "shut up." But he pushed that intention down as he took another bite of the toast. He could feel his heart beating heavier as he was being torn inside out. Their phrases and their looks were becoming hellish.

"Well, I'll apologize for everyone else, I'm sorry, dear," Glenn said.

He looked around for a few moments and then mumbled the word, "Thanks."

"Sorry that your sense of humor is even less entertaining than your sex life," Dave said.

That statement was followed by a cold laughter from the crowd.

There was a trembling reaching its way up to Rodger's throat. Their voices vibrated heavily, ripping into him. The friendly faces were becoming wolves that came to feed, and he was the corpse lying dead, bleeding into their hunger.

"So what if I hadn't had sex in a while." His voice became slightly defensive.

That brought out more laughter from the crowd.

"Honey," Glenn said, "don't worry about it, I haven't been laid in a century."

The laughter then died down as Rodger continued biting into his toast and slowly drinking the water.

"Well, right now, *I* need sex," Blake said.

"And when was the last time *you* had it?" Nora asked.

"What does that mean?"

"I think she's trying to say you have the libido of a bunny rabbit, honey," Glenn said.

They all smiled slightly at her remark, letting out only a small tone of their voices.

"Well," Blake said as he scratched his short, blond hair, "the option's always open." His green eyes were staring right at Nora.

She only smiled at him, as if it were a tease.

"Are you going to try and see how the other half lives?" Glenn asked.

"I guess we'll see if the right temptation ever comes along," Nora said before she bit into her burger.

Rodger exhaled, deeply. He made sure, though, that the exhalation was only light enough for him to hear.

They all walked through the littered street toward their cars. The wind was somewhat harsh, blowing items of trash to their feet. This created a sound of solitude. The sky remained cloudless and bled in a sheet of midnight blue.

"So, Rodger, what's wrong?" Nora asked.

"Nothing."

"You're lying," she said.

"Something's wrong?" Blake asked.

"Rodger, common, tell us. What's wrong with you? You've hardly spoken a word all night. We're your friends," Dave said.

He felt compelled to confess. But he had a fear that would lead to accusation. So, he only said, "Nothing's wrong. I'm perfect."

"No one can ever be perfect," Dave said.

Rodger exhaled once more. This time, it was loud enough for everyone to hear.

He felt a hand behind him. He turned around and saw Glenn. They were in an alleyway, now. Each side was built from vibrantly red bricks, and a dense fog was swallowing the far end of it.

He looked around, rapidly, and saw nothing but the continuation of the alleyway and a sign to the right with the name "Willfire" written on it.

He turned back around and asked, "Where did everyone else go?" His voice was a hushed whisper, as if the answer would only come if he was silent enough.

"They all went home, honey. I guess they needed to get away from each other."

"So, what did you want to talk about?"

Glenn put her hands on his shoulders and said, "Honey, you need to stop taking life so seriously. You're going to die a thousand times if you don't."

He pulled her hands off and said, "Is that all you have to say?"

She pressed her fingers together and pointed at herself. "Blaming me won't solve your problems, or blaming anyone else."

"Yeah, well, everyone seems to be putting a lot of blame on me."

"No one is blaming you for anything."

"Really? Didn't you think things got a little cold tonight?"

"Those people only acted like that because that is the way they are. If you are unhappy with the company you keep, then maybe you should find yourself a different circle of friends."

He stared at Glenn's face for a moment, looking at how it was shadowed by the dimly lit alleyway. The darkness blended with her porcelain beauty, resembling a beautiful nightmare.

"*You* seemed to have enjoyed laughing at me, as well."

She walked closer to him and said, "Are you so sure that I was laughing at *you*? You shouldn't take things at face value, hon. Because things are never as they seem."

His eyes roamed for a moment as she brushed her fingers through his bleached blond hair. She stopped her hand midway. "You're a nice lookin' kid. Try to take advantage of life while you still can, honey. Nothing lasts forever." She removed her hand and walked away from him.

"Hey, wait, please," he said. "I need to ask you something else."

She didn't say anything. She just continued walking; entering the dense, white fog.

He followed her into that mist. His eyes had trouble concentrating through the hauntingly white. He moved his hands through it, trying to cut into it, but its luminosity became progressively intense…until it came together like a ghost.

The fog faded slowly into a dark blue. As it faded, he was finding himself in a home doused within a midnight blue. It was a cluttered house with a sliding glass door to the right. End tables, lamps, couches, knick-knacks and many other items lay strewn throughout it.

He heard footsteps and looked to his left. He saw an entrance into a small hallway and a shadow was making its way through. Nora came out of it and looked at him.

"What are you doing!? Why are you here!?" she screamed at him.

He only shook his head slightly as he moved his hands outward in a lost motion, his voice just breaking through.

She ran toward him and then proceeded to shove him. "Why are you doing this!?" She shoved him again. "Why!? Why can't you just let things be!?" She began to cry profusely as she pushed him through the open door. She then slammed the door shut as it echoed into his ears.

His heart weighed inside a sorrow. The pressure was building inside his head. He wanted to knock on the door and ask her why she was so upset, but didn't. He ignored yet another emotion and turned around.

He was suddenly startled to see a woman standing in front of him. "Nora!"

"Rodger, what are you doing here?"

"I-I-I-I…um-m-m-m-m, ugh."

She smiled, slightly. "All right, look, we were a little harsh tonight, and I'm sorry, okay? You wanna come inside since you're here?"

He nodded his head.

"Okay." She stood for a moment while looking at him in an innocent expectancy. "Ca-a-an I get to my door so I can open it?"

"Oh, yeah, s-s-s-sorry," he said as he walked out of her way.

She put the key into the slot. He heard a click and the door opened. He walked inside as she went to find a light.

The home was still doused in a midnight blue, but there was no clutter. To the left stood a closed door to a closet where the sliding glass door should have been. He looked around as his shattered comprehension took in the scenery.

He saw a large couch that had an incredibly familiar presence. On either sides of the couch were two very tall lamps. They were colored in a light black.

"Shit! The lights aren't working...again. I thought the maintenance guy took care of that, already."

The place looked almost barren. Only a table stood in the dining room with a chair at each side of it. A television stood, centered, in the front of the living room.

"I know, I know," she said as she walked toward the entrance into the small hallway. She stopped and looked at him. "It looks pretty empty. But I'm redecorating. I've gotta bring in a new look to this house."

He nodded his head in agreement. "Aren't you going to call the maintenance guy?"

"No, don't you think it's a little late to be calling him?" she said as she tossed her coat into the hallway and walked toward him with a look of slight confusion. "So what was bugging you tonight? You hardly even spoke. Tell me what yo—"

"Why are you hitting on Blake?" he interrupted with a voice heightened in curiosity.

"Well, *you* certainly got to the point fast."

"You're not even supposed to be interested in Blake."

She crossed her arms while moving her body to the left side. "And why is that?"

A sudden remembrance came to him. "Because...you're a lesbian!"

"Oh, common, Rodger." She positioned her body to be erect while dropping her arms to her sides. "Maybe I'm a little curious...maybe I'm bisexual." She walked over to the couch and sat down.

"Yeah, well, does it have to be Blake?"

"First of all, where did you get the idea I was hitting on *Blake*?"

"Because of some of the things you said while we were at the diner. Or, actually, what you *didn't* say. I saw you giving him that look."

"Rodger, if I'm interested, so what? You should stop being so selfish."

"Selfish!? You know, Glenn was right, maybe I should—"

"Who's Glenn?" Nora asked, lifting up her hands in a moment of curious expression.

He looked at her in disbelief, his eyes expanding into two gaping holes as his eyebrows arched inward. His mouth dropped open before he spoke, his lips trembling to form the right words. "Glenn, you remember, Glenn."

She still continued to stare, blankly, at him.

"Glenn! The drag queen that was with us tonight!? Blake invited her!"

"There was no drag queen named Glenn with us this morning, Rodger." She leaned forward while putting her elbows to her knees and folding her hands together. "Are you okay, Rodge?"

"What is that supposed to mean?" he asked, his face and voice suddenly becoming accusatory.

"You're beginning to talk about people that weren't even there. Maybe you should get some sleep."

"I don't need sleep, I need answers," he said as he rapidly walked toward her. He sat next to her as she turned to him.

"Answers to what?"

"Well, to why you're so curious about Blake, for starters."

"Look, I don't know where you got—"

"Nora, stop it. Everyone could see it in your eyes, and you really acted the part. It's obvious that there is some sort of curiosity. Now tell me why." His voice trailed down to a demanding whisper.

She exhaled. "Well, it's not exactly a curiosity."

"What do you—"

"Anymore."

He widened his eyes, followed by him saying, "What?!" in a now grave and dismal whisper.

She looked down, delicately scuffing her feet upon the carpet. As she looked back up, there was a certain sorrow lightly painted into her eyes. "It already happened, Rodger. Blake and I...we slept together."

"Why? How? What could he have possibly said to entice you?"

"It was a bunch of cheesy lines; I don't know why I fell for it. 'Oh, Nora, I would never do anything to hurt you.' 'Oh, Nora, you're my only true friend.' 'Oh, Nora, please, it'll only be just this once.' I don't know, I guess it was all—"

He got up from the couch and stood before her. He then said, "You said that to me."

"What?"

"You said that to *me*."

"Rodger, what are you saying? I never said anything like that to you."

He bent down and grabbed Nora and desperately asked, "Nora, do you remember the painting? The one I painted of you? You were with me."

"What are you talking about!? Let go of me!?" she yelled as she began to push her hands against the stronghold of his arms.

"Nora! You were in my apartment! Are we still there now? Are we!?"

She pulled his hands off and got up from the couch.

"What are you saying?"

He got up, slowly. "Nora, what's going on? What's really going on?"

"Dave, and Blake, and, ugh, ugh...."

"Who? Who else, Nora?"

"Rodger, please."

"STOP CALLING ME RODGER! I *AM BLAKE*!"

She shook her head with sympathy. "No...you're not."

He began to find the lost emotion again. It sank deep inside him, cutting his heart. He became breathless for a moment as his body shivered. "Please, tell me, what's happening?" His voice was pleading.

She walked toward him and brushed her fingers through his hair. She pulled her fingers out and said, "You're not ready to know that."

"Why not?" His eyes were staring desperately into hers.

She gave a look of understanding. "You won't let me."

His eyebrows arched. "Why are you saying that?"

She lightly touched his arms. "Please, don't think right now. Just sit down." He followed the order and sat down in the couch. She walked up to him and stood before him. "What do you want?" she asked.

His mouth was beginning to quiver as his sanity was breaking inside his mind. "I wanna go back home, back to the studio apartment. I wanna go home."

"No," she said, almost sympathetically.

"Why not!?" he asked as he jolted his head forward. A heavy film was pulling over his eyes and the rims were growing heavy.

"Enjoy the moment. Close your eyes."

"Why?"

"Close your eyes and you'll find the place where you belong for the moment."

"For the moment?"

"Sh-h-h-h-h-h-h," she said as she lightly touched his lips. "Just close your eyes and rest. Don't think too much. Just try and find contentment."

He exhaled deeply. A choking fear was breaking his insides and released from his mouth as a shuddering breath. He slowly closed his eyes. He let the tears fall and he began entering darkness. He exhaled once more and tried to let go of what he was holding inside. But he could still feel that uncertainty. It was like a fist pounding in the pit of his stomach, taunting him by squeezing tighter.

He exhaled once more. His breath echoed in his ears. He could hear a voice becoming clear and there was music fading into existence, building itself inside his ears until it shook his hearing.

"Rodger!" He opened his eyes and saw Dave standing in front of him.

He looked around and saw that he was back in the night club. "Rodger, do you want to dance!?"

He looked back to Dave and said, "No, that's all right! You go on ahead!"

He stood straight up and said, "Fine! I'll just dance with someone else!"

As Dave walked away, he felt Blake tap him on his shoulder. He said, "You wanna go back out on the dance floor!?" He smiled mischievously.

"No, no that's-s-s okay," he said as he was entering a feeling of familiarity. "No, that's okay!"

"Oh, common, Rodge! Have some fun in your life and stop being such a dud!"

These phrases, these words had been repeated before. He knew the outcome of his defiance. He decided to be lighter with his words this time. "No! Really, that's okay! Why don't you try dancing with someone *else*! Besides, I think I need to regain my energy!"

Blake arched his eyebrow at him as his face began to show an obvious negativity. "You, know, this is not fair, Rodger! All I wanna do is have a little fun! That's it! Can't you ever put things in a platonic state of mind!?"

He looked at Blake for a moment. He wanted to break this cycle, somehow. He did not want to step out on that floor with Blake, again; he would just feel burned. However, he began to suspect if he didn't, this rage would repeat itself and he'd be pushed into a further state of solitude. He yearned to say the right words, but nothing seemed right to say.

He tried to swallow the bitterness that was rising up inside him and said, "Okay! Fine, let's go another round!"

Right after he got up from the chair and was about to walk out onto the floor, Blake put his hand against his chest and said, "You're not just saying that to appease me, are you!?"

He stared at Blake, annoyed. "Blake! Do you want to dance or not!?"

Blake put his hands up as he nodded his head, slightly. "Fine! Sure!"

Blake took his hand and led him through the crowd. He could feel his stomach growing smaller as he was being led. He looked around to all the other people dancing as they closed in on them. They were all laughing and having fun with each other. He listened to all of this and saw their faces express a joy.

Blake stopped and pulled him toward his body until there was no space between them.

"Let's do it again!" Blake said with a widening smile.

He only smirked as Blake began to dance with the music, moving against him. He followed Blake's motion. He tried to take in the moment, but as he listened to everyone pounding against the ground and saw them dance, radically, it was pushing him toward a fading existence. He was looking right into Blake's eyes, the reflections of all the people around them were inside those two slick pupils. They wouldn't stop pulling themselves toward this happiness. He began to see the faces turn to him, watching every move that he was making, feeling everyone else's eyes burn into his performance. Their judgments were grabbing tightly wound strings compressing the tensions in his head. The feeling seared inward and began to travel throughout the rest of his body.

Blake's arms were getting tighter, conflicting with the tension inside him. His body was beginning to move from an obligated emotion to satisfy the atmosphere.

He kept staring into Blake's eyes, struggling to find peace. But that peace was buried beneath everything else he had shoved down his head. He could sense a mockery expanding from everyone's perceptions. And even Blake's eyes seemed to be taunting him, telling him that nothing was going to be enough, that the only reason he was at this place, in Blake's arms, was because a space needed to be filled.

Blake's touch was feeling empty.

He leaned over to Blake's ear, and in a voice trying to control the despair reaching for his throat, he yelled, "Look! I'm going to go back to the bar! I need a drink!"

He tried to go back out, but Blake wouldn't let go. Blake put his head to his ear and yelled, "Why!? Just so you can guzzle down a beer that you won't even like the taste of!?"

"I just need to sit down! Please!"

"Oh, come on, Rodge! Stay out here with me!" he yelled, his face appearing to be of a subtle insistence.

He exhaled deeply. Everyone's laughter was beginning to combine and direct itself toward him. "I just need to sit down! I need to have a drink!"

"Rodge! Please!" Blake pleaded.

He looked into Blake's eyes, trying to find what would be the right thing to say. But as he was delving into the proper words, Blake's pupils began to expand.

"Bla—" He stopped himself as he saw that the pupils were expanding toward the color of his eyes. He could only watch in silence as they were rapidly becoming devoid of green and white.

He was now starring into two pools of complete black. He looked into this black and saw a mirror of everyone surrounding him as his reflection faded. All the other people were starting to turn their heads toward the dark, eye-shaped mirrors. They were laughing, mockingly. The laughter was sounding over the music. It was finding its way deep inside his mind as the severity of it was becoming a heavily demonic voice making fun of his broken emotions.

"I have to go to the fucking bar!" he said as he pushed himself away from Blake and turned away from his darkened eyes.

He ran toward the bar as if it were a salvation, and the beer becoming a prediction of relief. All he needed to do was taste it and everything would fall back into place.

He took hold of the beer bottle as he could feel Blake walking toward him. He tilted his head back and quickly guzzled a small intake of the foul liquid. He then slammed the bottle on the bar and looked up.

His face contorted into an expression of growing fear as he saw a large mirror behind the counter reflecting the interior of some sort of party. The room was designed in a Victorian taste and the people were elegantly dressed from a time long since passed . They danced next to each other as their fingers were holding up masks covering half their faces. He began to hear an echo of an eighteenth-century style of sound played from a piano.

He then felt a hand press against his right shoulder. Startled, he rapidly turned around and saw Blake standing in front him. He looked back behind him and saw that the mirror was gone and the drinks stood in their compartments.

"Rodger!"

He turned his head back around. Blake's eyes regained normalcy.

"Rodger, why did you do that!? I would've liked it if we continued dancing!"

"Yeah, well, maybe I just wanted to sit down!" he said as he did just that.

"You just wanna sit here!?"

"For now, yes!"

"Fine! Be in your little world!" Blake gave him a look of incredible disbelief as he angrily walked back out onto the floor.

He looked around the club and saw nothing but a blur of people. They all seemed to be characters he couldn't make sense of, and settings he couldn't quite place in an exact definition. Everything was becoming too much to possibly comprehend. All he could do was wrap his hands around his stomach and try to contain the fear growing inside of him.

Conflicting Realities

Slowly, spotlights came together by pairs of four, binding a circle. Each one was spaced at the same distance from one another, spinning throughout the nightclub to where the colors almost touched.

He turned back around and was thinking of having another drink of his beer, but didn't. He wanted to sit for the moment and concentrate on nothing. All he needed was a few moments alone, and then everything would make sense.

He started to tap his fingers on the counter top as they edged toward the beer bottle, but then pulled them away, knowing that he didn't need that bitter taste choking his throat. He remained focused in one direction and didn't even think about the pink neon that topped the counter. All thoughts and worry needed to be relieved to unravel the tight fist gripping the pit of his stomach. He breathed deeply a few times and slowly put the music out of his head.

His thought pattern was broken when someone tapped him on the shoulder. Annoyed by the interruption, he turned his head and was about to tell the person what he was thinking. But those words were stolen from him when he saw the person.

He was dressed in attire that wrapped tightly around his body. His shirt was a light brown on top and white from the middle of his chest down. The pants were of a black denim material. His eyes were perfectly angular. There was a dark brown surrounding his pupils, contributing to a mysteriously intriguing look. They reflected the lights within the club, giving an effect of glowing stars. His face had a defined shape that was intensely appealing. He curved his attractive lips upward to the right and said, "Hey! Never seen *you* here before!"

He smiled back and said, "Yeah, well, maybe you just never noticed me!"

"I find that hard to believe! Anyone could notice you from a mile away!"

"And why do you say that!?"

The young man brought his face close and said, "Because you're hot, simple as that!"

He smiled from an intimidation as the other man asked, "What's your name!?"

"Rodger, how about you?"

"Jack! So, Rodger, wanna go and dance?" Jack put his hands around Rodger's back as he asked the question.

"Sure! Why not?"

Jack led him out on the dance floor. And this time, Rodger didn't feel misery playing into his heart. This time it was a burning passion. He had finally encountered an occurrence he wanted to happen.

Jack led him to the middle of the floor and then pulled him closer. Their bodies left no space in between.

The spinning lights ran continuously as they moved to the beat of the music. Rodger let himself fall in Jack's hands as both their hearts were beating rapidly, engaging into a similar rhythm toward each other's chests. Their faces met as the lights spun in between them. Their noses were touching as their lips were delicately caressing.

Rodger continued to stare into Jack's dark eyes, watching himself in the reflection. He remembered every moment that occurred in which he found himself agreeing to. Every person, every friend that came to him was there just to take something. The men he wanted never wanted him. He remembered the depression that slowly surrounded him, forming the doubts in his mind. He remembered the nights that came closer and closer to crying into sleep. When that night finally happened, he let the tears guide him into another nightmarish hell waiting in the depths of his resting mind. He remembered the ghost that he had become, losing his soul to an emptiness craving a torn-and-tattered heart.

But now he had found a person that wanted him and that he wanted as well. He let this realization work into his mind as Jack brought his mouth toward his. Their lips became entrapped within an embrace. Rodger closed his eyes and felt the soft touch caressing his tongue. The passion began to boil inside and reach toward the center of his body. He began to feel stimulation as his tongue hugged Jack's.

He then opened his eyes and stared into *Jack's* eyes. As they continued to kiss, those eyes started to change into a murky brown, and the pupils had lost their glow. The perfect angle they had possessed slumped downward into an ordinary alliance. His face let go of its attractive features as his hair went from a short spike to being exactly combed.

He pushed himself away from Jack and saw that Jack was no longer the person that he was holding. He breathed heavily as he started to realize who this person was.

"Dave! Why are you here!?"

Dave gave him a look of confusion. "I just wanted to dance with you! You finally agree—"

He put his hand up. "Just stop! Everything just STOP!" He ran back toward the bar. "I don't want this! Why couldn't you have been Jack!?"

He slammed into the counter as his hands slapped its top. He felt the returning desperation pulling at his insides. "I don't want this!" he screamed. "I don't want any of this! I just want him to go away!"

He reached for the beer and put it to his mouth. He let the dense liquid strangle him and then put it down on the counter. "I don't want this," he whispered to himself as he sat in the chair.

He was about to turn around. Before he did, expectancy was forming in his head. He didn't want the music to be playing, or the people, or the club, or any of it. When he turned around, he wanted to see a setting he would be happy in.

Slowly, he started. Within the first second he was waiting for it all to fade. The same surroundings still clasped his eyes and the same music still latched onto his ears. Then, he stopped halfway. Everything remained the same, the patterns persisting to be stubborn and refusing to change. Somehow, this setting knew that it was taunting him, ripping into his sorrows. That must have been why it wasn't changing and continued in its cruel rage. With a needing hope reaching for his broken head, he quickly turned to complete the direction. For a second, everything blurred. Inside that brief moment, there was such anticipation crawling through his head, suffering for pleasure instead of pain.

Then he stopped. The music was still playing, the people were still there, the club still raged with everyone else's excitement.

He saw Dave walking toward him. His heart sank as he turned back around. He put his hands completely on top of the counter, surrendering to the neon pink.

He felt Dave's hand grab his right shoulder.

"Just go away, Dave!"

"Rodge, will you please stop all this!?"

"I said go away! I don't want to talk to you!"

"Damn it, Rodger!"

He didn't hear anything else from Dave and could sense that he was walking away, the sound of his footsteps imprinted with an infuriating, bitter sadness. He remained at the bar as he listened to the music play its words too loud to hear.

"Rodge, what are you doing?!" he heard a familiar voice ask. He looked to his left and saw Nora walking toward him.

"Just go away!"

She approached him and said, "No, I'm *not* going to go away! What the hell are you doing!?" she asked, standing beside him. Her face expressed a genuine curiosity, but it was buried inside obvious anger.

"What do you mean!?"

"I mean Dave's pissed at you! Blake's pissed at you! And I'm starting to feel the same! Are you just going to sit here and sulk all night!?"

"That's the plan!" he said as he turned back to face the bar.

Nora took a seat next to him. "Rodge, I'm worried about you! You're pushing everyone away! We're just trying to be your friends!"

"You know!" he said while still facing the bar. "I've told just about everyone tonight that I don't like being called Rodge! Funny how people forget things like that so simply!"

Nora nodded her head and asked, "What!?"

He looked back toward her, laughing with irony indelibly attached to his voice and said, "Nothing!", then turned back to the bar.

She crossed her arms and tilted her head, expressing her position as curiosity weighed heavily in demand. "You should be having fun! Celebrating your life, celebrating where you are right now!"

"And where *am* I Nora!?"

"You're here...with us!"

He exhaled, deeply. However, his exhalation was hiding inside the countless layers of raucous music. He arched an eyebrow and then said, "Yeah, well, maybe that's where you all *want* me to be!"

"Will you stop making it sound like we're the enemy!? We're just trying to help!"

He turned to look at her and stayed silent for a long moment. His eyes remained the same shape, his face suddenly becoming still, taking on the appearance of bitter stone. He said, "I think I'm going to try to find a place less noisy!"

He walked away from her as she looked at him in amazement. She appeared as if she was about to say something else, but then just sighed and walked away.

He stepped off the three elongated stairs, walking away from the dance floor and bar all together. He walked through an opened door that led into a pool room. The seat he chose was occupied by no one. The beer was not with him, but he didn't want to retrieve it. He lay back in the small booth seat that was a half circle. There were at least four wooden booth seats on the side that he was residing.

He saw that were there were four guys playing pool. Each of them was a configuration of external beauty. However, none of them looked his way. He wasn't very surprised by this. They were involved in their own game.

A light cloud of smoke surrounded them. It was from cigarettes still burning in the remains of ash trays.

He wanted to ask if he could join and was about to voice those words. But he lost the words to say when he saw one of the young men. "Jack," he whispered to himself. Jack didn't look up.

He listened in on their conversation:

"So, I don't know about you all tonight, but I am going to get laid," one of them said.

"How is that different from any other night?" another said.

"Yeah, I mean, that is just a continuous cycle for you. Practically every night is sex, sex, sex. And when it isn't sex, it's popping that shit in your mouth or up your nose."

"Hey, that 'shit' that you're referring to so kindly is very *good* shit. And besides, I don't do it often, only when I need to relax."

"You mean when you're not engaging in sex."

"Hey, I am just very active."

"Active, hell, you're more than active. You are a fuckin' rabbit. I can't believe you haven't died of a heart attack by now."

"Yeah, well, at least I don't date all the wrong guys like you."

"Hey," one said as the others reacted by acknowledging the harshness of that statement. "It's not that I date all the wrong guys, it's just that I haven't found the right one, yet."

"Yeah, well, you need to stop looking for Mr. Right and start concentrating on Mr. Right Now."

"There's a lot more to life than sex."

"That's all there is to life. That and food. Oh, and let's not forget money."

"What about friends? What about having fun? What about movies?"

"It's all just extra until you get to the sex."

"You can't define life by one little thing."

"What do you mean one little thing? Sex is nothing little."

"Yeah, well, it may feel good while you're doing it, and yes, I'd be lying if I said I didn't think of it as something wanted and needed, but it's not the only thing."

"Oh, hey, guys, listen, I think I'm going to become a model."

"And we've heard this about *how* many times?"

"I'm going to do it for real this time. My dream is going to become a reality."

"You've had so many dreams, I'm surprised you can still keep track."

"What's that supposed to mean? When I have a dream, I reach for it."

"Bull shit, every time you get halfway through, you become tired of *that* 'dream' and then move onto another one. I'm beginning to think that you just want to be known for something, but you're too lazy to do anything about it."

"That was kind of harsh."

"Don't listen to them, if you want to become a model, you go right ahead and do it. I guess I'll see you on the runway soon."

"That's not some kind of joke, is it?"

"No, it's not a joke. I'm being for real. If you want to do it, then go ahead and do it."

"Well, anyway I think I'm coming to a close on that novel I've been writing."

"You're just finishing that *now*?"

"Yeah, why?"

"Nothing, it's just that it's a little late. People have started in the business way younger than you. Do you know how long it takes to get to the top?"

"I'm not just attempting to get to the top. Anyway, what are you trying to say?"

"I believe what he's trying to say is that you're thirty."

"So? Who cares? You know, people have such a misconception when it comes to age. They think that just because you've hit thirty, forty, or even fifty, you should hang up your party clothes and wait to die."

"We never said anything like that."

"You never *had* to. The way you look at some people implicates they don't even belong here."

"We do not judge."

"Oh, common, everyone judges. I hate to say it, but bias is a very big part of life. We judge all the time, even when we don't know we're doing it. Don't tell me that none of you have ever looked at someone dressed so differently from everyone else and the thought of them being a freak jumps through your mind."

"Well, duh, tell me something that I don't know. Of course people do that, it's in their nature. I, however, try to be as open-minded as possible."

"Ha! You're not open-minded. You just open your mind to even further extensions of experiences you've had before. You think you have a complete vision of life just because you give someone the time of day. But you never got to know any of those people you talk to out of sympathy. In fact, the only reason you talk to them is because you think you're doing some kind of charity work. But you know what? Those people probably don't care what you think and are listening to you because they're too polite to tell you to shut up."

"Hey, listen; I don't do anything like that. You have no idea what kind of person I am. I have a real heart inside here. Just because the only times you see me are when I'm partying doesn't mean that that's the majority of my life."

"When are you *not* partying? There's not one time I've seen you without a drink in your hand, or dancing to some kind of music, or trying to seduce someone, or doing something that is not at all introspective. I mean, don't get me wrong: Sex, partying and having a good time is important to have in life, but so is thinking. When was the last time you sat down and read a book?"

"You have no right to judge me. You're here like the rest of us."

"Guys, you're taking things too seriously, just settle down."

"Why don't *you* settle down? You know what I don't like about you? You're always trying to be the voice of reason. Like you're some kind of fucking savior come to rescue us, you think by saying a few words, suddenly everything's going to be better and we'll all learn the error of our ways. Why don't you start figuring out your *own* life before you try to figure out everyone *else's*?"

"Look, just because you're bitter about yet another fuckin' drunk you've slept with died on you doesn't mean you have to take it out on me."

"What?!"

"You heard what I said. You only date these guys who can put you down in even more of a misery than you're already in. They're always some kind of drunk or dope addict, or they beat the hell out of you, or verbally abuse you, or something along those lines. You've never dated someone that was normal.

You're always after the danger and that danger changes into a normalcy anyway. One that is redundant and something you've had a million times before. You let them use you, abuse you, and just throw you away, because you're just too fucking weak to defend yourself and so you hide by disguising yourself with this false happiness, like you're actually happy seeing all these guys that don't even give a shit about you."

"I can't believe you just said that. Why don't you just go off and find some kind of sympathy case you can save."

"Fuck you."

"Well, I'm still going to be a model."

"I can't believe that you're still focused on being a model. All you care about is yourself."

"Well, you know what, it's better than being some sorry-ass loser like you."

"You will never reach your dreams. You know why? Because you're too…fucking…lost!"

They all stopped talking to each other. Each of them stood silent in the cloud of smoke. Their eyes had become empty and there were no expressions happily painting their faces. They only stared into each other, trying to find a solace but losing it as soon as they remembered a harsh remark.

One of them tossed their pool stick on the table, cutting through the smoke. He walked away from them. As each one left, the fog became more of a solitary presence.

Rodger turned his head back to the front and listened to the faded music echoing into the walls. The four men verbally tearing into each other stayed in his mind. His eyes roamed for a few moments as the smoke drifted through the dimly lit room. The only light source was a long rectangular object hanging over the pool table that provided a dim, luminescent shadow.

He inhaled deeply and tasted the smoke. He coughed as he exhaled.

Someone was walking into the pool room. He looked up and saw Blake. The only response he provided was an arched eyebrow as Blake walked toward him.

"Why don't you have a seat?" he asked in a nonchalant voice.

Blake sat down in front of him, casually. He looked at Rodger with a half-hearted sincerity, lessened by the apathy painted in his eyes. He asked, "Why? Why did you push me away on the dance floor, Rodge?"

He looked down as he pushed his lips slightly outward. He then faced Blake, again, his lips regaining their original shape. "Why do you keep insisting on dancing with me?"

"What is that supposed to mean? I'm trying to have a little fun," he said as he exaggerated his expression. "Rodge, you're my friend, and I like to have fun with my friends."

He slightly nodded his head. "No. Friends don't do that. They don't tease you like that. They don't make you think things like that."

"If you've been having thoughts like that, Rodger, then I'm sorry. That's not my fault. You need to learn a little self control."

"Fuck self control. Self control goes all to hell when someone like you comes my way and starts to practically feel me up."

"I never felt you up. If you perceived it that way, then you're dead wrong. It's just dancing, Rodge," he said as he lifted up his hands, as if that was the only comment he had to surrender. He then put his hands back down and curved a disbelieving smirk. "You should enjoy the moment, enjoy what you have."

"What do I have, Blake? Tell me."

Blake fixated his eyes on his for a long moment. He broke the silence by saying, "You have friends that care for you. You have nights where fun should be the main event. You have—"

"Friends that care for me? Is that what it is? I never would have guessed."

"Just what are you trying to get at, Rodge?"

"What do you think I'm trying to get at, Blake?"

"Are you trying to play some kind of mind game with me?"

"The only reason minds are played with is because they are vulnerable."

"Are you saying that I'm vulnerable?"

He only stared at Blake and didn't answer.

"Rodge, I wish you'd talk to me. Make some sense."

"You never made sense throughout our entire friendship. You're just a fucking hypocrite."

Blake looked at him with a cold expression. An eyebrow arched, harshly, as if it were cracking into concrete. He then got up and walked away, leaving him alone once more.

He lay back against the seat and began to think. He ran his finger in circles on top of the table. Its reflective shadow swirled beneath his finger, following his motions.

He looked down and began to watch his mirror image while still running his finger in the same redundant motion. He became lost in his own eyes, staring at their color, wondering if his looks were worth anything. The doubts were peaking in his mind and he couldn't find the courage to go back out on that floor.

He heard heavy steps coming toward the opened door. He ignored them, figuring that it would be just another person that would ignore him. The steps came closer until they reached the interior of the room. Still he didn't look up as the film was forming on top of his eyes and the quivering motion was edging toward his throat. He could feel his needs slowly die as the steps were coming toward him, probably the bartender, probably someone else to yell at him. He could feel the liquid filling his eyelids and soon it would have to be released.

He then saw the reflection of another coming toward the table. When it was completely hovering atop the polished wood, he could see that it was Dave, and his face looked pained. Rodger narrowed his eyes as the film blurred his vision. The tears were released. When his vision became clear, again, he saw that there was a small circle of red to the right of the table. He rubbed his eyes and looked again. The reddened circle was still there. Wondering what it was, he went to touch the substance. It felt slick, and it clung to his flesh when he brought his finger up from it.

He arched his eyebrows in confusion as another drop of red fell on his finger, followed by a trickle. It spilled over and was beginning to spread. In a fit of worry he moved his head up and saw Dave looking at him. His mouth was open and the red liquid was spilling over his bottom lip.

"Dave, wha-what happened?" Rodger asked as he reached out to him. When he touched Dave's arm, he tried to speak.

"Ro-o-o-o-o-dg-g-ger." His voice was masked with a gurgling sound. Dave then closed his mouth; the liquid was falling from it, covering his chin in thickened streams. It dripped periodically on the table. His face grimaced as his eyes squinted from a hopeless misery. His voice edged outward in only small whines. His mouth then popped open and screamed as the red jumped out of his mouth and splattered, landing on the table and Rodger in a light shower.

Dave dropped on his knees and fell over on the seat.

"Oh, my God!" he cried as he edged himself away from Dave and crouched in the middle of the booth. He saw that the back of Dave's neck had been ripped open. The walls of the gash were freshly wounded and the blood was beginning to form a pool of itself around his head.

He looked up as he heard someone running toward the room. Nora came through the door, her eyes filled with tears.

"Rodge," she managed to say in a quivered whisper. "Rodge, Rodge I saw him." Her body was moving in a confusion of motions.

He got up on the seat and walked around on it until he reached the end.

"Nora," he said before he stepped down. He walked toward her, "Nora, what happened?"

She put her hand up to her forehead and it quivered through her hair. "The glass," she said. "The glass."

"What glass?" he asked in a pushing voice. He walked closer to her as she spoke.

She looked directly into his eyes. "The glass, the glass of the mirror…in the bathroom." Her lips were moving fast and her words were blending together.

He took hold of her by the arms. "Just calm down," he said in an uneasy voice. "Just calm down and explain."

She closed her eyes for a few moments as the streams of tears poured over the dried ones previously cried. She breathed deeply a few times. Her lips shook before she spoke. She then opened her eyes. "I heard a sound in the men's room as I came out of the ladies'." Her voice was still quivering as she tried to release the information. "It was a very loud sound. I became worried and I ran to open the door. I saw Dave grabbing his throat as he tried to speak. I saw that one of the mirrors was broken and there was blood all around the glass. He ran out of the bathroom and pushed me out the way, leaving a trail of blood behind. I chased after him."

"That's when you came here?"

"Yes."

He looked down a few times. "But why would he push you out of the way? Why did he just come over to me?"

"I don't know, he just did." She shook her head slightly as it tilted to the left.

"But why? And didn't you go in there and look to see if anyone was in the bathroom?"

"I was in a state of shock, Rodge! Did you expect me to think of everything?!" He let go of her. She stopped. Her eyes became suspicious. "However…I could ask you why he's here, with you, and his blood is all over you."

"Nora, you came running in here right after you saw Dave run out of the bathroom. Now, unless I can be in two places at once, then your suspicions are shot all to hell."

Still looking at him, she said, "Yes, but that doesn't mean the police won't suspect you."

"Someone's called the police?" he asked as he began to walk backward.

"If they haven't been called yet, then someone's bound to. It's inevitable." She began walking toward him.

"Nora, Nora are you telling me everything?" He stopped. She continued to walk toward him. "Yes, I'm telling you everything. Someone is going to walk into that bathroom. Someone is going to see that mess. What's going to happen next?"

"Yes, but they'll suspect me as much as you."

"Maybe...maybe not." She then stopped, as well.

"You know, for someone so innocent you're sounding awfully malicious."

"Why do you say I'm sounding malicious, Rodge?"

"All right, look," he said as he put his hands up. "Arguing is going to get us nowhere." He put his hands down and looked back at Dave's body. He saw how his arms were hanging, lifelessly, and how the blood was still coming out of the opening. He tried to think of how painful it must have been and suddenly remembered when he said he wanted Dave to go away.

He slowly looked back at Nora and asked, "So, what are we going to do?" His voice came out as a cracked whisper.

"I don't know." Nora then formed a look of confusion.

"What is it?" he asked.

"I'm just thinking," she said as her eyes looked downward.

"What?"

"If the back of Dave's throat was slashed, then how could he have had trouble speaking?"

Rodger opened his mouth, slightly. "How did you know the back of his throat was slashed?"

"He *was* running away from me. I could see it."

"Are you sure?"

They heard footsteps coming toward the open door.

"Go see who that is," Nora directed.

"You're the one closest to the door."

She rolled her eyes as she went to go see. He saw her place her hands on the right edge of the door while she pushed it forward. She then poked her head outside of it. He heard conversation, but the voices were too light to hear.

His breathing became heavy again, and the smoke was being tasted with each breath. He didn't cough, he let it strain his throat and tear up his eyes. He thought about what must have happened in that bathroom. How Dave had to have struggled for his life. How he must have felt death becoming more and more inevitable. He wondered who came into that bathroom, how he could have died, how no one else was walking past the door. The questions were festering in his mind, growing at a pace faster than he could manage.

"Well, why!?" he heard a voice yell. "I want to know why I can't go in there! I just want to play a game of fucking pool!"

He walked closer as he heard Nora's voice becoming clearer. "Because, sir, it's broken. It's no use."

"So! Just let me in there!"

He then saw Nora being pushed. She was pushing back as he walked rapidly toward her.

"I'm sorry, sir," he said as he went to help Nora push the door. Her long hair swayed radically as both their hands clasped the edge of the door, tightly. "You can't come in here."

"I want to know why, damn it!"

"Please," Nora said. "Please." Their breath became relentless as their bodies continued to push harder, heartbeats were growing faster with each second. Their worries were beginning to cloud their minds. This man showed no intentions of stopping.

"WHAT THE HELL IS GOING ON IN THERE!?"

"Please!" Rodger said. "Just go! This is none of your concern!"

Nora suddenly said, "If you know what's good for you, you'll leave right now!"

Rodger's eyes widened with astonishment. Was that the wisest thing to say?

They felt the man's resistance lessen. He saw the outline of his body beneath the shadows as he walked backward through the short hallway. "I don't know what's going on here." He stopped. They wondered what he was going to say next. "But you know what, what goes around comes around." The man then walked away and out of the night club.

Rodger became confused. "Where's the bouncer?"

"Get back in the room!" Nora whispered.

They both hurriedly walked back inside. "Now what?" she asked.

"The bouncer, where is he?"

"I don't know, why? What's so important about that?"

"Because he's always there, he's the only way in or out of this club. It wouldn't make sense for him not to be there."

"Rodger, let's just think."

"No, let's just go."

"What?"

"I think we should leave, Nora."

She walked toward him. Her face dropped to a grave seriousness. "Rodger,

I think we should stay here until we think of what we can do with Dave's body." She stopped.

"Look, someone is eventually going to come in here. I suggest it would be a good idea if we weren't here when that happens. I think we should go now while we still have the chance."

"What about Blake?"

"Fuck Blake. Let's save ourselves. You can stay here if you want, but I'm leaving."

As he walked toward the door, she stopped him with her hand on his left shoulder. She said, "Let me come with you."

"What?" he asked as his face backed away.

"Let me come with you."

"Nora, I don't think so, that's going to look very suspicious," he said as he put his face forward again.

"I don't care. I just want to come with you. I don't feel safe right now."

"Didn't you bring your car here?"

"No, I rode with Blake, remember?"

He shook his head as he sighed. "Why do you want to come with me?"

"Rodge, please. I want to leave, too. I can't tell Blake what happened. Dave is dead. Do you know what that means?" She brought her face forward while a film was forming over her eyes. The evident sadness and desperation were breaking coldly into her face, masking it in a fearful shadow. "Our friend is dead. I can't tell Blake that. What if he suspects one of us? Will he still trust us?"

He looked at her for a few moments. Suspicion clasped his eyes as a multitude of thoughts confused themselves in the saddening madness corroding his head. "I think the question right now is…does at least one of us trust the other?"

"Rodge, just let me come with you. I want to get out of this situation, please."

The film on her eyes became heavier. She pulled her arms around the width of his body and buried her face in his left arm as her head began to shake from crying. He could feel her becoming vulnerable. She squeezed his arm, holding onto it as if it were her life. The cries were genuine, and cut through her trembling shivers like a razor blade running across a wrist.

He sighed once more. He didn't say anything for a few moments as she cried on his arm. He then asked, "So do you want to drive or should I?"

She looked back up as she weakly attempted to smile through the tears.

"Thank you," she said in a cracking whisper resembling a desert wind brushing coldly against the sands.

"Let's just go." He spoke the words quickly and without much thought. Right now he was just trying to escape all thought. But that seemed impossible, as they were imprisoning his head.

They walked out of the room and toward the exit. He still didn't see the bouncer anywhere near the exit and wondered why.

"So, I guess you should drive," Nora said, breaking his train of thought.

"Huh? Oh, yeah."

He tried to retrieve what he had been thinking only moments before, but couldn't remember.

They walked through the doors. The streets were desolately populated. Nothing seemed to be a threat at the moment. They walked toward the end of the building and turned to the parking lot beside it. A multitude of cars littered the lot, each one appearing dead and cold from completely darkened headlights and lifeless interiors.

As they walked toward his car, he noticed a light fog from somewhere within the lot. There was also the sound of an exhaust pipe running. When they reached his car, they saw it was on, and the engine was grappling with shuddered reverberations.

"Did I turn the car on?" he asked.

"Why would it be on? Why would you have left the car on if you were going to be inside the club for such a long time?"

He shook his head, slightly. "I don't know. Have I done it before?"

"Yes."

He looked at her. "When?"

"About a year ago. In fact it was this same club, don't you remember?"

"And it didn't overheat?"

"Someone reminded you before it did."

"Wouldn't it overheat if it was out here for this long?" he asked as he turned his head back toward the car.

"I don't know why it wouldn't."

They heard a phone ring and looked toward the direction the sound was coming from. A pay phone was standing against the outside brick wall of the nightclub.

"Was that phone always there?" he asked as they continued to look at it.

It rang again. Its echo shattered through the faint winds, cutting into their ears. The sound solidified its image, bringing its black-as-night exterior into a sudden reality.

"Yes," she answered, "that phone has always been there."

"What are we going to do?"

"You should go answer it."

"What!?" he asked as his face contorted to a look of disbelief.

"You should go answer it," she said again before the phone rang for a third time.

"All right, then come with me."

As he started to walk, he felt that she wasn't moving. He turned to look at her.

"No, you go."

"What!?"

"I said you go. Go and see who it is."

"All right," he said as the phone rang a fourth time. "Let me get this straight. Dave has just dropped dead, the car is on and nobody knows why, and you want me to go over there alone and answer the phone?"

"Well," she said while nodding her head, slightly. "Yeah."

"I can't believe you."

She put her hands up to her head while forming a look of exasperation. "Rodger!" she said as the phone rang for a fifth time. "Just go over there and answer the damn thing!"

Against his better judgment, he turned and began walking toward the phone. While he was walking, he attempted to find comfort in this decision. However, his mind remained fearful, cracking his skull in a mind-numbing apprehension.

The phone rang for a sixth time. Its sound was louder. A new unforgiving and relentless shade of black was made vibrant beneath the systematic rings breaking its surface.

He then picked it up, cutting off the sixth ring. He put the phone to his ear and said, "Hello?"

"*Just get in the car*," a voice said.

His eyebrows arched upward, maddeningly, as his eyes widened. "Who is this?"

"*Just get inside the car, please.*" The voice was a general whisper. It was one that couldn't be identified and had sounded like nothing he heard before. "*Just get in the car and drive. The journey you are about to take will have to be.*"

"And why is that?"

"Don't ask too many questions right now. Don't think too much about it, just do it. This time, you're decision has to be your own."

"I don't understand what you're trying to tell me. Who the hell is this!?"

"Just refer to me as...the caller."

He then heard a click. Slowly, he hung the phone back up. He turned around and ran toward Nora. There was a grasping fear trembling through her stance. He stopped in front of her and said, "Let's get in the car."

"First of all, who was that on the phone?"

"I don't know, but they certainly have a sense for the dramatic. Anyway, let's go."

"Are you sure that's a good decision?"

He thought for a moment, and then said with complete confidence, "Yes."

They began walking toward the car. Their footsteps echoed for a distance, trembling atop the ground. There was a sound close to silence enclosing them, and the streetlights hung lifelessly from the power lines as only a few cars drove by, illuminating the lonely road for brief moments. He focused on their reflections within the midnight blue of his automobile as they went for the handles. Before they opened the doors, they looked at each other.

"You know," he said, "this almost seems laughable."

"Are you going to start laughing?" she asked. Her voice was genuinely curious.

"No," he said.

They both got in and shut the doors. He released the emergency break and looked to the back of him as he drove in reverse. When he was facing the street, he waited to see if any cars were coming on either side and turned left.

As he drove, he noticed that the roads were completely empty of any other cars and became fascinated from how his headlights were shining on the barren streets. He drove through an intersection and didn't even look to see if anyone was near. He noticed some of the buildings that dotted each side of the four-lane highway and saw only empty parking lots and places that were dark inside.

"I'm just waiting for someone to jump out of the backseat and kill us both," she said.

"Stop worrying. Besides, you are the one that wanted to tag along."

"Right."

She looked around the car for a few moments, an obvious question collecting in her head. She asked, "So, what do we do now?"

"About what?"

"About the fact that Dave is dead, Rodge. I mean, aren't we supposed to grieve? He was one of our friends and now he's dead."

He looked to the road for a few moments. He pressed his hands on the wheel tighter as he thought about that question. The thought of the life leaving his body as the blood escaped from his open wound entered his mind. Broken words struggled for completion in speech suddenly haunted him.

"Let's not talk about that," he said.

"But, Rodge—"

"I said let's forget about it!" he said as he rapidly turned his head toward hers.

She quickly responded by saying, "Look, Rodge, I know it's hard to deal with, but you have to get it out."

"You're making this into more than it is."

"Rodge, please."

He sighed with one long breath. It echoed into a long silence as it died down. She could hear the rasping of his breath screaming in her ears. For a long moment, not a word was said. She felt compelled to speak of something, but didn't. Only the sound of the engine could be heard as the car kept traveling through the dark streets. The headlights became ghosts revealing an abandoned, yet intriguing night. The streets, themselves, were of a hard concrete topped with a cold, gray tone. Deepened cracks bled through its surface.

Then he spoke. "Listen, let's not say anything for a while. A lot has happened in the past few hours. In fact, why don't we listen to the radio and just ride?"

"Okay," she said rapidly, afraid to evoke any kind of sadness from him.

He went for the dial of the radio and switched it on. There was somewhat of a technically powered sound becoming louder as he turned it up. It had a soft resonance hidden beneath its notes. A palpable image of a rain forest made from circuitry was embedded into its music. It played with purity into their ears as he let go of the dial. He put his right hand back on the wheel and continued to drive.

They could see that it was a cloudless night just below the top of the windshield. There was only a valley of burning stars splashed into an eternally darkened sky. Only she looked long enough to try and connect constellations. There were so many of them that it was almost too confusing to do so. But she started to focus in on only a few and tried to make her own connections.

Slowly, pictures started to show through the woven strings of small dotted lights. They were formations that were nothing like what a constellation should be, just shapes defined through the need of her imagination. She wanted to burn each star in her mind, so as to be rid of the apprehensions this situation was bringing. Her eyes began to circle in on groups of these pin-sized lights that she knew were large balls of gasses rolling throughout the galaxy, violently dancing with their nearly volcanic bodies. These realizations were allowed to amaze her thoughts for a moment, just long enough to forget what was really happening.

He was concentrating on the road. It was moving toward him at a fast rate. He was fascinated by the fact that the only sound was that of the engine voicing itself beneath the hood. It was like a low grumble exhausted from its continuous, overlapping motions. He wondered if he had pressed the accelerator a little more, would anyone be around to stop him? Everything around him seemed so empty, not a soul was seen walking through the roads. However, it was this emptiness that made the night seem even more intriguing. There was almost a danger to it. He felt safe because he believed he could control it. His malicious intentions could reach as far as he'd like, and there wouldn't be a person around to witness any of it. He wanted to press the pedal more, feel the car's speed drill itself into his flesh. There was nothing to crash into, nothing on the road. He smiled. It was a smile of villainous intentions just beneath his mind. He imagined his own face showing through the shadows of light reflected from the front of the car.

Then the thoughts of the past occurrences came back to him. It slowly took away the happiness that malice had brought him. He remembered being inside the night club and how it seemed to last forever. His mind was replaying all of the spinning lights. His role as an outcast haunted his head, again. But the guilt from David's life coming to such an end cried into his misery of being ousted. The two emotions were conflicting. He could hear the laughter on the dance floor, laughing for each other, laughing at him.

He wondered if any of them would have cared that Dave died, that a friend was lost. He even wondered if Blake would feel any kind of sympathy. He could see Dave falling on the seat again and again, struggling to speak beneath the physical pain crushing his body. The blood was coming back, rapidly escaping from his ripped and torn skin. He remembered how it flowed, carelessly. It was a river that had no understanding of suffering. It came fast and vengeful with its release, leaving him to feel the cold approach of death's shadow. He could imagine how cold Dave must have felt as his interior warmth was losing itself through the wound. He could see the red liquid reaching for him, taunting him, its vibrant color only confirming his strong emotions of wanting things and people to disappear. It began to pour over the pool room. The people laughing in the dance club, at him and at Dave's death, the spinning lights screaming through a blood red, it all collaborated in a controlled chaos. The people dancing carelessly held the blood in their hands as it spilled out onto the floor, spreading its body further into the cruel abyss of pulsating lights. They relished the death of another person no one knew. His thoughts were drowning in layered rivers of a bloodthirsty hopelessness.

He wanted to see Dave again, but the only Dave was the one that was dead.

He needed to run away from these taunting thoughts. His sudden escape route appeared as the bar heavily colored in a neon pink. All of the people were taken out of his head and he was suddenly thinking of only the bar and that radically bright shade. He didn't want to think of a color that he detested. But the more he tried to resist, the more vivid the remembrance became. Each bottle was still placed so perfectly within that structure and the counter's top, standing within that black-and-pink construction.

The bartender then faded into existence. He was wiping the counter top slowly with a red rag. He just wiped in small circles, its streaks trailing translucent silhouettes left over from the moisture. Charley's face was cradled in the pink luminosity and a thin layer of an underlying darkness. He smiled, slightly, as he continued to wipe the counter.

He could then hear Charley say within the faded sounds of his head, *"When are you going to leave this place?"* The rag's ink started to leak and it sweat with red. Its color was coming toward a darker existence and continued to dim its shade as it flowed over the neon pink trapped inside the top of the counter.

He gradually exited his mind as he put his concentration on the road. The deepening cracks branched outward on its surface, the motion of the car gliding on top of it, his foot pressing against the pedal. It almost felt as if he was flying off the road.

He could see a shape from far off. It was white and rectangular. The rectangle began to have dimensions, becoming something that he could identify. He kept looking, trying to see what it was. It was getting closer. The white was moving. But it seemed to be moving in exact alliance with him. The lights were beginning to show its physical definition. He suddenly realized what it was, and before he could slow down, the back of a car broke into the radiance of his headlights and was rapidly approaching the front of his automobile.

"RODGER, SLOW DOWN!" he heard Nora's voice scream as he pressed his foot against the brake. The car's tires cried against the pavement.

Their hearts sank as the hood came in close contact with the car in front of them.

"Shit!" he screamed as he swerved toward the right and their car spun into a half circle. They were suddenly thrust into an unstable circling of velocity until the tires hit the grass beside the road. The black rubber dug, quickly, into the grass with its spinning motion, tearing through into the earth. The automobile jolted to a stop as they were almost propelled forward.

They breathed, rapidly. They couldn't speak for the next few moments because their voices had not yet been found. They let their hearts come as close as it could to a normal rate. Nora then slammed her hand against his arm. "What the fuck were you doing!?"

He moved his head from side to side as his eyes widened in confusion. "I don't know, I didn't even see it."

"I kept telling you to slow down!" she yelled as her eyes burned into his.

He looked at her for a moment and said, "I didn't even hear you."

She sat back in her chair. "I don't know what the fuck has gotten into you."

"I'm sorry!" he said as he threw his hands up in the air before grasping the wheel again. "I...I didn't hear you."

She sighed, heavily. It was a pushed sound that ripped its way through her throat.

"You know what," she said in a voice that sounded as if it were giving up, "you should just let me drive."

"What?!" he said, grasping the wheel. He suddenly felt a new fear inside him. "Nora, I can't let you do that, this is my car," he said in a pleading voice.

"Yeah, well, it doesn't seem like you can drive it."

"So, what? I was out of focus for a second. It won't happe—"

"A second is all it takes, Rodge!" she screamed as she neared him. Her hands were grappling the sides of the seat as she peered at him, an intense anger in her eyes.

His voice became soft and submissive as he looked at her with eyes cast in a reflection of pleading. "Nora, I can do—"

"Rodger!" she yelled, her voice expanding in a furious insistence, "You are not going to get us killed! Now, get the fuck out of the car and let...me...drive!"

He exhaled deeply as he backed into the seat. His left eyebrow arched as his mouth became tight lipped. He grasped the driving wheel once more as he opened his mouth to speak. An insistence of his own was burning inside of him. However, it could sway at any moment. The power that it had was one that it could only cling to, almost lifelessly. It was as if he were expecting to surrender at any moment.

"I can drive," Rodger said as he pressed the pedal and slowly began to get away from the grass.

Surprisingly, Nora remained silent as she crossed her arms and lay back in the seat.

"Okay, why don't we just drive until we hit a rest area or a hotel or something?"

"Okay, then." He spoke rapidly.

"And please don't get us killed on the way."

He got the car back on the road and continued to drive. He then said, "I don't know what happened."

"Yeah, well, just don't do it again."

"I won't."

He started to think. "I wonder, why didn't the other car stop? Why didn't the driver complain or yell or scream?"

"Who cares," she said. "Let's just find some place to stay for the night."

"Why can't we go home?"

She looked to him with amazement. He looked at her with a slight curiosity. "What?' he asked.

"Rodge, Dave is dead and we are witnesses. We have to disappear and this will hopefully blow over."

"Then let's go to the police."

"No! We left him, Rodge, we left his body. Do you have any idea how suspicious that makes us look?"

He exhaled with an annoyance. "I think that we should go to the police and tell them the truth."

"Rodge, please, listen to me." Her voice was pleading. "There is a very big chance that we could be arrested for this. We could be facing a life sentence here."

He laughed. "Oh, common, Nora, you're making too much out of this."

"Rodge, let's find some place to rest, okay? The police are a very bad idea. Do you want to go to prison, Rodge? Huh?"

He thought for a moment. Her words were very convincing. He then said, "No, I guess not."

She sat back. "Okay, then. Let's just—"

"Find a place to crash? Like you've suggested for about the third or fourth time, now?"

"Well, at least we're on the same wave length."

"Can we go back to not talking, please? I know we've just experienced quite a situation," he turned his head toward hers, "but can we plea___"

"Rodge?" she said while looking to the front.

"What!?" he demanded.

"It's the car."

He looked to his front and saw the back of the white car. "I don't feel good about this situation," he said.

She looked to him and said, "Look for an exit."

"What do you think I'm doing?"

He then saw another pair of headlights in the rearview mirror. They were far off at the moment.

"Something's going to happen," he said. "We have to get off this road, now."

She began to breathe, deeply. "That certainly calms me down. Damn it! When is there going to be an actual peaceful moment, tonight!?"

He saw the pair of headlights coming closer. He felt an impulse. He began to edge his car toward the left end of the road.

"Rodge, what are you doing!?"

With the fear of hitting the grass again taking hold of his mind, he put his car back in alliance with the road. "I don't know!" he yelled. "I just need to get out of this situation!"

The headlights in the back were closing in on his bumper as the front car began to slow down.

"What is going on here, Rodge?" she asked.

"I don't know," he said as he saw an exit to the left. "But I am not going to stick around to find out."

He swerved the car toward the exit as they felt their bodies react to the sudden movement. He pressed the pedal further inward, making the car's speed heighten.

"Rodge, you can stop now!" Nora yelled once they went past the exit sign.

He slowed his car and looked behind him. There were no other automobiles in sight. He turned back around. "That was odd."

"Let's find a place to rest, okay? I don't care if it's in a fucking shit hole. All I want is to calm down."

"Then calm down."

She looked at him with skepticism. "That seems so rational, Rodge." Her voice was on an animated tone of sarcasm. "You know, because ever since Dave has died on us, everything that's happened so far has been some sort of heart-stopping experience like we were in some kind of movie! Yeah, I'll just calm down. Tonight has given us plenty of time to do that."

He sighed. "All right, so nothing normal has happened on this night."

"That puts it mildly."

"Let's just try and find some kind of comfort. Worrying about everything isn't going to make things better. Like I suggested before, why don't we go back to not talking?"

"After everything that's happened? We have to talk about it to let go."

"Not everyone can let things go through talking, Nora. So, please, let's be silent for now."

"Ro—"

He pressed his fingers harder against the wheel and felt a sudden burst of anger. He contorted his face into a raging expression and interrupted Nora by yelling, "JUST SHUT THE FUCK UP, OKAY!? THINGS ARE SCREWED UP ENOUGH!" He sat back in his seat as he continued to drive. He could feel his heart drilling into his chest as his stomach ached inside a devouring fury.

"Rodge, I'm sorry, bu—"

"Nora, please."

"No, you please, Rodge. I've been through a traumatic experience and I have to talk about it."

"I'm sure you've experienced worse."

"When was the last time one of our friends died?"

"Look, it's not as if David was that important anyway."

"What?" She arched her eyebrows in confusion and formed a sympathetically perturbed face.

"Let's face it—Dave was just someone that followed us around. He was a third wheel. When was the last time you ever even talked to Dave because you really wanted to? He pressed things too much, he wanted too much."

"Rodge, what are you trying to say?" she asked with a note of worried suspicion.

"Not what you're thinking. Yes, it's a tragedy that Dave died, but it wasn't that much of a loss." He then silenced himself. He tried to make sense of the words he just spoke, struggling to force them into the sorrow he had for David's death.

"Rodge, if you're saddened by this, the—"

"Nora, just shut up, okay? Please."

She only looked at him with concern. She sat back in her seat and exhaled deeply. Not another word was said. However, there was a tension forming between the two of them, one that they didn't attempt to break.

He began to wonder if Nora was worried about him or suspected him. He wanted to say something to dispel such theories, but he couldn't bring himself to speak. He was unnerved from the apprehension of making things sound worse. So, he let everything conflict inside his mind. The worries breathed into his body like a cancer eating his insides. Nothing seemed like the right thing to do.

To their left, they saw a small motel. It was blackened and the walls were worn to a point where they were decaying. There were few cars parked in the lot, and each of them were rusted and aged. The ground around it was covered in gravel.

"No," he said. "I don't care how much trouble we're in. We are not going to go into a hotel that closely resembles something Norman Bates would invest in."

She didn't say anything.

"We'll just try to find a nice, decent place to stay."

Still, she didn't say anything. Her silence was knifing into him. He didn't say anything else, thinking that it would only enhance her current behavior. He kept driving and was starting to frantically look for a decent place, one that wouldn't exemplify a feeling of discomfort.

They both then saw a small motel on a hill to their right. It looked to be mediocre and was only a structure of about six or seven rooms. It looked somewhat peaceful.

There was a beige sign standing next to the entranceway. It had the words "The Wishing Motel" painted onto it in crude, black letters.

"Do you want to go there?" he asked. Still, she said nothing. "Damn it, Nora, talk to me."

"I thought you said you didn't want to talk."

"Stop playing around, this is not the time for that. Now do you want to go here or not?"

"Fine."

Even though he was disappointed in her one-word answer, he proceeded to drive up the small hill. He turned toward the first parking space and stopped the car once he situated it and turned it off.

They both got out of the car and walked toward the motel. Once they got closer to it, they saw that it was more of a curiosity. After walking up the steps, they could see that the structure was somewhat old-fashioned. The exterior looked to be as desolate as the surrounding area. The windows were completely darkened and it formed an interior of a country-western setting in their minds. However, the western motif was defined by the possibility of naïve and disturbed people. They looked up ahead and saw that a door was open. There was a rippling glow from what sounded to be television. The sound of a twanging song was off in the distance. It played into their ears as if it were a tormented ghost.

Feeling a simultaneous eeriness, they rapidly turned around. Once they did, a man appeared in front of them and they both felt their nerves jump.

"Hello," the man said. He wasn't dressed from how they thought the occupants of this place would be. He was an attractive man who was clothed in fashionable attire. His shirt was a sleek black that showed the shape of his chest and his pants were a light gray tone that complimented the black very well. His light brown hair was combed to a physical perfection, completing his caramel eyes. "I'm Winston; I'm the owner of this little establishment." He extended his hand.

They both shook it as obvious interest crossed their eyes.

"I assume you'll need a room."

"Yes," Rodger said. "Yes, that assumption would be correct."

Winston smiled with a particular look toward him.

"So, you have one, right?" she asked.

"Oh, of course," Winston said while lifting up his hands. "Newlyweds, right?"

They both looked at each other and laughed. "No, no," he said.

"We're not together. We're just, um…."

"Friends."

"Yeah."

"Okay," Winston said with a curiosity in his face. "Follow me; I'll give you two a key."

They followed him into the last room with the open door. As they walked into the room, Winston said, "You'll have to forgive the twangy tone, it's just sometimes I like to listen to this kind of music. If it bothers you, please just tell me. I'll turn it down."

After they all got into the room, he said, "Please, have a seat." They looked to the left of the king-sized bed, where there were two chairs sitting in front of a desk. The desk, itself, was in front of the wall opposite the bed and looked like it belonged in an office. There were papers scattered throughout the surface of it. As they sat on the bed, they looked around the room.

The majority of the room resembled a front lobby. To the left of the television was a board built into the wall. Along it were eight keys, one of which, the biggest one, looked to be the skeleton key. There was a podium standing in front of the board as well, supporting a sign-in book that looked to be very thick.

They listened to the television as he went for one of the keys. It showed a man singing in a rainstorm. His voice was screeching with a high tone, telling of stories that were desperate and lost. The singer was standing in the middle of an alley with reddening bricks on either side. To the back of him, on the right, stood a sign that read "Willfire." This caught Rodger's attention and he began to listen to the words the man was singing:

"...I've been trapped inside these bricks,
My only love is the death of dreams that lay me down to sleep,
When I wake, it is this nightmare that we call life,
I'm trapped inside my own head,
It's going to break and I'll be dead,
Whisper to me your convictions,
Tell me how much I don't matter,
It don't mean a thing,
Because I can't even stand my own ground..."

Winston walked back toward them holding a key. They looked at it with curiosity. "It's blue," Nora said.

"Yes, um, sorry about that. It fell into some paint."

"Why didn't you just clean it?" Rodger asked.

"It's a long story," he said with an evasive smile. And as if to divert them from any more questioning, he shoved the key into Nora's hand. "Well, you two must be tired." His voice sounded pushed.

"I guess we are," Nora said. "We've had quite a night."

"Really?" Winston asked with some suspicion.

"Not that kind of night," Rodger said.

Winston then smiled with interest at him. Nora got up and said, "Well, I am very tired. Listen, I'm going to go to bed. Rodger, why don't you and Winston stay here and talk?"

Rodger had an astonished look. As Nora walked toward the door, he said, "Hold on, Nora, there's something that I have to say first." He looked to Winston and said, "Excuse me."

"Of course," he responded.

He walked rapidly up to Nora as they both exited out of the room and stood right by the door way. They conversed in whispers.

"Why are you going to leave me here with him? I don't even *know* him. He could be dangerous."

She laughed, lightly. "Don't be silly, Rodge. Besides, he obviously seems interested."

"After the night that we've just had, I don't think it's a good idea for us to part."

"I'm going to be fine, Rodge. Don't worry about me; I can defend myself. You have a good intuition about you. I'm sure that you'll know when to get out."

"He listens to country western music, and not even the good kind; he doesn't really say much. Basically, there is a lot of mystery about him."

"There's a lot of mystery about a lot of people. Listen, just talk to him. What's the worst that could happen?"

"That question is like the phrase, 'Knock on wood,' or 'What else could possibly go wrong?'. It's not a good sign when someone asks that."

She rolled her eyes, "Please, just get to know him. Like I said before, he seems very interested."

"Yeah, but in what, my body or how to dissect it?"

"I'd like to close my door sometime tonight," Winston's voice said.

They both were surprised as they turned around, quickly. Nora then said, "Rodge is going to keep you company. I'm going to go to bed. Night, Rodge."

Rodger was going to say something, but Nora left him before he could. He then turned to Winston and said, "She's very insistent, it's her nature."

"I can see that. Well, you'd better come inside, anyhow. It's going to be awfully cold out here and you need at least some kind of shelter."

He was intrigued by Winston's offer, and even excited. But there was also a fear as to what intentions Winston had. He ignored that fear and walked inside his room as Winston closed the door behind him.

"Are all the rooms like this?" he asked.

"Well, except for the desk, keys, podium and space, yeah." He laughed after his own answer.

Rodger smiled as he turned around. He then felt compelled to ask, "How far away is this from Restless Falls?"

"Oh, you guys are miles away from Restless Falls."

"How many miles?"

"Oh, I'd probably say about eighty, ninety. Why? Is that where you guys live?"

With amazement in his eyes, he said, "Yeah, it is." It didn't feel like that long a trip to Rodger. It only felt like just over thirty, but ninety was something that he would've never conceived of.

Winston then sat on the edge of the bed and proceeded to ask, "Wanna seat?"

Rodger waited for a moment, wondering if that would be the right decision. But then he realized he was already inside Winston's room and sat next to him.

"So, why did you two travel all the way out here?" he asked as he turned his head toward Rodger.

"We don't know, really. It was just a split-second decision. I guess we were bored and decided to do something."

As they conversed, the music still sang with its desperate tone. Rodger looked to the television and still saw the man in the alley. The rain continued to come down and he remained to stand in the same position. The only body part that was moving was his mouth. The singer continued to tell the story of his life:

"...Don't ask me what I should say
Because I just don't know,
Maybe it's time I move on
But time is being too cruel..."

"I hope you at least like it here," Winston's voice interrupted.

Rodger looked to him as he was torn away from the television. "Huh?"

Winston laughed, slightly. "I hope you at least like it here. Do you?"

"Oh, um, yeah, yeah I do. It's...really nice."

"You sound like you're just saying that."

"Oh, no, no I'm not, really. I just don't have much to say about this place is all."

"Oh, I see." He smiled, mischievously.

Rodger looked down for a moment, caressing his fingers on the mattress in small circles. "So, you call this place 'The Wishing Motel'?" he asked to break the tension that was beginning to form inside him.

"Yeah, nice name, huh?"

"Yeah, did you think of that?"

They were both beginning to feel more comfortable. They acted out the comfort by letting their positions become more relaxed.

"Well, actually, no. My ex came up with it."

110

"Your ex? Did you two own this place?"

"Yeah, we both invested in it. He's the one that had the idea."

Rodger's face showed a surprised look.

Winston smiled, knowingly. "Oh, common, it's not like you didn't know. Besides, isn't that why you're here?"

He looked at Winston with misunderstanding. "What exactly do you mean?"

"I don't think I have to explain myself. You already have a pretty good idea, and you're already intrigued. In fact, I would say more than that."

He tried to hold down a smile, but didn't succeed. He then asked with an intimidated voice, "Could, ugh, co-o-oould you be more, well…blunt?"

He laughed, slightly. "The reason that you are here, Rodger, is because you want us to fuck."

He widened his eyes in shy wanting.

"But not just yet," Winston said while looking at Rodger up and down, once. He then said, "Before I sleep with someone, I at least want to get to know them first."

"What do you want to know?" he asked as he laughed with obvious giddiness.

"Not so fast, there. We should at least try to take things slow, even if it is one night. After all, one night can last a lifetime." Winston positioned his face to evoke a passionate curiosity from Rodger.

"So I see."

"I guess you do. Anyway, one of the things I really do want to know, though, was what did you think of this little place and the people in it when you first got here?"

"Why do you want to know that?"

"Because when I first saw you two, you both looked like you were very ready to leave this place, almost as if you were afraid of it."

"How honest do you want me to be?"

"Brutally."

"Well, if you really want that much honesty, then, I thought that this place was kind of, well … disturbing. In fact when we heard that country music in this room, and it wall all the way down that hallway, and very faint, the first thought that popped into my head was, well, for people to be running out with chainsaws and wearing the flesh of human victims."

Winston laughed. "Really? So you thought that this place was just crawling with chainsaw-carrying hicks?"

"You wanted me to be brutally honest."

"And I got it," Winston said while looking at Rodger in a contented intrigue.

"Hey, I wonder, have you ever gotten any weird customers here, before?"

"To tell you the truth, we don't get very many people, here. Or should I say *I* don't get very many people here, since it's just me, now, anyway. But, yes, out of the few people that actually do stop by, I've seen some weird ones. Like there was this one family who was completely perfect. Everything about them was perfect: perfect hair, perfect teeth, perfect clothes, perfect everything. They seemed like they were all in the same state of mind. It was like watching this television family from the fifties jump into reality. They didn't swear, and they even thought 'heck' was a bad word. One of their boys said that and the father gave them a very stern look. They were just so together, and too well dressed. It really gave me the creeps."

"So you don't like normalcy either."

"Well, what *is* normalcy? That, in itself, is an age-old question. People have asked themselves and each other that for years. Normalcy is not something that gets to me, it just irritates me when people—"

"Try and achieve what they think it is?"

"You took the words right out of my mouth," Winston said, curving a smile within the same contentment. His eyes were calmly shaped and looked at Rodger in a reserved wanting.

"I don't like that, either. People try and understand what normal is, but they try and see their own vision of it. Those kinds of people are striving to be like that just to satisfy others because they think everyone else expects that of them. They think if they act a certain way, or talk a certain way—"

"Then they'll blend in with everyone else and their own individuality just slips away."

Rodger laughed, lightly. "Exactly."

Rodger was suddenly becoming calm as well, affected by Winston's tranquility. He felt very cool and comfortable to be in this place. Rodger wanted to just touch Winston's hand with his fingertips, and even began moving them toward his hand. But then he stopped himself, wanting to believe he had all night.

"We seem to be on the same wave length, Rodger."

"I'm sensing that."

They both laughed slightly at that statement.

"So, how did you get into the motel business?"

"Well, I was actually kind of pushed into it."

"And how would one get 'pushed' into this kind of business?" Rodger asked with a playful smile.

Winston returned the smile. "It's a long story with a string of broken hearts."

"Well, that's nothing new to me, since I am the broken-hearted."

"So you've been damaged as well."

"With supposed friends that like to use me for their own purposes and entertainment, not to mention the fact that I'm usually the one pushed into the shadows at social events, yeah, I guess you could say I am, just a little."

"Maybe you just like to think of your life that way."

Rodger arched his eyebrows as his comfort suddenly suffered a small puncture. He reacted with a voice that broke away from its serenity and sounded briefly tense. "How do you mean?"

"From what it sounds like to me, you've let things go this far."

"You're not going to start criticizing me, are you? I don't think that that's going to be a very good mood setter," he said, slightly laughing from a different intimidation, one that feared the end of this sexual comfort.

He laughed, slightly. "You're right, I'm sorry. I kind of have the habit of jumping into other people's lives."

"I see," Rodger said, suddenly relieved. "So, are you going to tell me your long story that left a string of broken hearts?"

"No, not really. Tonight should not be meant for reflecting on our miseries. There should be some sort of positive tone with this moment."

Rodger laughed. "There is no positive tone in my life. If I'm lucky, I get to experience a brief shining moment of acceptance here and there."

He then looked at Rodger for a long moment. His eyes were piercing and his face was inquisitive.

"What is it?" Rodger asked.

"Tell me, Rodger, how do you feel?"

"Why do you ask that?"

"I just want to know. Haven't you ever met someone that just wanted to know?"

"About me?"

"About anything. Tell me."

"Truthfully?"

"Yes."

"Well, I feel kind of good. However, I also feel like what's happening right now isn't real. Like it's some kind of dream, and like the cruel trickery of one's dream, I'll wake up just before we kiss."

Winston then rapidly pulled himself toward Rodger's lips. He pressed his lips onto Rodger's before he could react. They became caught in the moment and were beginning to feel as if they were losing their breath to one another while their tongues delicately twisted. Winston then let go of his lips and pulled back. "Did you wake up?" Winston asked.

He smiled. "Maybe this dream will be a little more sympathetic."

Rodger pulled his face toward Winston's. He could feel the need to regain touch become palpable across his lips. He then felt what seemed like two finger tips cover his mouth. Rodger looked to Winston as he said, "Not just yet. I don't jump into bed with complete strangers."

Rodger smirked as Winston put his fingers down. "If we have sex before the night is through, I'll still be someone that you met only tonight. And besides, I could always lie about myself."

Winston laughed. "I can tell when someone isn't telling the truth."

"Maybe I'm a really good liar."

Winston gave him a knowing look. He put his hands over Rodger's and said, "No...you're not. I can tell."

"And why do you say that?"

"I can tell just from looking at you. You're eyes seem to be begging for something. I can feel that your skin is shaking. I know your heart has got to be beating a million miles an hour."

Rodger started to lose his smile.

"You haven't had sex in a lo-o-o-o-ong time, have you, Rodger? Of course you wouldn't lie, you're too nervous to. You don't want to say or do anything to possibly ruin this moment."

He arched his left eyebrow. "You can read people well. Should I be insulted by this?" he asked as his comfort was brought down more. Tranquility began to release him, quickly, leaving only the cold touch of rejection.

Winston pursed his lips while forming what seemed like a sarcastically sympathetic reply. "I'm sorry if I sounded too harsh. I tend to be a little blunt."

"That puts it mildly."

"You're not upset with me, are you?"

He looked back to the television for a moment. The man was still in the alleyway with reddened bricks. He continued to sing his story:

"...I'm bleeding, can't you see?
It's not the fact that you didn't care,

Because my heart was bound to be broken,
I'm walking on broken glass,
Thinking I'll find relief,
My apprehensions
Have become my false beliefs..."

"Rodger?"

He turned back towards Winston's voice. "Huh?"

"Are you upset with me?" Winston's face wasn't worried. He only showed a light concern. His eyes weren't remorseful, only curious, as if he wanted to know the answer to a simpler question.

"No," he said, suddenly, while moving his head back and forth. "No, I'm not."

The truth burned him as he spoke that. The words, themselves, felt like knives slicing his tongue. He wanted to speak the truth, but couldn't. The fear of rejection was too much of a deterrent.

Winston smiled. "Good. Then maybe we can continue talking?"

"About what?"

"About anything."

He was showing an irritation. "Why should we even talk at all? Do you really want to get to know me?"

Winston let go of a breath with a pushed voice of small laughter. "Of course I do. I want to know as much as I possibly can about you. Why do you ask?"

"Do you enjoy fucking with people's heads, too?"

"What?" Winston grimaced. His voice was suddenly shoved down into a gruff, demanding tone.

"Let me tell you a little story, Winston. It's a really short one. It's about a guy named Rodger. And you see, Rodger had encountered many people in his life who he thought he could consider a friend. But he had yet to meet someone that was who they said they really were. And you know what, he still hasn't." Rodger's voice was becoming agitated as he looked to Winston in an irritation. The true rage within him hid beneath that familiar fear of rejection. He could not show the entirety of his anger, for something that complete would ruin such an incomplete situation.

Winston moved his head a little from side to side while trying to form words. He then said, "Look, Rodger, I'm sorry if I gave you the wrong impression or if I upset you in anyway. I didn't mean to, really. You shouldn't get so defensive."

"Defensive?" His tone was becoming accusatory. "Defensive? You know, maybe I should start getting a little defensive, it's better than not defending yourself at all. I stood by all my life and just let things happen. Maybe I should start trying to leave all of the upsetting things in my life behind instead of trying to make sense of them so much."

Winston grabbed onto his shoulders. "Look, Rodger, I'm sorry, please don't do this. Yes, maybe it's true that you've let things happen for too long. Maybe it's true that you should start defending yourself more. But, please, I am just trying to be your friend. Even if sex is the goal for tonight, that doesn't mean that we shouldn't try to understand each other. Besides, it doesn't matter how this night will end, all that matters is how we get there."

He let out an exasperated breath while looking to Winston for a sign of truth. He then said, "Perhaps you're right."

Winston smiled. "Great. Listen, there's a diner not that far from here. Maybe we should go to it. Try to talk about things."

"Why?"

"Well, it might help us try and understand each other more. And besides, it's a great diner, neat as hell. What do you say?"

"I don't even know you. How do I know you won't just drive me to some remote place and dismember me?"

"Then follow me in *your* car. That way, if you suspect that I'm leading you off some place far away, or if you feel uncomfortable, you can drive off. I won't be offended, really. And you can even bring your friend along with you."

He tilted his head, slightly while thinking. "No, that's okay. Nora might only complicate things. I'll follow you then."

Winston smiled. "Glad to hear it."

Rodger looked back to the television screen. The man continued to sing in the alleyway within the rain:

"...I never had a voice of my own,
I've become the ghost that you created,
My devotion is hopeless,
And still,
I have yet to find anything in this journey of empty souls,
I'm beginning to wonder if I should just wait for death."

The television faded to black. The song was over.

The pink shade doused the material completely. It covered her body in a style reminiscent of the fifties. Their seat was a half-circle shape and embroidered in a deathly yellow color. The floor was held within a design of checkers. A jukebox stood against the left wall, it was mainly shaded in a ruby red. Around the top half of this machine was a surrounding of at least three neon strings of color. There were bubbles swimming inside each string, almost like the continuing cycle of a lava lamp.

They sat next to a large window. Their reflections were cast against a night atmosphere with not a cloud in the sky. The scenery was only of a street with a few houses dotted on each side. The street itself lay littered in crumpled papers and random garbage.

"Will that be all, hon?" the waitress asked as she finished writing down the last order.

"Huh? Yeah, sure, that's fine," he responded.

She put the pamphlet in the pocket of her apron and went toward the kitchen in the back.

"So, how do you like it?" Winston asked.

"What?" he asked as he brought his head forward.

"The diner, what do you think of the diner?"

"It, um," he looked around. There was a vivid sense of similarity creeping into his mind. "It…seems familiar."

Winston tilted his head, slightly, to the right. "Really? Have you been here before?" he asked as he straightened his head back to where it was.

"I don't know."

"Maybe it's déjà vu."

"Perhaps, I don't know," he said while he turned his head down as if looking for something. His voice became a loud whisper. He looked back up and said in his normal voice, "Is this where you take all your one-night stands?" He wanted to change the subject.

Winston smiled slightly at him. It was almost a smirk. "No, this is where I take all the people that I plan to have a relationship with and then break their heart."

"You know, a broken heart is nothing to laugh at," he said with a comical tone.

"It can be. It all depends on how it can get broken."

"Enough about broken hearts, let's talk about whatever you want to talk about."

"Well, it's not really what I want to talk about; it's mainly what *we* want to talk about."

He laughed lightly as he looked to the window behind him. There was someone standing behind it outside the diner. He wore a tuxedo and had white gloves. His hair was a dark brown and perfectly combed. He held a mask up to his face that just covered half of it. The mask had a small pole connected to it so that he could hold it. It had a smooth texture and went over the tip of his nose, extending around the nostrils. The sides were segmented into curved triangular shapes going upward. There were perfectly large circles where the eyes should have been. The circles had a sleek texture of a pitch black and were pushed outward. It almost looked as if a significantly large marble was severed in half and placed into two holes of the exact shape.

The masked man stood perfectly erect. He wasn't sure if this man's shrouded face was staring at him or elsewhere. He also noticed how there was a heavy rainstorm outside, and the material of his clothes, his hair, every part of him remained to be unaffected from the moisture of the rain.

"Rodger, Rodger what is it?" he heard Winston's voice ask.

"There's a man standing outside." His tone was a light whisper.

"What man standing outside?"

He looked to Winston. "Right there," he said as he pointed to the window. When he looked back, he saw that the man had become a reflection in the glass. He looked to the back and tried to see if the masked man was standing anywhere inside the restaurant.

"Rodger, I don't see any man standing outside."

He looked back to the window and saw that Winston was staring right at it. There was now nothing there: not a reflection, not a person, nothing but the rain tapping against the glass. He looked back to Winston as Winston looked back at him.

"Are you okay?" Winston asked with concerned eyes.

"Yeah, yeah, I'm fine."

"Are you sure?"

"I'm fine," he said while laughing. "I guess it was just something else."

"Oh, well, anyway, so, I assume that you drove all the way here."

He smiled at Winston, then said, "You would assume correctly."

Winston leaned toward him and asked, "Did you just decide to take a trip off somewhere?"

"Yeah, I guess you could say that. You know, I think you already *asked* that question."

"Where were you when you decided to leave?"

He curved the right side of his mouth upward while giving Winston a look of suspicion. "Why the third degree all of a sudden?"

He laughed, "Sorry. I guess I just have a habit of asking too many questions. It's in my nature."

"So, I see. Why are you always so inquisitive?"

"I don't know, I guess it's because I find other people's lives so much more intriguing. Just the stories that they tell, and the experiences they've endured along the way."

"So, I guess one could say that you are a voyeur."

"Yeah, well, maybe I just want to try to see what the people around me are like."

"That sounds an awful lot like a voyeur."

Winston smiled, once more. It almost seemed to be one of intrigue. "Haven't you ever wanted to know what other people are like, even people that were never that interesting to you? Haven't you ever just wanted to know?"

He had a calm look on his face. He was contented by Winston's questions, by his voice, by just him. He wanted to answer the questions instead of just avoiding them. "There's enough shit going on in my life, I don't need someone else's thoughts making it worse." His voice was very smooth as his tongue formed the words in a leisurely perfection.

"Maybe you need to jump into someone else for a while, to put things in place."

"I am my own person. And this person can't pretend to be something else. This person doesn't have the luxury of make believe."

"Everyone has that luxury. Sometimes, people bury themselves in too much truth to find it."

He spread his mouth out into a broadened, attractive smile while exhaling once with a pushed laughter. He let go of the smile and said, "Okay, let me turn the tables here. Have you found the person that you are?"

Winston rapidly moved his head back while widening his eyes to express the obviously unexpected emotion he felt. He brought his head forward, again, and said, "Wow, where did that one come from? You just jumped right out there."

"It's rare, but sometimes I do take chances. So answer my question."

Winston laughed, lightly. "Awfully demanding, aren't you?"

He only stared at Winston with an expectant look.

"All right, okay. Well, yes and no. I really don't think that anyone can find who they are. I believe that that's not what life is about. Life is about experiencing. It's supposed to be fun and sad and intense and happy and pleasurable and exciting and erotic and depressing and just so many emotions on so many different levels. Introspection is a good thing, but it's nothing to get lost in."

"Why's that?"

Winston smiled, kiddingly, and said, "You'll get a headache."

They laughed, collectively.

He then said, "That was a really good answer."

"Oh, you're pleased, are you?" Winston asked, a tranquil comfort masked his face.

"Very. Now…"

"You have more?"

"Of course, a person can never ask too many questions. Anyway, why do you think you live in a place where the people never stay the same?"

"Well, like I said, I was pushed into it."

"Did you have to stay there?"

"I don't know. I guess. I felt as if I had to care for it. It was what was left behind to me and I couldn't throw it away. In fact, I invite all these different people into my space. It gives me a variety of understanding and a broader sense of society. I've always welcomed that kind of change in my life."

Rodger's smile somewhat faded. He could feel that a little of his serenity had been lost. "I see," he said while moving his eyes down to the table. There was a new confusion imprinting on his mind. His stare became lost upon the table for a moment while his mind moved into different directions, all suddenly needing answers from a painful wanting. When he faced Winston again, he looked to be more than curious; rather, like he desperately needed to know.

He then asked, "If you were narrating a story that happened in your life, would you ever include your own name in the telling of it?" He didn't know why he had to ask that question, he just felt he needed to know such an answer to gain his serenity back.

Winston only arched his left eyebrow and stared at him for a long moment. Winston's face became devoid of any emotion. The smiles and laughter were gone. He then said, "Maybe you should try some of these questions on yourself."

The waitress came back to their table and lay the plates down toward each of them while announcing the food. "You got the burger and fries and you got the … toast." She smiled and walked away.

He didn't even focus on the waitress. He could feel that his contentment had been stolen from him again and he became lost in pushed, unstable breathing. His eyes became sorrowful as he could feel his heart rattle from a multitude of beats.

Winston's eyes were sympathetic. "Rodger? Rodger, are you okay?" Winston then reached out to him. At that instant, he became afraid of Winston's touch. He could already sense the burning of Winston's fingers against his flesh.

As Winston reached out, the formation of his body changed. His eyes became doused in a green; his hair fell into slightly longer strands, his face became that of another.

When he went to touch his cheek, Winston had disappeared. "Rodge, are you okay?"

He leaned back into his seat and exhaled with one long exasperated breath. "Blake."

Blake put his hand down next to his lap. He then said, "Look, I know this is all overwhelming for you."

"You bet it is. Nothing's staying the same." His voice hid inside a delicate protest as his head ached with a multitude of passing thoughts, all of which took the form of daggers ripping his sense of security and safety.

"That's expected in a situation like this. Sometimes people are just meant to be no more."

"That doesn't mean that they can just disappear whenever they feel like it."

"Well, shit happens. I'm sorry, but it does."

"I need more of an explanation than that. I deserve more than that."

Blake put his head forward while looking around. He whispered, "It's just as much your fault as it is ours."

"I don't think that I can take responsibility for this."

Blake put his body back against the seat. "What?" He had a pushed whisper.

"I never meant for any of this to happen."

Blake tilted his head while forming a look of understanding. "Look," Blake said, "I know you feel guilty about this, of—"

"Guilty about what?"

He looked over Blake's shoulder as he saw Nora walk through the entrance door. He looked back to Blake as if he could be the savior with just one explanation.

"About killing Dave."

He pushed both of his eyebrows down while widening his eyes. In a voice of overemphasized shock, he said, "What?"

"I'm sorry, Rodge, but it happened. We had to do it."

He shook his head, slightly. He then stopped and stared right into Blake's eyes. With the same sorrowful look, he asked in a softly broken voice, "Why?" as the thoughtful daggers multiplied throughout the already tormented corners buried inside his head.

"It had to happen, Rodge, I'm sorry. Sometimes things just are."

Nora came to the table. Blake moved in so she could sit next to him. She looked to Blake and asked, "Is he still upset?"

"It's a pretty traumatic experience to lose a friend, Nora," Blake said.

She then looked over to him. Her eyes were cold. "He's dead, honey, get over it."

"Nora!" Blake said in a light whisper.

"I'm sorry, Blake, but if Rodge here can't deal, then he's worthless. I'm not going to get life in prison over a guilt trip."

"I'm sorry to disturb your plans," he said with a sarcastic anger, pulling his voice out of the disturbing and puzzling abyss gradually swallowing him.

"You know, you should also be worried about yourself, Rodge," Nora said. "You could be facing imprisonment just like the rest of us."

"I'm already imprisoned."

"Don't get symbolic on me, now." Nora said. "There is nothing but simple truth at this table, so stop trying to sound so profound and just be the pathetic, fearful loser you are."

He stared at her with a burning fury as he breathed in, deeply, and exhaled with a long, pushed breath.

"Don't expect me to say anything, Rodge," Nora said. "If you're expecting an apology, then you're just going to have to wait until I see you in hell."

"Nora, you are being incredibly vicious. You're not the only one going through this," Blake said. His face sought some sort of emotion from her, but he couldn't find any. "Why don't you calm down, all right? Shit happens, we know this. Dave died, I'm sorry if that makes you feel upset, bu—"

"Will you please shut up, Blake?" she said as she turned her head rapidly toward his. "You're not my fucking savior."

Blake looked to the front while arching his left eyebrow as she turned away from him. "Listen, Rodge," she said, "it had to happen. Dave was really pushing it and he was about to die, anyway. We just helped him get there faster."

He only stared at Nora in a momentary disbelief of which quickly changed to an angrily expressive face. He could feel his heart sinking as a trembling resurfaced in his throat.

"Don't even start to cry," she said.

"Nora, he's been affected," Blake said. "We all have. *I* could break down in tears, right now."

"Oh, please. If you two start to go all emotional on me, I swear, I am going to leave. I'll just let the cops take you two away."

Blake looked to Nora. He edged his face toward her. She could feel his breath against her hair; it was pushed with a shuddering rage. He whispered the words in a raspy and unforgiving tone, "If we're going down...you are going down *with* us."

A smile crossed her lips. It was smug and more than knowing. "Whatever you say, Blake, but just remember, I can get myself out of any situation."

"That's just what you think," Blake said. "Be careful, being too confident can bury you."

Rodger brought himself forward to both of them and asked, "Why did we kill Dave?"

"It's not as if you weren't there," Nora said. "You saw what happened."

"Rodge, you're one of my best friends, and you know that I appreciate you, but I can't go on like this, explaining everything to you. You've asked this umpteen times tonight. Please, just give it a rest. Think about something else, something that makes you feel more content."

"How can I feel comfortable? Dave died, and we're responsible."

"Get over it, Rodge," Nora said. "Besides, he really wasn't that important, anyway. It's not as if he was that big of a loss. He just hung around everyone. He didn't really say much. He had no life, and no real friends. I mean, we pretty much did him a favor."

"You know, you've got some nerve," Blake said. "I can't believe you can just sit there and spout things like that. How can you feel happy with yourself?"

"I feel just fine about myself," Nora answered. "I look into the mirror every day and I still like what I see. There's no guilt here."

"Obviously not," he said.

Blake smiled slightly at his comment.

"Yeah, and that's because I don't let things get to me. I'll admit it, I've done some shit in my life that I'm not too proud of. But I don't let it get me down. You have to live your life and if you let all the regrets you've had continue to eat you away inside, then you might as well just blow your fucking brains out."

"I see."

"Look, Rodge, why don't you just go back to the motel?" Blake asked. "I think you might need some time alone."

"I feel fine."

"Are you sure?"

"Yes, I'm sure."

"I can't believe you," Nora said to him. "You've lived twenty-four years of your life, and you still can't get over shit."

"Nora, will you please just leave him alone?" Blake asked. "I am getting really sick and tired of your mouth."

"I speak nothing but the truth."

"Yeah, well, *your* truths seem to be a little detached from reality," he said.

"The truth hurts. That's just a fact of life. Deal with it."

"The truth may hurt, Nora, but you know what?" he asked.

"What?" Nora said with a mockery in her voice.

"I think that the only reason you're being as cold as you are is just so you can fool yourself into some sort of satisfaction with what you're doing. You're trying to hide the fact that you feel just as guilty as we do."

"I think you're just saying that so that you can feel superior."

"Look, Dave's dead," Blake said. "It happened; we have to try to move on. Arguing about it, and tearing each other apart over it isn't going to make things any better or easier. So, we should just try to leave it behind and move one with our lives."

None of them said anything for a long moment. They tried to find agreement in that statement but this death was placing itself against their emotions.

"Just like that?" he asked. "How can we leave it behind the same night it happens?"

"We can try," Blake said. "We can just try. I know you feel bad about this, believe me, so do I. But we can't let this eat away at us. People fuck up. I mean, yeah, killing someone isn't exactly excused, but it happened, anyway. I say we try to have our dinners and calm down."

They stared at each other. They each remembered the kind of person Dave was, trying to find some sort of explanation to rationalize his death. All they could see was the person they spent time with, the person that was with them, the person that was just as much of a friend as they were to each other. They tried to forget their current emotions. Nora took a bite from Blake's plate. It followed into a chain reaction of everyone eating.

It was silent now. All that could be heard was the rain outside and the faint conversations behind the kitchen. They concentrated on the food and let its taste melt into their thoughts. As they swallowed, they could feel Dave becoming more of a memory. He still remained a strong presence in their minds, and their stomachs still felt like stones that had sunk into a watery abyss, but this would at least put some solace in the night.

Rodger went for his toast. He bit into it as the sound of it trembled in his ears. Its flavor was slightly stale, and it grinded against his teeth as he bit into it. He took a drink of his water and gulped three times as it rolled in tumbles within the glass. The thin ice cubes swam inside the deepening ripples as they clanged against the glass. Each intake of water went quickly down his throat as it closed in on the liquid and thirsted for it like it was a redeeming addiction. He put the glass down lightly and continued eating his toast, letting the crumbs fall to the plate, covering it in plain brown confetti.

Blake chewed his fries with caution. The heat floated inside his mouth as a dense fog dampened his taste. He proceeded to salt his fries. They were already coated in a heavy film, but he still wanted more, more of a taste, more of a bitterness to just keep it alive. He put the salt back down on the table and went for his burger, trying to hold its insides. He could feel them sliding out from its breaded body, so he held tighter. He took one large bite out of it and had to condense the bite of food because it was slipping in between his lips, almost coating them. He chewed with a quivering effort. Slowly, this food was lessening its size as his cheeks expanded as he continued to eat away at it, feeling as if they were coming closer to being ripped apart.

Nora ate lightly. She didn't take bites that were too small or too big. She just ate at her own pace and with ease. She almost taunted the food by slowly taking away from its body. Her fries were inserted without being blown on and she just let the heat burn inside. She didn't take any drinks of water or eat slower. The surface of her tongue raged with a fire. She didn't react to it; she wouldn't let it pull her expressions into a bitter face, letting what naturally should have been happening, which was letting the fire burn.

After he finished his second piece of toast, he took one more drink of water and then said, "Why don't we put on a song?" as he put the glass back down.

"Why?" Nora asked. "I don't want to hear music right now."

"Don't you want to at least hear something?"

"I'd like to hear some music," Blake said. "Anything to break this silence."

"I thought you said we should move on," Nora said in her mocking tone.

"I did. Silence can be broken with more than words."

"Is Rodge's introspection beginning to affect your way of thinking, now?"

"Nora," he said, "shut up."

"Is there something you're trying to tell me, Rodge?"

Disbelief shadowed his face. "I just said it, you stupid bitch."

Blake was trying, desperately, to contain a smile; however, it still broke through his defenses. Nora turned to him and saw that his lips were quivering upward.

"I don't think that was very funny," she said as she turned away from Blake and back to him.

"That's mainly because someone has just proven you to be an actual person that makes mistakes," he said.

"Why don't you turn the fucking jukebox on?" Nora said to him.

He smiled at her before he did so and then walked over to the machine to look down at the glass for a specific song. Everything that he came by was something that had been heard before. They were all good songs, but his ears begged for something different. He then spotted one that said, "*Life Is Coming for Me*" by Willfire. It sparked an interest in his head and he went for it. As he turned back around and walked toward the table, he heard a heavy sound emanating from the machine. It was a sound that beat profusely in its own vibrations and played out like a demon's cry. As he sat down, the words began:

"*I'm inside my room
And I like it here,
The walls are large and white,
And the doors are permanently closed,
I feel safe inside this small space,
I feel like I could live my whole life
Staring at my reflection in the window,
But now something is wrong,
Something has disturbed the process,
I can feel it running inside my veins,
It's pulling somewhere away from this room,
Life is coming for me,
I can feel it,
Life is coming for me,
I can see it,
It won't be long before
The others come into my life,
The ones called friends,*

Already my room is breaking apart,
The walls are cracking,
The doors are crying with the noise
Of twisted screws,
I don't want to be alone,
But I don't want to be accepted,
My life is fine where it is,
I don't need anyone else,
I don't need someone there
To tell me when I'm crying,
I don't need anyone
Just so I can be a savior's story,
I want to lock the door,
Never come out,
The ceiling is crumbling now,
And I can't do anything about it,
Life is coming for me,
I can feel it,
Life is coming for me,
I can see it,
It won't be long before
The others come into my life,
The ones called friends,
Already my room is breaking apart,
The walls are cracking,
The doors are crying with the noise
Of twisted screws,
I can't lie and say
I want to be by myself,
But no one can help my problems,
I can deal with myself just fine,
Don't need your help,
I just want to burn in hell,
But life is coming for me,
I can feel it,
It's coming for me,
I can see it,
This room will be gone,
And I will have to live."

The song ended on one last note that screamed in the sufferings of guitar strings.

"They call that fifties music?" Blake asked.

"I though it was a good song," Rodger said.

"Yeah, well, you're just fucked up, Rodge, you always have been. The only reason you like that song is because you *have* no life." Nora's voice weighed with a bold seriousness. She looked at him with a consistent stare. Her eyes were completely focused, almost as if she were dead.

"Why do you have to be so cold?" he asked.

"I'm not being cold, Rodge. I only speak the truth. I tell people what they deserve to hear. It may not be something they *want* to hear, but I think it's important to inform others of their mistakes."

"You know, Nora, you're not so perfect yourself," Blake said.

"No shit. I know I'm flawed, but at least I try to tell people what I've learned from my own flaws."

"Then why don't you just tell people what you've learned from your own flaws?" he asked.

"They have to hear it from how they've lived *their* life."

"Nora," Blake said, "that has got to be…the stupidest piece of bullshit I have ever heard in my life. I think you say that just so you can rationalize being a nasty bitch."

"You may think I'm a bitch—"

"We do," he said.

"But," she said with an insistence, "I am the person that I am, and if you don't like it, then don't talk to me."

"If everyone followed that rule, practically no one would be around you," he said.

"You know, I think you both are sharing the same opinion because you're both men. Yeah, one may be gay, but still, I think you two are just trying to look superior."

"That's not true," he said.

"I'm sure," she said right after he voiced his statement. "You two are trying to suppress me because neither of you want to hear that your lives are headed for shit, and only I can tell you how to save it. But you don't want to listen because both of you want to die in your own little worlds."

He nodded his head, and then laughed with one quick exhalation. "You are some piece of work, you know that?"

"More like a Picasso," Blake said.

He saw the waitress walking towards their table. She was walking with a rapid motion, almost as if she had something that had to be relieved as soon as possible. She stopped right at their table and they all looked at her.

"Who turned that song on in the jukebox?" she asked. Her voice was demanding and strict.

"Why do you ask?" Nora said.

"Because that is one of the restricted songs on there, that wasn't even supposed to play, who broke the restriction?"

"Why didn't you just come over here while it was playing?" Blake asked. "Didn't you hear it?"

"I was busy, but that is beside the point. Who broke the rules?"

"Well, *I'm* the one that went over there," Rodger said.

The waitress turned her head toward him in one swift motion. "How did you get past the restriction? How did you get it to play?"

"I turned it on. Nothing stopped me. Listen, if you don't want that song on there, then why don't you just—"

"That is beside the point. It does not fit the image of this diner. No one is supposed to be playing that song. It can't be played and will not be allowed in this diner. This is a place where families come. What about all the other people?"

They all looked around the diner, it was empty. Blake then asked, "What other people?"

"Are you trying to get smart with me!?" the waitress said while quickly turning her head towards Blake.

"No, I'm no—"

"This is a place of good, clean music. Not that filth!" She began to look at all of them in quick, jerking motions as she spoke. "I can't believe you people! You all should know better! All of you are immoral and a disgrace to society! I hope you all burn in hell where you belong! All of you fuckers deserve to burn! Now get the hell out of this diner! NOW!"

They all looked at her with questionable expressions. "What is wrong with you?" Nora asked.

"Get out!" she screamed as she directed her finger to the exit.

"Fine," Rodger said with gritty irritation.

Blake was about to put money down on the table when the waitress said, "No! I don't any of your filthy money! Just get out! Get the hell out of my diner! This is a wholesome place with wholesome people!" As they walked away, she proceeded to yell at them. "All of you are sick! You're all just sick sons a bitches! Fuck every one of you! You can all just go fuck yourselves and die! Just eat shit and die!"

They all walked out the door. They could hear her voice screaming through it as it closed. She then walked up to the glass and continued to scream. Her voice vibrated through the window as she began pounding it with a fury. Nora, Blake and Rodger just stared at her with disbelief. They turned around and walked toward the car. As they did, they broke out in laughter, her voice still pounding as harshly as her hands against the window.

The waitress's pounding faded away as he looked at the car they were walking towards. His walking slowed. Both Blake and Nora turned around and Nora asked, "What's wrong, Rodge?"

He saw that the car had a white color. He then focused on the broad shape. He looked to the center of the car where the back windshield was located. The trunk was completely two-dimensional on the surface, giving it a flat look. For some reason, he recognized this car, but not from anyone he knew of driving it.

"Rodge, let's go," Blake said.

He looked up and said, "Huh?"

"Let's go," he said.

They could still hear the waitress pounding against the glass as they got into the car. After Nora ignited the engine and drove out of the parking lot, they started to converse about the situation.

"Can you believe her?" Nora asked.

"She must be on some kind of medication. There is something seriously fucked up with that woman," Blake said.

"I think that puts it mildly," Nora said.

He looked out onto the road from the back seat. He noticed that there were no deepening cracks. The concrete was smooth. It felt as if they were riding on a cloud.

"What did you think of her, Rodge?" Blake asked.

"What?" he asked.

"The waitress," Nora said. "What did you think of her?"

He moved his body upward and looked at the two of them sitting in the front seats. They were almost like silhouettes. He could only see parts of their facial features from beneath the shadows whenever they turned their heads, giving him an allowance to see such features.

"Rodge! The fucking waitress! What did you think of her!?" Blake yelled.

"She was, ugh, out there," he answered as nervousness entered his stomach, along with a tearful, saddening rage he carried over for Blake yelling at him like that. Blake had seemed so careless for his emotions in that moment. However, he hid the rage deep inside and let it torment him.

"Yeah, she was," Nora said. "I can't believe she actually proceeded to scream at us like that."

"I can't believe she screamed at us at all," Blake said.

Rodger's concentration was being pulled away from the road and the car. He put his body closer to the front seats, trying to listen in on their conversation over the car's noises.

"If she has a problem with it, why doesn't she just take the song off there?" Nora asked.

"I know."

He pulled himself a little closer while trying to think of something to say, something that would catch their attention. He wanted to have fun at the waitress's expense as well but wanted to say something that was witty and different. He wanted his words to reach out to both of them in such a way that they would take notice with an entertained and surprised laughter.

"She was just so messed up. Maybe she's delusional," Nora said.

He searched for phrases throughout his mind, frantically, desperately clutching for a string of innovative words.

"I think she just wanted to yell at us," Blake said.

"I think she just wanted to yell," Nora said.

He could feel his mind coming closer to it. His thoughts were just touching the right thing to say, the one thing that would redeem him from this place Nora and Blake put him in.

"She was just incredibly screwed up," Blake said.

He could feel it like a fire on his tongue. He only needed to find it. Then, it finally jolted his mind: *"She just needs a good fuck. That would loosen her crazed sanity."* It was perfect, not only humorous, but an oxymoron to make it more ironic. Now he just needed to say it.

"Could you see how angry she was?" Blake asked.

"I know. She was like a demon from hell. Especially how she was talking about it being a wholesome place—"

"And then she swears up a storm?"

"Yeah, exactly!"

He wanted to say these words, they would be his savior. He just needed to release them.

"She's probably mentally unstable," Blake said.

"Oh, my God! That reminds me of this person that I used to work with."

The subject couldn't be changed. It would completely ruin his intent. If he needed to say it, he needed to say it now, before Nora told her story. He wouldn't want to interrupt, but his mouth was quivering to speak. His heart was screaming and his veins were on fire. He focused completely on his words and how they would react. Now was the time.

"She just needs a good fuck. That would loosen her crazed sanity."

Blake turned toward him while Nora eyed him in the window as the frantic need of acceptance took complete hold of him.

"What?" Blake asked.

He could feel his heart begin to sink.

Suddenly, they felt a jolt throughout the car. They looked behind them and saw a pink car within scant space behind them.

"What the fuck!?" Nora said.

Blake turned back around as Nora pressed the pedal.

They felt another slam into the car. She pressed harder as the wheels began to fly on the pavement. The scenery became a blur. Another slam jolted them, once more. Their hearts were quickening in pace. A growing fear was creeping inside them. Again, the car behind them rammed the trunk. Their flesh was tingling with suspended emotion. Death was coming closer to inevitability. Again, there was another slam.

"Is this fucker crazy?!" Nora screamed.

"I don't know!" Blake yelled. "Just keep driving!"

"The motel isn't that far now!" Rodger yelled.

They saw the motel nearing. She swerved the car into the lot. The pink car slammed itself into their side. They abruptly found themselves in a spinning motion. She pressed the pedal as the tires screamed on the concrete. They could see themselves edging towards a street light. She grasped the wheel with a tight grip as the blood pumped heavier beneath her fingers. They stopped.

They collected themselves.

She quickly parked the car and said, "Quick! Inside!"

"I can't believe no one is out here yet!" he said as they all got out of the car.

They all ran toward the door. One of them was about to open it. "Shit!" Blake said. "The key, it's inside the car!"

"Why didn't one of you get it?!" Nora asked.

"Don't try to blame me!" Blake said.

"I can't believe you."

They heard a car door slam.

"I'll get the key," he said. "We'll all be dead before you two finish arguing."

He quickly walked toward the car. He was about to open the door, but it wouldn't budge. "Keys!" he yelled.

Nora frantically looked in her purse.

He then looked inside the car and saw that they were in the ignition. "*Fuck me!*" he yelled. He looked around on the ground.

"What are you doing!?" Blake asked.

"Shut up!" he yelled.

"Rodge!" Nora said.

"Shut up!"

"Rodge!" Blake yelled.

"Shut the fuck up!"

He saw a stick. He picked it up and began slamming it against the window to the driver's seat until it broke.

"Rodge!" Nora yelled.

He didn't even answer. He reached through the window and opened the door.

"RODGER!" they both said in unison.

He pulled his body out of the car and shut the door. Then, he saw the waitress's reflection on the other window. It looked as if she was holding a gun. He turned around and saw that she was.

"Shit."

"You can say that again," the waitress said as her grayish blue eyes had become indifferent. She pointed the gun at him and said, "Get in the room," in a voice that was just as indifferent.

He didn't protest. He just walked up to the room with her holding the gun up to his head.

"And don't try anything funny, I'm not afraid to use this."

He unlocked the door as the three of them reluctantly walked inside the room.

The waitress followed them and then closed the door behind her. "Now," she said, "we are going to get to the *real* truth."

Hypocrisy with a Gun

A tension weighed densely in the air dominated by the cold steel of the gun. The waitress held her hands closely together just to hold it. There was an intrigue shadowing her face as she looked to the three people that she made captives in only seconds.

The room was deathly silent for the moment, and the only sounds were rushed breathing and pumping hearts. They watched how she held the gun so tightly, as if she were afraid to let it go. They wondered what was coming, what she would demand of them. There heads were made nearly restless by the continuous questions knifing through their thoughts.

However, there was a faded calm in the back of their minds. It held their hearts delicately within its grasp, confusing the anxiety already clasping their veins.

"I'm surprised none of you are talking," the waitress said. "I assume from how much you all had to say at the diner you would be screaming by now. Maybe you're all more brave than I thought." She watched their eyes and saw that their look was gripped within a potent fascination. "Or maybe you're all too scared to speak."

"Just what do you want?" Rodger asked.

The waitress turned her head toward him and said, "Shouldn't you be asking your*self* that question?"

"What do you want?" Blake asked.

She then turned her head toward Blake. "I want nothing more than what

134

anyone else would want—truth, just simple truth. I want everyone to understand that the world is not dominated by a few people. No one is terribly important on this earth. Their words, their phrases, everything people say and do are segmented into a series of movements, actions, and spoken languages."

"Are you using this as an excuse to preach to us?" Nora asked.

"Well," the waitress said as she looked to Nora, "I think we've found our brave one."

"You didn't answer my question."

"Is that all any of you have? Questions? When will it be that society knows enough? Why do they have to move on and find out more?"

"I think the only reason you have that gun is because you know that you wouldn't have been heard without it." As Nora said this, she could feel her fear breaking away. Slowly, she was being drawn into the calmness that was growing inside her.

"You're the first one to show true bravery," the waitress said. "It's always the women first. Why do you hang out with these two guys? Why do you even waste your time with them?"

She didn't answer.

"Now, you're not going to answer me. Tell me, what's stopping me from shooting any one of you right now and just ending your life like that?"

"Nothing," Rodger said, "nothing at all."

"And now the men follow," the waitress said.

"Nothing is stopping you from just killing us right here and now," Rodger said.

"Are you trying to encourage me?"

"We all have to die sometime."

"Do you want to die?"

He arched his left eyebrow. "No, I don't want to die. But I don't think any of us have much choice in this matter, do we?"

"Very good observation, young man. Tell me, what is your name?"

"Rodger. Some of my friends call me Rodge, even though I don't like it."

"Is there a reason why you added that little detail? What do you prefer to be called Rodge or Rodger?"

"You're the one with the gun. You can call me whatever you'd like."

The waitress stared at him. She pursed her lips while tightening her eyebrows. "Make a decision."

"Rodger," he said without hesitation.

"Don't you want to know our names?" Blake asked.

"If I do, I will ask for them. You're freedoms are very constricted right now, so don't fuck with me."

The waitress then moved her head as if weighed with disgrace. "I can't believe that you three act the way you do. I can't believe you actually had the nerve to turn that song on, Rodger. I am a God-fearing woman, and I go to my church every single week and I listen to our preacher speak the truth. When was the last time any of you heard the truth?"

"Are you going to recite excerpts from the Bible now?" Nora asked.

"No, I'm not. It's not my job to remember what the Bible says. We leave *that* to our preacher. You see, people like me, we have respect for others. We don't go running around shitting on everyone else."

"And how would one shit on another?" Nora asked.

"Are you getting smart with me?" the waitress asked. "This is not the time for that. Like Rodger said, I am the one with the gun. I suggest you try not to get too brave."

"Are you going to at least answer?"

"I don't need to tell you that. You should already know that, you all should. In fact, I'm sure you all do know, but ignore it, because not one of you has respect for anyone else."

"So, what is your name?" he asked.

She looked at him with a long, piercing stare. "Why do you want to know my name?"

"Because I ju—"

"Well, I'm not telling you!" the waitress blurted. "You don't deserve to know my name."

He tried to look for a name tag, but remembered that she never had one on.

"Very sneaky, Rodger," the waitress said. "Very sneaky, indeed. I'm not wearing a name tag," she said in a childishly taunting voice. "I will never tell any of you that. That is something that belongs to me and you can't have it, none of you."

"I never thought you were giving us anything," Blake said, "since you are the one that's threatening our lives and all."

"Do you really feel threatened?"

"Well, it would usually seem threatening if someone was waving a gun around," Nora said.

"You all certainly aren't acting like it. You're too busy making wise cracks and telling me that I'm some lunatic with a gun."

"None of us said that," Nora said.

"Well, you implied it, and I don't want to hear you didn't. Anyway, just wait. If you're not afraid of me by now…you will be. And I don't mean just sticking a gun in your faces either, oh, no. I've seen things, I've done things, things that none of you could even imagine. Thinking of unfortunate fates to come is much worse than actually experiencing them, believe me. Wondering what will happen next, if you'll still be breathing, if you'll still feel comfortable in your own skin."

"So, if you've done these things, seen them, heard them, whatever. Then why are you such a church goer? Why are you preaching to us about your life and about how to be respectful?" Blake asked.

"That is not for you to know. Some things should be left unanswered. You can't know everything, and I'm certainly not going to give you answers you want to know."

"Is that gun really loaded?" he asked.

The waitress smiled, mischievously. She pointed the gun toward the pillow of the bed behind them and pulled the trigger. The bullet shot out with a flash of lightning. The noise ripped into their hearing with one quick sound. It penetrated the pillow, searing a hole into its skin as it bled of feathers. They landed softly all throughout the hotel room like snow. She then pointed the gun back at them. "What do you think?"

They were still trying to collect themselves from the sudden shock that shattered their nerves. Their minds started racing again with a thousand different fates that could be waiting for them. Breathing became almost painful as the exhalations pressed against their chests like led and was released in the feeling of needles crawling out of their throats.

Slowly they let their hearts slow and everything else followed.

"Pay attention, Rodger," the waitress said.

He rapidly turned his head toward the waitress. "I'm listening to you."

"I'd like you to look at me while you're listening. I demand your respect."

The feathers still lightly rained. However, there was far less now. Only about seven pieces from the insides of the pillow swooped back and forth through the air, swinging themselves down to the ground.

"So, do any of you live here?" the waitress asked.

They all shook their heads in unison.

"Then what are you doing in a place like this? Where are you all from?"

"Restless Falls," Nora said. "We're all from Restless Falls."

"Restless Falls?" the waitress asked in a dismayed voice along with a face of the same emotion. "All of you are from Restless Falls? So you decided to leave your place of sin and sexual desires and unappreciative standards and loose morals and decided to infect us with it? This is not the place for it. Sexualism is not a town that takes lightly to filthy people like you. You are all horrid examples of our society. I'm just glad that you're all going to hell, and I'll be in heaven where I belong."

"If you believe in God's word so much, then why don't you take time to read that Bible of yours?" Rodger asked.

"Didn't I say not to get smart with me? That's just not getting through any of your heads is it? Do I have to make myself clearer?"

Rodger felt something pulling at him inside, an urge that was latching onto his head as he could feel it turn to the left. He looked to the mirror. Inside it, the waitress was holding the gun to her head. She was still staring at all of them with her stern eyes, but the gun was pointed against the right side of her skull. He turned his head back and saw that she was still holding the gun out, pointing it towards them.

"Why did you do that, Rodger?" the waitress asked.

"What?"

"Look at the mirror. Why did you decide to do that?"

"Are you going to kill me for looking at a mirror?"

"Did you see something? Did you see someone? What? What did you see? *Who* did you see? Tell me."

"I didn't see anyone, I just decided to look."

"DAMN IT, TELL ME!" she screamed her words through a widely opened mouth and shuddering body movements. Her eyes became obsessively focused.

"I didn't see anyone or anything, I just decided to look, that's all."

"LIAR!"

They could feel another suspended emotion forming inside them. Her mood was becoming hostile. Something had to happen.

She pointed the gun at the bottom right of Blake's stomach. "Tell me, or I'll shoot him, tell me now!"

"Look, please, calm down! I didn't see anything!" He moved his body desperately.

Nora's breathing deepened.

Blake just stood, frozen in his own trepidation.

"I'm going to count to three!"

"I didn't see anything!"

"One!"

138

"You're just going to have to believe me! Shooting people isn't going to get you the answer you're looking for!"

"Two! I'm not going to believe you! I don't trust you!" she said rapidly. "Tell me before I count to three or he'll bleed to death!"

"All right! Fine!" he said as he quickly tried to think of something to make up. "I'll tell you."

"Do it now, you're wasting time!"

"I thought I saw someone outside the window by looking at the mirror. I thought I saw a shadow of someone."

"What were you planning to do?"

"What?"

"Don't make me count to three!"

"All right, all right. I was going to ask for help, okay? Please don't shoot him, please."

She looked at him while still having the gun pointed at Blake. She stared at him for a long while. They could all feel their minds being torn apart by the apprehensions. The waitress exhaled and inhaled deeply, looking as if she was trying to reach a decision. While still keeping a tight grasp on the gun, she directed it toward the middle of them, where it was, originally. She then said, "Don't fuck with me."

He desperately tried to lessen his sudden distress. As it faded, he thought about the motel and wondered if people were around. The sounds that were made, the screaming, he knew someone should have noticed. There should have been a knock at the door. The stillness outside this room was eerie. No one even peered through the window. He remembered the other cars parked in the lot, and it would be too unrealistic for everyone else to be out at the same time, even the people driving through the road ahead of the motel. Something should have happened by now, but it didn't, and that fed the fear taking hold of his stomach.

"You must realize," the waitress said, "that what I say is understood, and what I demand will happen. If you acknowledge this, then everything will go smoothly, and we won't have to get into these little tiffs. After all, I really don't want to kill any of you. All I want is for you to just understand, and for you to know what I know. I want you to see the truth."

"What is this truth you keep talking about?!" Nora asked. "Is it worth threatening people's lives for?"

"There you go with that '*threatening*' word again," the waitress said. "Right now, you are all perfectly safe, and on some level you all understand and know that. A lot of people have used guns in the past for many different reasons. Sometimes, it was just for the sheer pleasure of murdering someone. Sometimes, it was to take something. Sometimes, it was just to scare others. But, in all those instances, guns have instilled order more than murdered. They have made people obey more than they normally would. Guns have a lot of power, and that power is more than just the possibility of death."

"But you would still use a gun with the intent of doing some sort of harm," Blake said, still attempting to calm his anxieties.

"Harm? What harm is it to teach someone to respect and obey a higher power?" the waitress asked.

"Not just physical harm," Nora said, her voice reaching an aggravating level. "It could also harm someone emotionally, mentally. A person would never be the same after they've had a gun held on them."

"Exactly," the waitress said. "They wouldn't. Rude people would learn to have manners. Loud people would learn to speak less. It would do more good than harm. That is what society has lost today. The respect they should have, the manners, the everything. The earth has become chaotic. There is no order."

"So you think a gun is going to help?" Rodger asked.

"How else are people going to listen? Most people would ignore what you have to say if you don't have a gun in their face. If this is what I have to resort to, then so be it."

"Do you feel as if you're on some kind of mission or something?" Rodger asked. "Like, do you think that you were sent here to make people learn, to force them?"

"Everyone has a purpose," the waitress said. "Everyone is here for a reason. However, others really are here just to take up space. Like you three. But not after I get done with you."

"So, what's the moral here?" Nora asked.

"If it were that simple, I would have told you, but it's not. Morals just don't come to you, you have to earn them. It's almost like that song said, 'Life is coming for me, I can feel it, life is coming for me, I can see it.' Life will direct you; let life be your guide."

"You know, for someone that doesn't like that song, you feel awfully passionate about it," he said.

"No! I'm not going to let you do that!" the waitress said. "I'm not going to let you make me out to be someone that's just saying things. There is an order to my words, a real order. I will not have them questioned. I am the one that's right here, *I* am the true one. Just because you haven't found the serenity that I have does not mean you can take your disappointments out on me."

"So why don't you just take the damn song off there?" Blake asked.

"Hey! Watch your mouth! You are not going to fucking swear at me! And I am not going to answer that question. You should have known not to play it. It wasn't there to be played. You must resist temptation."

"We didn't know it was a temptation to resist," Blake said.

"That's because every one of you has become so infected by the sin around you that you have lost sight of what the true temptations are. Don't think you can get away by just saying you don't know them, either. Excuses have no place, here. I'm sure you know what they really are, too. You've just chosen to forget them. You've decided that they were never that important to begin with. But believe me; they are just as important as your lives. You've buried them, but you are going to dig inside yourselves, and I will make you. You will pull out everything that you've forgotten, everything that you've chosen to forget. Now, tell me, when was the last time any of you have prayed?"

"I've never prayed," Nora said.

"I can't remember," Blake said.

"I pray every night," Rodger said.

"I believe you two, but I *don't* believe you, Rodger."

"What? Do you want us to pray, now?" Rodger asked.

"No, you're not ready yet," the waitress said quickly, almost with an evasive voice.

"Well, then why did you bring it up?" Blake asked.

"Because you are going to prepare yourselves, prepare yourselves to be moral, to be perfect. And I am going to teach you."

"So what do you think is so imperfect about us?" Nora asked

"You should already know that. You've sinned; you should know the sins that you've committed. But don't fret; forgiveness is on its way. You just have to see."

"See what?!" Nora asked.

"The truth, the fucking truth! You remember the *truth* don't you, or have you all lied so much that you've forgotten that as well."

"Don't you mean *chosen* to forget?" Nora asked.

"Don't get smart with me, don't do it."

"Come on," Blake said, "you're telling us that we're imperfect, but, yet, you're not telling us what we're doing that is so wrong. You want to teach us, but you won't tell us a thing. The only things you are saying is all about the world and how it's just so bad—"

"Shut up!" the waitress said as she pointed the gun back at Blake's stomach, facing, once again, the bottom right-hand side. "Just shut up!" She then shot the gun.

The bullet discharged from the gun. It flew with its unforgiving speed toward Blake's right side. He could feel the bullet puncturing his flesh. His skin expanded inward until it had to let go and begin to rip. The bullet's head was piercing, forcing its way into his stomach. It severed through vital blood vessels while biting into his organs and sped through the interior until it lodged itself within the self-made hole, finding a place inside. The broken vessels leaked through the wound as he had to put his hand on it. He felt the sudden pain knifing into his nerves. He had to bend over slightly to reach some sort of comfort. His face squinted as the pain pulled his expression toward a grimace.

"What the fuck!? Why did you do that!?" Nora asked.

"What the hell are you thinking!?" Rodger asked.

They both rushed over to Blake. Nora helped him back up.

"Don't swear at me! Now you see I mean business!"

They both helped him toward the bed.

"Let him be! He can walk!"

Nora turned to the waitress. "What!?"

"I said let him be! He's learning his lesson!"

"You're just going to have to shoot me!" she said.

"Don't make me do that. Just let him be. I swear to you, we'll get him help…after we're through here. I will leave when I've done what I'm supposed to do."

Blake painfully walked over to the bed as she spoke. He was practically reaching for it.

"You are all supposed to learn. I'm not leaving here until you do. He's just going to have to suffer through it for now."

Blake placed his left hand on the sheets as his fingers pulled at the material. He reluctantly put his other hand on the bed. He pulled himself on it as the blood leaked on the side. He pushed his legs so that he could lie on it without falling off, pressing the aching of his stomach further inward. He had to at least lie down. When he reached that point, he turned his entire body upward, facing the ceiling. His left hand lay on the bed and his right on the wound. Both of his hands were stained with the internal substance. He breathed heavily as the red liquid seeped into the sheets, expanding itself through them.

"You can't just let him lay there like that!" Rodger said while he had his hands directed toward Blake. "Please, do something!" He reached out to Blake as he was watching the color of Blake's attire stain in a quickening red.

Nora quickly turned toward her and screamed, "I should just kill you right now! I don't care if you have a gun or not!"

The waitress looked at her with knowing in her eyes. She said, "No, you won't, because if you do, I'll just finish him off. Let him lay down. He should think about his life, about what he's done and how he can redeem himself."

"Redeem!?" Rodger asked. "Redeem!? How can he redeem himself if he's dead!?"

"Okay, first of all, stop the screaming, I don't appreciate it. Second of all, if he is truly meant to see the error of his ways, he'll live. That is the way it really is. That is the truth of the matter."

Nora sat down on the bed and looked down at Blake. Blake looked up at her with a searing pain. His eyes were widened in dying gaze and his mouth quivered, appearing as if it were trying to form words. "Blake, please," Nora whispered to him. "Please tell me what you want." Her voice was just beneath a cracking surface. She could feel the tears begin to scream beneath her eyelids.

"Let him be," the waitress said. "You can't do anything for him, now. His time of judgment has arrived."

Nora looked at her with an embittered anger. She could feel her heart begin to burn with a passionate fury.

"Please," Blake said in a voice that was forced out. "Please, just let things be. I don't want … either of you to get hurt."

"But, Blake," Nora said.

"You heard him," the waitress said. "So get up off the fucking bed."

All the waitress had was a gun. This, he obviously noticed. What was stopping either of them just from jumping on her and taking it away? He was wondering why she had so much power, and how this situation should have been over long before it started. There were so many things that could have prevented it, so many things that could stop it, now. But it all seemed impossible.

"Why can't you go off and try to save someone else from their supposed sins?" Nora asked. "Why don't you go, period?" Her face was beginning to pull itself inward, forming a pleading look. Her voice was choking on the piercing sadness that clasped her throat.

"You are the ones that need the most guidance, *I* believe. You are all in trouble," the waitress said. "I can see how your lives are going to play themselves out. If this night hadn't have happened, you would have learned nothing, and you would have been lost forever, trying to find some sort of serenity in that hell hole you call a life."

Nora touched Blake's right hand, of which was laying on the wound. She could feel the blood escape through the crevices in between her fingers.

"You think that killing people is going to help you save them?" he asked.

"He's not dead, yet. You see life still in his eyes. Besides, people have to learn, you all have to learn."

"I can't believe you did this," Nora said to the waitress while looking down at Blake. He tried to form an understanding in his eyes.

"Will you get up off the bed!" the waitress demanded. "He has to lay there by himself and think about what he's done."

Absolute compassion took hold of Nora's face. She didn't want to see Blake suffering like this. Her heart slowly began to break as she looked at his eyes and how he tried to appear as if he could handle the pain. Thinning liquid began to spread over his eyes, he was very close to screaming.

Blake said to her, "Please...just do what she says. I assure you...we'll...make it...through this."

She opened her lips. Her head slightly moved back and forth as she let go of quick exhalations laden with her weeping voice. She reluctantly pulled herself away from him. She still had her hand out to him, now stained with red.

"Turn around," the waitress said.

She put her hand to her side and turned around while still lightly crying.

Rodger could feel the sadness poking into his heart as well. He tried to hold it down, not letting it surface, not letting the waitress see his tears.

"Both of you can feel it, can't you?" the waitress asked. "The sadness, the utter sadness for the misfortune of your friend. You can feel the fear of him possibly slipping away, can't you? You can feel it in your hearts. I can see it. But this is all apart of what has to be. Things have to be this way, there's no other way. The sadness will come to pass, I can guarantee you that. People die, it happens every day."

They only stared at her with solemn eyes while Blake remained just as real in their minds' eye. The sounds of his exasperated breathing only pushed the misery harder into their maddening grief.

"You can't possibly know what it feels like to see people waste their lives every day," the waitress said. "To see them throw everything away for a few cheap thrills. People that have had so much going for them, people that could have been better, but they let themselves fall into that trap, the trap that tempts us all. I can see that in all of you. You've been doing nothing but spending day to day in your little, insignificant worlds. Like you have been, Rodger, and you, and, yes, especially the one now laying, bleeding on the bed. I can see it in all of you, just like I could see it in Dave."

Nora stopped her sobbing as she almost lost her voice in the sudden gasp. Rodger widened his eyes in disbelief.

"Oh, yes, I knew Dave. I knew Dave very well. I knew the nights he spent at that club, I knew the friends he hung out with. I knew where his life was headed. I also know that he is now dead. Don't ask me how; I really don't want to say. And I know who he died at the hands of."

"How did you know Dave?" he asked.

"How does anyone know anyone else? That is none of your business and I am not about to tell any of you. Dave was a very tortured soul, I tried to help him, tried to make him see the error of his ways. I tried so hard to make him live a happy life, but he was not happy, not at all. He had to die."

"What do you mean?" he asked.

"I mean just that. He had to be rid of. He had to die, and I had to make that happen."

"What are you talking about?" Nora asked.

"Are you saying that I didn't kill Dave?" the waitress asked.

"We saw it ourselves," Nora said.

"Think back," the waitress said. "Do you really think that Dave died at your hands? Just try and think of what really did happen. Things happen every day, especially things we care not to remember, things we block out. The mind is a very funny thing. It can lead into certain beliefs; it can remember things that were never there to begin with."

"No," Nora said. "No, you're just fucking with us!"

"Hey! What did I say about that damn swearing?!" the waitress screamed as she jolted the gun forward.

"Fine, I'm sorry," Nora said. "But how do you know all this? I don't believe you. I don't believe you at all. You've gotta be some kind of stalker, or something. Did someone hire you? Or are you just some sick individual who likes to follow people and then mess with their heads?"

"You're just saying that so you can be rid of the fear that you might be losing your sanity. Is Blake really suffering, is he really bleeding on the bed? Is Nora really crying?"

"So, you do know our names," Rodger said.

"No shit."

"What the hell is going on here?" Nora asked. "Okay, if things are really as you say they are, then how do we know that *you're* real?"

"Oh, believe me; I'm as real as they come. I don't think you want to find out, either. I still have the gun, and I am still in this room with you. This gun is just as real as I am. Just look behind you and see."

They both slowly turned their heads to the back. They could feel their emotions begin to confuse each other. They could hear Blake's heavy breaths, but would he be there when they looked? That question taunted their minds as they saw the room pass by their vision. Their thoughts were overloading with possibilities as their sense of reality was starting to be questioned.

Then they saw him; they saw Blake still on the bed, still holding onto his wound. He didn't say anything. He just lay there, looking up at the ceiling. They turned their heads back around, rapidly.

"What are you doing to us? How did you know about Dave?" Rodger asked.

"Why should I answer you?"

"Look, one of our friends is dead, the other's *dying*. We would just like to know some truth here, at least give us that," Nora said.

"Do I really have to go into my little speech about truth, again?"

"Please, just tell us," Rodger said. "We're already at your mercy, you can obviously see that. You've done what you wanted to do. So, please, tell us this."

"Do you really want to know? Do you really want to see the reality of this situation? Once you have the answer to this question, you're not going to be able to go back."

Nora sighed. "Fine, whatever. Just tell us."

"All right, then," the waitress said. "Close your eyes. Both of you."

"Why? What are you going to do?" he asked.

"It's not what I'm going to do; it's what you're going to see."

Even with their suspicions, both of them closed their eyes and their sight faded into black. They waited for her to tell them when to open their eyes as Blake's breathing became the only sound they heard. They concentrated on his breathing. It began to weigh heavily, like the sound of an echo, one that seemed to fill a space bigger than what they were in. Then, it was suddenly silenced as if it were nothing more than a tape recorder that had been turned off. They wondered what had happened. They began to worry if Blake had just died.

"Hey, hon," they heard the waitress's voice say.

They opened their eyes and found themselves in the diner. They stood in the middle of it, looking to the booth seats. They saw Dave sitting in one and the waitress was standing up, facing him and smiling.

"What is going on here, Rodge?" Nora asked him.

"I don't know," he said as he looked around as well. "I'm not sure."

"I've got to get out of here," Nora said. But right before she could make a move, he grabbed her arm. She looked to him and said, "Why did you do that?"

"Don't leave, not yet. We don't know what's going on and we don't know why we're here. I don't think it's a good idea to just walk away."

"And why not?"

"Because we don't know what is going to happen. I don't know what is happening either, bu—"

"So how have you been?" the waitress said, interrupting their conversation. They both looked to Dave and the waitress, suddenly becoming attentive.

"I've been doing well, Rebecca. How about yourself?"

She tilted her head and smiled. "Same here, Dave. Do you want your usual, tonight?"

"Sure, why not?"

"Okay," she said as she wrote on the pad in her hand.

Nora held her right arm while bringing herself close to him. "I'm scared, Rodge."

He continued to look at Dave and the waitress with eyes staring blankly. "So am I, but let's just let this play out, see what happens. It looks like the only way," he said as they could both feel themselves falling victim to the surroundings.

Right before the waitress left, she turned back to Dave and said, "Honey, are you okay?"

Dave didn't answer; he just continued to look down.

"Honey, what's the matter?" the waitress asked as she sat down in front of him.

Slowly, Dave looked up. There was obvious depression in his face.

"What happened, tell me," the waitress said as she slid her hands across the table to him.

He exhaled with one long breath. "Things, things happened. Things that make life worth living for," he said sarcastically.

There was a clattering sound in the kitchen from utensils falling. All eyes quickly turned to the kitchen. Nora and Rodger turned back around as did the waitress and Dave.

Nora could feel her nerves shaking just beneath the surface. She held onto him as close as she could, trying to find some sense of reality.

"What sort of things?" the waitress asked.

Dave looked right at the waitress. "His name is Rodger."

The waitress formed a look of confusion. "You mean a friend of yours?"

"He's the man that I have fallen for."

A surprised look crossed her face. "You mean you're…gay?" she asked as she looked at him with a deeper concern that seemed to carry a light anger.

"I thought you knew."

"No, no I didn't. Tell me, what is it about this man named Rodger that depresses you so much."

"He is the man that I have wanted for a long time, but he doesn't want me."

She took her hand and held his tightly. "Dave," she said with sympathy, "you should know that you can never find happiness with another man. That's just not the way."

Dave pulled his hand away as he arched his left eyebrow. He then said, "Great, so you *are* homophobic."

"I'm not homophobic. I just don't think it's right. Dave, please, don't do this."

"What do you know about this? You're not gay. You think it's a sin. You're sitting there trying to judge me?" Dave asked as he put his face near hers. His lips became tight as his eyes widened in a sudden rage.

"I'm not judging you, its ju—"

"Don't, please."

"Look, I'm sorry, all right? I really am. I didn't mean to upset you." She looked down at the table. As she looked back up, she made an attempt to change her face to a more sympathetic look. "Just tell me why you don't think he doesn't like you?"

"He makes it obvious."

"Dave," she said as she quickly held his hands, once more. "Dave, please, tell me about him, tell me why you feel this way."

"I *am*."

"Take me to them."

"What!?"

"What!?" both Nora and he said in unison.

"Take me to them, take me to these people. They won't even have to know I'm there."

There was a pleading in the waitress's face. She held onto Dave's hands tighter as her eyes sunk into desperation.

"Now why would I do a thing like that?" Dave asked, a look of misunderstanding forming on his face.

"Let me help you, let me help you with this, please. I can help you; I can help you reach happiness."

"No!" Nora said as she reached out to them both.

"Nora, don't!" he pleaded.

She put her hand out toward the air. Once she did, the surrounding in front of them broke like a mirror, shattering pieces of a seeming reality. It vanished into nothingness as she pulled away. Nora and he held each other as the diner's construction faded into another existence. Slowly, they were finding themselves back in the motel room as its construction ripped through the shattering.

They let go of each other.

"What just happened!?" Nora demanded.

They looked to the waitress, then behind them. Blake was still on the bed, bleeding.

"What the fuck is happening?!" Rodger asked.

"Just what you think is happening," the waitress said.

They turned back to her.

"So, your name is Rebecca," he said

"No, it's not."

"But, Dave—"

"I know what Dave said," the waitresses said, interrupting Nora. "I know what happened in that situation. But the question is do you know the rest?"

"I should just leave, I should just leave right now," Nora said.

"You can't. You have to stay, you all must stay," the waitress said. "You're not going to be able to leave."

Nora felt the urge to walk towards the door. She tried to follow that urge and could feel her legs burning, her arms begging for movement. She could see the door, it was just a few steps away, but her feet were like stones. There was resistance within her, something instilling her with the want not to go, a resistance that weighed, heavily inside her.

"I told you that you weren't going to be able to leave."

He looked to the waitress. He needed an answer to this. The lost emotions inside him had to find a place, somewhere. "Why?" he asked.

"No," the waitress said, "no, you can't know the answer to that. I can't tell you, and I'm not going to. The words that I am saying are very important to you. They will guide you, let them guide you."

"We don't want guidance, we want to leave this place," Nora said. "Everyone wants to go. No one wants to stay anymore. Life has become this repetition to you people. You never want to stay and listen to the real answer. You want everything now, quick and fast. Well, not everything can be so easy."

"So, Dave came here, to Sexualism? He was one of your ordinary customers?" he asked.

"How do you know he was in Sexualism?" the waitress asked.

"We were inside the diner, we saw it," Nora said. "We saw it. Please, tell me that this is some kind of nightmare." She asked this question with a cracking voice that begged for some sort of truth.

"Reality is a nightmare," the waitress said. "Yes, Dave and I knew each other, you already know this. He came to me, he smiled to me. He became a very important part of my life. I had to make sure that he was on the right path, to make sure that he wouldn't be diverted by certain influences. Obviously, I was wrong. He couldn't live the rest of his life like he was."

"You are full of so much bullshit," Rodger said.

"Don't make me shoot you. I've already shot Blake."

"So, how did you know us?" Nora asked. "Did he lead you to us?"

"'Lead,'" the waitress laughed. "What a funny word. Did he '*lead*' me?" She laughed again. "He didn't '*lead*' me anywhere. We went to places together. He showed me things, I showed him things. It was a counterbalanced relationship. However, you don't know what happened after we left the diner, do you? No, you wanted to find out, you wanted to reach out to a person that doesn't even exist anymore. You wanted to know more than you should have known."

"Stop," Nora said. "Stop playing with our heads."

"It's getting cold," Blake said. They both turned quickly and walked up to him.

"What?" Nora asked.

"It's getting cold," he said, once again, in his shuddering voice.

"Don't! Don't step near him!" the waitress said.

Against her words, they walked over to him with a quick motion.

"Stop!"

They sat down on the bed with him and looked down.

"What are you saying, Blake?" Nora asked, trying to deny the thought of possible death.

Blake didn't say anything else. He just looked to both of them, almost as if trying to reach out to them. His breathing became more of a rasp.

"Blake," Rodger said, touching Blake's left shoulder, lightly.

"Blake, talk to us."

He only stared at them. His mouth moved lightly, but no words were coming out. Only the sound of trembling breath escaped through his lips.

"Blake?" Nora said as she touched his hand that lay on the wound.

"Get up off the bed!" the waitress demanded.

Blake then took in a deep breath as there was a sudden look of shock in his eyes. His body convulsed as if he had experienced something that was coming near. He exhaled for a long moment.

"Blake, what's wrong?" Rodger asked.

Both their eyes looked down at Blake in a pleading manner. There was a suspicion coming to their minds, something that they didn't want to happen. They could feel it weigh inside their fears, like an uninvited ghost.

His mouth was beginning to move differently, he was trying to form words. His lips curved inward and outward as small sounds of his voice were breaking through. "I-i-i-i-i," air broke through, interrupting the word.

"Blake, tell us what's wrong," Rodger said rapidly.

"I-i-i-i-i-i-it's ge-ge-ge-get-t-t-ting c-c-c-cold."

"Blake, no," Nora said, holding Blake's hand with a tighter grip.

Blake inhaled, again, with a gasp.

"Blake!?" Rodger said.

He let go his breath with another long exhalation. His eyes pleaded for something. He narrowed his eyes as a light film began to spread over them like a shadow escaping into the light.

He went to touch Blake's chest, to feel his heart. He pressed his hand harder, the rhythm was practically non-existent.

"Blake!" he exclaimed. "Blake, please don't!"

The exhalation was coming to an end. The sound of his breath was dying down. His eyes were losing movement. His face was becoming motionless. Nora held tighter onto his hand. Her cries begged for his life, but she could feel his hand losing its grasp.

He looked away from Blake and to the mirror. Inside the mirror, Blake got off the bed. There was no blood on his clothes, no red stains on either of his hands. He walked by the waitress and exited the room.

He looked back to Blake. His eyes had lost movement, completely.

"Blake!" Nora yelled. She rapidly turned her head toward the waitress. "You bitch!"

The waitress pointed the gun at Nora's head and pulled the trigger. The bullet hit her forehead with incredible force. Her body jolted. Her blood escaped through the back of her head as it splashed into the air. She fell down onto the bed, and the blood came running out onto the sheets, exhaling its formation through the material.

"Nora!" he yelled. He rapidly looked back to the mirror, and saw that Nora was leaving the room as well.

He looked back at the waitress. He got up off the bed and slowly walked toward her.

"What are you doing to us?" he asked.

She looked at him with a kindness. She smiled, pleasantly. "I'm saving you," she said. Her breath began to shudder. She then said, as tears were forming in her eyes, "You don't want to become like me." She pulled the trigger.

He saw the bullet flying toward him. Its pointed edge reached out to his vision. The bullet then escaped his sight, reaching above his eyes. He felt it pierce through his forehead. It almost felt as if an emphasized migraine was suddenly screaming through his brain. He could feel himself falling as he watched the surroundings float past his vision. Everything slowed. As he was falling, he could see the ceiling change. It became a smoother white. The walls were deepening. The original shape of the entire room faded into another transformation.

He fell on a shiny checkered floor. The pain inside his head was gone. He rapidly took his hand and put it to his forehead—there was no wound. He got up and saw that he was, once again, in the diner.

He then heard a familiar voice say, "Kid."

He turned around and saw a person in a waitress uniform. The hair was long and jet black.

"Glenn," he said, with relief.

A Small Transition

He walked towards Glenn. "What are you doing here?"

"I'm just here," Glenn said, standing behind the counter. He walked up to it and put his elbows on it.

"What just happened?"

"Didn't you listen to her? She didn't want you to become like her. You're scared, kid, I know it." There was tranquility in her face as she looked at him with calmness and spoke in a reassuring, slow voice.

"I don't know what to do, Glenn. Please tell me what to do," he said with a pleading voice.

"Only you can decide that for yourself. Life is going to be a long, depressing experience if you don't stop."

"Stop what?"

"You haven't had a confident thought about yourself in a long time, kid. You're going to bury yourself."

"I don't want to stay here."

Glenn moved toward him. "Then don't."

A phone began to ring. He looked toward the sound and saw a pay phone against the wall left to the entrance. He then looked back to Glenn.

"I think it's for you," Glenn said.

"What should I do?" he asked as the phone rang a second time.

"Whatever you want."

He looked back to the phone. "But I don't understand," he said as he looked back the other way. His voice suddenly trailed off when he saw that Glenn was gone.

He exhaled with a laden breath. He went over to the phone and picked it up.

"Hello?"

"*You're going to have to go back to the night club.*" He heard the same general whisper he did last time.

"What?"

"*It won't be for long. Just enough so you know when to leave.*"

"Who is this?"

"*You're going to have to leave him very soon.*"

"Who?"

"*Rodger. He's breaking away from you; this truth will be lost into fiction.*"

"What about Dave?"

"*Dave is gone.*"

"What the hell are you talking about?"

"*You have to go back to the night club just for a little while.*"

"I don't want to go back to the night club."

"*Turn around.*"

He followed the order and saw a pink spotlight gliding through the diner.

"No," he said. "No, I don't want to go back."

"*You have to. You're going to have to go through a lot more before you know.*"

"Before I know what?"

The spotlight then came up to his face, clouding his vision. The music faded in and the spotlight left from his eyes.

The nightclub surrounded him. He looked around. The music blared in his ears and the strobe lights convulsed like lightning.

"Hey!" he heard a voice say as a hand grabbed his shoulder. He turned around and saw Blake.

"Blake!" he said with excitement. "What are you doing here!?"

"I took you here, remember!?"

He looked around. "Where's Nora?"

"She's somewhere back there!" he yelled, pointing his thumb behind him.

"And Dave! Where's Dave?"

Blake looked at him with confusion. "Who's Dave?"

He looked back at Blake with a maddening sadness.

"What's wrong?"

"Nothing!"

"All right, well listen, it's time for us to leave!" Blake said as he took the coat he was holding and put it on.

He looked at Blake's coat with a sudden astonishment. A vague remembrance appeared inside his mind, one that was shaking his sense of fear. "Your coat!" he said, breathlessly.

"Yeah, what about it!?"

"What color is it!?"

Blake leaned his face forward and said, "Midnight blue!"

He backed away from Blake.

"Rodge, what the hell is *wrong* with you!?"

He turned to the bar and ran across it while his fingers glided over the surface of the counter. The bartender grabbed his hand. He looked up and asked, "What do you want, Charley!?"

The music around him faded into nothing. The motion slowed. Charley and he were the only ones possessing normal movement. Charley leaned toward him and said with a demanding voice, "It's time for you to go." Charley gave him an unopened beer bottle.

Everything regained its speed, and the music came back into his ears, flooding them with sound. He slowly walked away from the bar. His breathing became heavy as it echoed in his hearing. He raised the beer bottle with his right hand. He then screamed, letting out a burning madness through his lungs. He threw the bottle towards the wall behind the bar. When the bottle and the wall met, everything around him broke like glass. The surroundings segregated into shards of a one-sided mirror. He could feel himself falling, there was a weightlessness taking over the interior of his body. Slowly, he was fading into nothing. His heart was beginning to pound with a desperate fear. He felt himself fall on a floor.

He got up and found himself in the studio apartment.

"Where am I!?" he screamed.

The storm was still raging outside.

"Go through the door," he heard Nora's voice say.

He turned around and saw her. Her pupils flashed with lightning.

"Why? Is there another place I'm going to suddenly appear in?"

"This is just a transition," she said. "The only one getting lost is you. Go."

He exhaled, deeply. His throat began to quiver. There was a desperate need to know growing inside him. "I just want to know what's happening."

"Go," Nora said.

Reluctantly, he turned to the door. He began walking toward it; despair was taking over with each step. He was getting closer to wanting to fall off the face of the earth.

He put his hand on the knob and turned. He quickly opened the door as a blinding flash of three colors masked his sight: midnight blue, pink and white. The colors slowly vanished. Another surrounding began to appear.

When everything cleared, he saw that he was inside a library. He looked around him. He was in the entranceway of this library. It was of a massive size. He was standing on a staircase that was of a towering height. He looked down for a second. There were no banisters on either side. This grasped his sense of acrophobia, making it slither beneath his skin like a true fear. He cautiously walked on the first step, which resulted in him slowly walking down the stairs. There was a dread heavily playing in his mind. He could feel his heart pressing itself against his chest. It felt like a fist hitting at his insides. He began to sweat as he sensed the possibility of death coming near.

As he came closer to the ground, he saw that there were hallways of books on either side. They reached above the staircase. Their height almost seemed absurd.

He then ran down the stairs, quickly. He hoped he wouldn't trip or fall off either side. His legs burned like fire as his feet pressed harshly in to the stairs. His hands were condensed into fists. He wanted to close his eyes and never open them again, but he fought this temptation. His eyes remained open and became two gaping holes staring outward.

He reached the ground while walking off the last step. There was a large desk in front of him. Its height was half that of the hallways of books. It was a dusty brown and looked as if something a judge would reside at. Nora was sitting behind it, reading a book. He looked around him and saw other people sitting, reading their books that lay on long desks. One of the people that he saw was Blake. They all turned a page, simultaneously, the sound was emphasized in his head, as if someone had turned a page inside his mind and the sound exited through his ears.

He walked up to Nora, having to look up just to see her face. He had to stop halfway, and already the back of his neck was pressing into his shoulder blades.

"Nora," he whispered, his bottom lip pulled downward as the front of his neck was stretched.

Nora looked up. "What are you doing here?"

"I'm just here."

"Oh, well, I thought you were still at home."

"No, I'm here."

He then looked around. There was a question forming in his mind. One that he felt he had to ask. He looked to Nora again and asked, "Where's Dave?"

Nora looked at him as if confused. She then said, "You are Dave, honey."

A Storied Hell

He continued to look at Nora in confusion while slightly moving his head back and forth and asked, "Dave?"

She looked back up from her book and leaned toward him. "Yes, that's right, you're Dave, I am Nora, he is Blake," she said while pointing toward him. "And if I were you, I would read something."

"Why?" he asked while blinking his eyes.

"Dave, you have to read something. If you're going to be here, that's the way it has to be."

He still looked at her with confusion.

"Damn, it Dave!" she whispered. "Will you please just go read something? I don't even know why you came here. It's not as if anyone pays that much attention to you anyway."

He walked away from her, rapidly, while turning his head back a few times.

As he made his way through the rows of desks, he looked around the library. The environment was embellished surrealistically. Just looking up at the hallways of books brought back the feeling of acrophobia.

He saw that he was walking toward a desk covered in cobwebs. There was a pile of books laying on it. Each one looked as if it was aged from many years. The hardback covers were cracked and stained and the pages were yellowed. He brought his hand toward to one of the books, the one laying on the very top of the pile. He pulled it off as lines of cobweb stretched until the connected strings broke, slowly. They were pulled apart like soft, mildewed gum. He took the book in his hands and walked to one of the desks.

Once again he looked around. The majority of the library was shrouded in shadows. The only place with the proper amount of light was in the middle. This delicate luminescence made everything appear as if it was on a stage and things would be moved at any second.

He sat in the same desk Blake was at. He decided to sit close enough to Blake so that he would be within hearing range.

He went to open the book. A voice stopped him—Blake's voice. He whispered, "You don't want to start with that one, you want the one on the bottom."

He looked to Blake. "What?" he asked.

Blake looked up. "What?" Blake asked.

"What did you say to me?"

"I didn't say anything to *you*," he answered in an irritated voice. "Mind your own fucking business." Blake looked to him almost as if he didn't recognize him. There was a deep annoyance in his face, like him asking Blake any sort of question was an insult.

He put his head back, dismayed at what Blake said as he looked back down at his book.

He got back up from the desk and decided to follow the direction. He then saw every one turn a page, simultaneously again, hearing it emphasized in his head. He quickly walked back to the desk and brought his right hand to the bottom. He wasn't sure which one to get; his fingers were running across the table, trying to decide.

"Pick the one that is the most aged," Nora's voice said.

He looked at Nora, still reading her book. He turned his head back around and looked for a book that seemed to be the oldest. He saw one that looked to be more stained with age than the others. He pulled it out and walked back toward the desk.

After he sat down, Blake looked up and moved his head toward him. Blake asked, "Why do you have to sit near me?"

He looked back up at Blake as he looked to his book again. He wasn't sure what to make of this situation, but then he just opened his book and began reading it.

This book was comprised of short stories. It was entitled *From Heavenly to Hellish*. He looked at the first short story that was called "Perfect Lives."

He began to read the story:

Once upon a time, there was a man with no name, for he could not remember it. His life had been a sequence of events that he could not identify. He believed that there was no real purpose to his life; he was just a person that existed on the earth. He could usually be found walking on lonely roads, looking as if he'd be searching for something. However, he felt that he was never lost to begin with, because he was never meant to be found.

So, on one night, when the rain fell hard and the lightning screamed through the sky, he was walking beside a road. The cars that drove by were few and far between. The few drivers that were on the road gave him glances that were not too favorable. But he didn't care, all he cared about was the walking, but he didn't know where he was walking to.

He was past the point of cold. His skin was numbing as it endured the falling temperatures of the night's weather. He had experienced many nights like these before. He had also experienced days where the heat could burn right through his flesh. But this was his supposed purpose, to walk, aimlessly, with no destination, no ending.

Then he saw a pair of headlights coming toward him. He figured this person would drive on like the rest. But, if it was a free ride, he might as well take it.

The car slowed as it neared him. The driver rolled down his window as he went to the side to see who this person was. It was a man dressed in business attire. It was obvious that this was a wealthy man, for his car was extravagant.

"Need a ride?" the driver asked.

Without hesitation, the nameless man got in the car with him and closed the door.

"Where you headed?" the driver asked.

"No where," the man said.

"That's a general goal," the drive said, sarcastically. "Better buckle up. I wouldn't want a dying life on my hands."

The man buckled his seat belt as the driver continued on the road.

There was nothing on this road but concrete, dirt, and power lines. It was very open and very desolate.

"So, what's your name?" the driver asked.

"Don't have one."

"You don't have one?" the driver said with astonishment. "What, like, you can't remember it or something?"

"No, I just don't have one," the man lied.

"Well, I'll tell you mine, then. Phil!" he exclaimed. "Phil! What an ordinary name, huh? Phil."

"Are you dissatisfied with it?" the man asked.

"No, not necessarily, just dissatisfied with my life in general." The driver laughed as if there was an inside joke he was sharing with the man. He then said, "I'm a business tycoon. I make the money, I have the life, I have everything."

"But you're lonely, correct? You don't have love in your life?"

"Oh, no, I have plenty of love. It's just, my life is perfect; there are no problems, no nothing. Everything is just so together. It's like I'm living in a suburban nightmare, you know?"

"No, not really," the man said.

"So, tell me, where are you from? How did you get here? What's your life all about?"

"Life?" the man asked with skepticism in his voice. "I have no life. All I have are days and nights that just blend into one another, lonely roads, and hotels, and cold nights, and hot days, and the occasional free ride. My life is very simple, and very general. There is no purpose, nothing to complete, nothing to really live for. I am just a man...walking."

"That's a pretty dismal picture," the driver said. "How can you live like that?"

"How can you live your life the way it is? If you're so dissatisfied with your life, you have no right to accuse my way of living."

"Okay, sorry," the driver said. "Sorry that I upset you."

"I wasn't upset, just astonished by how hypocritical some people can be."

After that, there were no words. It wasn't a tense silence, they had just reached a moment where words weren't important. The road was all they needed right now; a big, open space such as this left room for thoughts, instead of the clutter of life.

The clutter of life was not something that the nameless man had to deal with. The hellish screams of beeping horns, the demands of corporate America, the massive houses that only a few people lived in. He didn't need that, all he needed were silent moments, or moments with conversation that actually meant something. Not just words that were spoken for the sake to have words. As far as he was concerned, words were overrated. They got too complicated, and got in the way of people's thinking.

"Are you hungry?" the driver asked.

"Are you paying?"

The driver laughed, "Of course I am. Where do you want to go?"

"Wherever there's food."

They stopped at an all-night diner. They walked in the entrance and saw that there were booth seats on either side of it. The counter lay in front of them, stretching to either side of this place. The driver walked up to the counter first. There was a waitress wiping it down. She wiped the rag in small circles, continuously. It looked as if she had been doing it all night.

The waitress looked up and said, "What'll it be?" The driver looked to the man behind him.

"Whatever," the man said.

The driver turned back around and said, "We'll have two hamburgers, please, with water."

They both sat at the counter and waited for their meal.

The driver looked at the man, really, he began staring at him. It wasn't a stare of infatuation, more of curiosity. His stare was slowly burning into the man's eyes. It was as if the driver wanted to know something, he wanted to see something that wasn't visible on the surface. The man stared back, trying to answer the wordless question. There was silence gathering around them, until everything faded. It felt like everything was falling away, and all they could see was each other. Their stares became more aggressive, their eyes started to pierce more into one another. Their eyebrows were arching, and it slowly became like two beasts ripping into each other.

They were disturbed by the plate slamming on the counter. They looked to the waitress. "Have a nice meal," she said in a cold voice.

They looked down and saw two plates with a hamburger on each along with two glasses of water.

The man picked up the burger and began to eat it. The driver watched him bite and chew and drink.

"Aren't you going to eat?" the man asked.

"Not right now, I'm going to wait. Would you like to hear more about my life?"

"You mean your perfect nightmare?" the man asked while swallowing his food.

"Yes."

"Why? Why would I want to hear more about that?"

"It might humor you."

The man looked down for a moment. "True, it might. Go ahead."

The driver stared at him for a few moments, preparing his words. His stare pulled the man into his train of thought. The driver then began to speak:

"I wake up every morning in a bed of silk sheets. The alarm clock sounds like a beast driving metallic nails into my brain. I then wake up into this horribly perfect world. Everything is in its place, and everything is clean and neat. There isn't a speck of dirt, anywhere. I always look to my right and see no one, mainly because I don't want anyone, romantically, in my life.

"So, I get up out of bed, I take my shower, and I get ready for work. Everyone there respects me. We're almost like this suburban family who live extravagantly and one always tries to look better than the other. My day is filled with supposedly important meetings, but it's nothing but the same thing over and over, just something to make more money.

"After my work day, I usually stop by my family's. My mother has always been supportive of everything I do and my father has shown nothing but unconditional love. We have never had one problem, and everything just seems…redundant."

The man looked at him with curiosity. "Why did you tell me that?" the man asked. "Why did you describe that to me?"

"Why do you think?" the driver said.

The man nodded his head from side to side. "I don't know."

"Yes, you do." The driver pushed his face toward the man.

The man began to feel something inside him. There was a connection forming with the driver, a connection that somewhat scared him. He put the remainder of his burger down and looked at the man. His hands began to shake, and an apprehension was forming inside his mind.

"You need to wake up, now," the man said. "You need to wake up and feel the silk sheets against your skin."

"No," the man said, as everything faded to black.

He suddenly felt himself laying on a padded surface. He opened his eyes and saw that he was inside a spacious bedroom. He suddenly got up as the reality was forming inside his mind.

The bedroom was perfectly designed. There were blinds covering a long, tall window to the left. And extravagant designs and items lay all throughout the room, put in a specific order.

"Shit!" Phil said.

He got up out of bed and walked toward the door, toward his perfect life.

He closed the book with a slam, echoing through the library as everyone looked at him. He could see everyone blaming him for the sudden noise, their eyes expressing a sudden and extreme annoyance.

"Sorry," he said, sheepishly.

They all looked back down to their books.

He looked down to his and saw how small it was. The space between the cover and the back was very thin. However, to read it all seemed to be a trying experience. The first story had an effect on his mind. It played with his thoughts and introduced him to a world he didn't want.

"You're going to have to finish the book," a familiar voice said.

He looked up and saw a person sitting in front of him.

"Charley," he said. "What are you doing here?"

"I practically live here, don't you remember?" Charley asked.

"Oh."

"Anyway, you're going to have to finish the book, finish it, read it."

"Why do you say that?"

Charley formed an exasperated look. "Just finish the damn book, Dave. It's not like you have a choice. Either read or get the fuck out, it's that simple. And trust me, I have no problem throwing someone like you out." Charley said this while looking at him with indifference, forming his words rather nonchalantly.

Dave gave Charley a look of disbelief. "Why do you say that?" he asked in a dismayed voice.

"Stop acting like the victim, Dave," he said in an angry tone, hidden in whispers. He looked as if he had been tiring of this for a while. "No one's buying it. Besides, it's not as if you really matter to anyone, anyway. Just read the book, you're dragging everyone down by talking."

"Why is my talking dragging everyone down?"

"It's your voice. No one wants to feel like you. Don't infect us with your despair and loneliness. Just read the fucking book, the faster you're out of here, the better."

Reluctantly, he looked back down at the book. He could feel a strong desire to leave. However, he didn't follow it. He got up and walked away from the desk and into one of the hallways and opened his book. Even with the resistance screaming inside him, he turned toward the next story called, "Sex in My Head:"

I am a man whose life is just days spent in my little apartment. It is a very small apartment, though. However, the walls aren't decaying and it's not roach-infested. It's not what one would picture, immediately when the word "small" is mentioned. It *is* inside the city, though, but it's a very fashionable part of the city. This is a place where even the street lights are fashionably sensitive. You have to be on top of the clothing world to get noticed around here, and if you're just an average guy, just someone walking through life, you might as well be dead. I live in the only plain apartment in my building. Everything else has elegant designs and just a mix of cultures all in one room. All I have are things, important materials for everyday life.

This was not my plan when I moved here. I had a plan, I had a big plan. I wanted to be a writer, even though I had never written a word in my life. I was tired of the small town that I was living in, with everything just so picturesque. So, I decided to take a big step and move out here to the city. I had envisioned that I would meet people, I would make friends, and I would finally have the city life that I had always dreamed of.

When I got off the bus, I had stars in my eyes. One of the first places I went to was a café. The people there looked intriguing. I decided to sit in my seat and just start writing. I looked around me and tried to think of words and phrases to describe the situation I was in. There was nothing coming to mind, I had drawn a blank. I needed some assistance. Maybe I would eventually meet someone who would help me with this. Wrong.

The rest of that day, I just walked through the streets. Everyone walked past me as if in a hurry. They rushed by me like they didn't even notice me. Everyone's clothes looked to be much more stylish than mine.

The next day, I decided to get a job, but the only one I could find was at a factory. There wasn't a more depressing place I could be. Everything around me was of these dismal colors, and even the machines sounded as if they cried.

After my first day of work, I fell into this depression. I needed something to make me feel better. Since no one was offering to give me a few kind words, I took the option of which seemed to me like a last resort: an adult store.

Inside this store there were so many attractive men splattered on paper. Their bodies just lay exposed to my eyes, they had no shame. They begged for my attention, and I decided to give it. I picked the one magazine that caught my attention. The man on the cover was unbearably attractive. My eyes were pained just by looking at him. I had to have it.

I immediately took this magazine home. I ripped it open and searched, frantically for the man. Dark brown hair, dark eyes, perfectly tanned flesh, a body that was constructed from a solid formation of muscle. Not the muscle that seemed to look difficult to carry, but the kind that was lean. The shape of him looked as if he had been sculpted from skilled hands. I could only imagine what it was like just to have his skin below my fingers.

I looked to him, and slid my right hand down my stomach. I saw his eyes looking at me. I pictured imagery inside my mind. He was kissing me, seducing me, he wanted me. Slowly, he put his lips over mine. I could feel his mouth pulling at my upper lip. We engaged in this kissing, gradually deepening into a passion. Our lips began to glide against one another. He straddled my breath with his tongue.

I could feel his hands on my top button. He was pushing it through the slit. I could feel my shirt opening, my flesh being exposed to the air around me. He gently moved his fingers down to the second button.

A harsh sensation was forming inside me. It was tickling my flesh, pressing itself against my body, centering down below my waist. My breathing became rapid, and my heart began to race.

The tickles then jolted into a shuddering, it remained constant for only seconds, but it seemed like an eternity.

I immediately went to the bathroom and washed my hands. I

then began to picture other fantasies I could have with this man. I could imagine us in sexual congress in many places, and in extravagant settings, maybe in a waterfall in the middle of a forest, or maybe in the rain within a steamy back alley. We would begin to share a romance. We would become more than people that just fucked, but people that had a bond. I could already feel the sentimentality with him. He would treat me with endless love, we would be…happy.

I then walked back inside the living room with this thought in my mind. It weighed with a tearful bliss. I looked down and saw the man, the man on paper. I looked up and felt the bliss fade. This man that I could imagine loving, that I could imagine being with, he was a man on paper, and this all depleted into nothing more than sex in my head.

He slammed the book again. This time, he didn't care who he interrupted. He continued walking through the hallway. It seemed endless.

This story played into his mind, as well as the gravity of the situation, the realization of being alone; it clutched his heart and pained his throat. He couldn't open another page. It was already burning his soul. He could feel his mind wanting to break away.

He opened the book up and flipped through the pages. There were only two more stories. But he felt resistant to read them. He couldn't find it in himself to open it back up. But he felt that there was temptation inside him, and eventually he would continue, but not now.

He heard the sound, once more, of a page turning inside his head. It clasped his skull with a resonance that was too close to comprehend.

He looked up and saw that the hallway was ending and decided to walk toward it. He could see am image just beyond the end.

When he walked through it, he saw that he was back inside the middle. Nora was sitting at the front desk, and Blake and Charley were reading their books.

He then saw a masked man when he looked to the front of him of who was standing a few feet away. The man was dressed in a tuxedo and held a mask to his face by a small pole that was connected to it. This man seemed familiar and he decided to walk up to him. He saw big, black circles covering the eyes and saw his reflection collapsed inside their shape. "Who are you?" he asked the man.

The man did not answer. He just stood there, as if frozen. He went to touch the man's hand when he felt someone slap him on the shoulder. He rapidly turned around and saw Charley.

"What?" he asked.

"Don't touch that. He is one of our most valuable mannequins. Do you know how much it cost for us to get him here?"

He looked down and then said, breathlessly, "Mannequin, of course it would be a mannequin."

"Just go read your damn book," Charley said. "Go read it so you can leave. I don't even know why you wasted the time coming here. We worked hard on this library, and we don't need people like you in it. Just read your book and leave." Charley's voice was stern and demanding. His eyes were still in an embittered stare. He then left.

He watched Charley walk to one of the tables as echoes of his voice seared into his mind. Charley had sounded so harsh and insistent, as if he were ashamed of him. He saw him talking to Blake. While doing this, Charley periodically looked back at him. They then quietly began to laugh as if sharing some sort of joke.

He walked back into another hallway, desperately attempting to put what he just saw out of his mind. He looked down at the book and thought about opening it. He could just put it away and walk out. All he had to do was leave it behind, but he couldn't. He felt himself being pulled toward the curiosity of what story would be revealed next.

The next story was entitled, "A Deceptive Friendship."

> I was alone that night. I sat inside the all-night diner and momentarily looked to the counter that stretched to both sides then back.
>
> My emotions were piercing inside me this night. I was reflecting back on my life, as short as it was. I remembered the fear the played inside me every day I went to school. I was afraid to say things, do things, because everything that I did was looked upon as a joke. I had become the entertainment for everyone's stone-cold hearts. These people, the ones that rose to the top of popularity, they saw nothing inside me but what remained on the surface. Their assumptions lead to the accusations that my life was one of insignificance and that I was their property, property they could damage any way they pleased.
>
> I had people that I thought were friends, people that I thought I

could turn to. But they left me very soon. I thought that they had befriended me, but it was only temporary. When the realization came that they were hanging out with the school nerd, they left out of fear for their reputations.

Slowly, as the days had passed, I could feel them coming to me, expecting them, like wolves coming to feed. They ripped into me, clawing at my weaknesses, exposing me to their starving need to demean. I stood, naked, many times, as their words tore at everything I could hold onto in my life.

The only thing I could possess was my parents' love, but that couldn't follow me inside the scholastic hell. What lay ahead for me was a tormented existence, where nothing was reliable. Everything and everyone was against me, and I could feel a burning need to end my life with the passing years.

Now a sophomore in high school, I felt that need stronger than ever. And when I saw Kevin Douglas walk through the door, that feeling was pushed even further. This was a guy that was popular in my school, the respected jock. However, he was the only one that actually acknowledged me. Even though it was segmented into a few short phrases here and there, they were still words, and they were still directed towards me.

I hoped that he wouldn't see me, which was the last thing I needed, to find out that a possible friend was nothing more than another disappointment.

I looked up, and he saw me. He nodded to me and began walking over to my table. I could feel the fear growing inside my head like a crying beast. It howled beyond my thoughts and was lodging itself in my throat. I tried to smile, but my lips quivered. His eyebrows arched in concern, and I could feel my eyes burning, now. The heavy film weighed against my eyelids, and soon, I'd have to let go. I tried to hold it in at least before he sat down, but this water was like lead. My right eyelid gave way and I had to bow my head to hide it.

I heard him sit in front of me. I heard his voice. "Hey, Jake, what's wrong?" His voice was laden with concern.

I looked up, my entire body was shivering. Both sides of my face were now running with streams.

"What happened, did that dick, Carter, pick on you again?"

"No," I said as I nodded my head, "no, not at all."

"Well, what happened?" His eyes were begging for the truth. I had to tell him, or I was going to cave in.

"Life," I said as I looked into the night outside the window. I looked back. "Life is what's wrong, it's fucked and I'm right in the middle of it."

"What do you mean?"

"What do I mean?" I asked in disbelief. "Kevin, look around you, I'm not exactly the most popular guy in school. I try to live my life, but they won't let me. Day after day, it's all the same thing, just harsh words and harsh intentions to match. All the other kids, they feel like they can just say whatever to me. It's like I don't even matter, and you know what? I'm coming to believe it."

"Hey," Kevin said. "Don't say that." He looked to me with compassion. He extended his hand and put it over mine. "*I'm* you're friend."

His face was sincere. I looked to him with a relief. My entire body was suddenly lifted from its sadness. I could feel my emotions lighten as I smiled. A painful happiness was edging itself inside me. This acceptance clasped my heart and, for the first time in my life, I felt important.

Then, they walked through the door, the rest of his friends, or at least a few of them. They were the jocks and the cheerleaders. And their impression was that they were the leaders of the school, and what they were defined everyone else. Anyone who didn't follow was punished.

They saw Kevin holding my hand. He quickly retracted.

Bobby Carter then walked up to us while saying, "Hey Kevin, you and Jake here have a little something going on?" His voice was mocking and his face was reveling in the cruelty of his sarcasm.

"No, no, man, of course not."

I could quickly feel myself falling again.

Bobby put his hands on our table, slowly, as if planning something. He turned to Kevin. Bobby asked, "Why are you hanging out with him? Why do you waste your time with him?"

Kevin's face was lost in his words. He constructed his features in a series of confusing expressions as his voice periodically broke through. He then said, "I don't know."

My heart was losing its happiness, and I could feel the pit of my stomach quickly emptying into a burning disappointment.

Bobby's face drew close to his. He then said, "I want you to say it."

"Say what?"

He waited until he said the words. My apprehensions were piercing my skull. "That he's a loser."

Suddenly, I felt a pang inside my entire body. There was a curiosity inflaming my mind, asking if those words would cross his lips.

Kevin looked at me. He could see a fresh tear falling on my face. There was a hesitation in his appearance, I could see it burn into his skin. He inhaled deeply, and exhaled like something was tiring him. While closing his eyes, he opened his lips. "He's a loser."

"Good," Bobby said, "Now say it with your eyes open."

Kevin opened his eyes, a screaming sadness was ravaging through my insides. He then said, with eyes staring into mine, "He's a loser."

I looked up at Bobby and said, "Fuck you."

Bobby rapidly turned his head. "What!?" He took his fist and swung it through the air. His knuckles slammed into the right side of my face. My body was thrown onto the floor. I could still feel the impression of his fist against my skin. He branded his knuckles into my flesh.

Bobby laughed, coldly. The laughter echoed in my head, biting my brain, letting it bleed a saddening flow of imprisoning thoughts. I could hear him and Kevin leaving. I only lay on the ground, like a victim giving into his prey. My stomach pained from the jolting movements of my crying. I cried silently, so they wouldn't hear. I was afraid to get up and walk away, letting them see their victory. All I could do was lie on the ground and let the grim fear clasp my dying heart.

He closed the book, this time shutting it harder. It echoed throughout the library. His mind had absorbed the three stories with a passionate regret. There was a desire to read the last one, just to get it over with. He knew he'd eventually come to that decision, but he had to wait a little longer, just a littler longer and he would be ready again.

He walked through the end of the hallway, and found himself back in the middle, with Nora at the front desk, and Dave and Blake at the *middle* desks. He looked back to the mannequin, and was astonished at its life-like qualities. He didn't know why such a mannequin would be in a library, but he didn't want to question things any further.

He looked back to the front and saw Blake rapidly walking toward him. He wasn't sure what Blake was going to say, but he knew that it would be something harsh.

"Read the rest," Blake demanded as he walked up to him. "Read the rest and just get out of here."

He nodded his head back and forth as his eyes pleaded. "I don't want to read the rest right now. I can only take so much." His heart was burning with a desire for some sort of understanding.

"I don't give a fuck, Dave, no one does. Just read the last story and get out," he said, stopping in front of me.

"How did you know I was on the last story?" he asked in a light, submissive voice.

"Who *wouldn't* know, you're like an open book. Everyone knows every move you make because you're so predictable. You're just an average person with no individuality whatsoever. As far as I'm concerned, you were put on this earth to take up space."

He spoke with a harshness that weighed with a certain tiring. Blake sounded as if what he was saying was righteous, as if he were speaking to someone with villainous intentions, and he was the one that would save the day.

He arched his eyebrows in a hurt expression. He tilted his head to the left and shook out the words, "How can you say that?" with his breath.

"Dave, it's just so easy to put you down. You have no will inside you, no independence. If you did, you would have left by now. So just read the fucking story and leave."

He could feel a scream inside him. It was flaming a trail toward his throat. "Bu—"

"JUST READ IT!" he yelled as everyone else looked up.

He looked to all the other people. They all had irritated faces, and they were directed toward him. They put their heads back down.

His skin began to shiver. He looked down and opened the book while feeling his mind being raped by the demands of others.

He turned to the last story. The only word that was on the page was "You." It was placed as a title, but the rest was blank. He flipped through the rest of the pages and saw nothing but yellowed paper. He slowly looked back up to Blake.

"These pages are blank."

Blake grabbed the book out of his hand and put it on the table behind him. As he jolted his head to the right, he said, "Get out of here!"

"But, Blake—"

"Get out!" Blake grabbed his right arm and began to force him toward a door left of the staircase. "I don't know why you persist on being such a little asshole about things."

As he was being dragged along, he tried to speak. "Blake, please, why are you doing this?" His words were shaken from the rapid body movements he had to perform in order to keep up with Blake's force.

"Just leave, you don't belong here, you don't belong anywhere."

Blake opened the door and pushed him outside of it, then closed it behind him.

He looked to the back of him. The actual building of the library looked to be of a normal size, like it couldn't even contain the interior. It was just the back of a long, rectangular building constructed from charcoal-black bricks. He turned back around and saw that he was standing on an empty parking lot. Beyond the lot was a small patch of grass that vertically extended the length of the library. There was a road in front of that grass, a four-lane highway. It was nearly empty, and only a few cars drove through it. From the under-populated environment, he judged that it must have been sometime after midnight.

He began walking toward the road. As he did, thunder sounded throughout the sky. However, it didn't sound like normal thunder. It was like a demonic growl voicing itself through the clouds. He was startled by this as the growl echoed through the night.

He then saw a car drive by. The driver rolled down the window and screamed the words, "It's coming for you, Dave!" in a mocking tone. He was somewhat confused by the comment, but decided to continue walking.

He began walking on the grass. He wasn't sure where he was going. This area didn't look familiar to him at all. He felt a little scared by the fact that he had no destination, that he was just walking. He noticed, though, that there was no lightning striking down from the clouds. He wondered if there was a storm at all, or if it was just a storm about to happen.

As he neared the end of the grass, another car was slowing to a stop. The driver rolled down his window and put his head toward it. "Are you looking for somewhere to go?" the driver asked.

"Why do you ask?" He wasn't sure if he could trust this situation, he had to ask some sort of question to feel secure.

"You look lost. You look like you want to go somewhere. Now do you or not? I have other places that I can go to."

He arched his left eyebrow. He wondered if he should wait for a person with less rude manners, but then he thought about how everyone here behaved. He felt as if he had no choice, he had to go somewhere.

He walked toward the car as the driver opened the door. He got inside and closed it.

"So, what's you're name?" he asked.

"Jack."

As he buckled his seat belt, he asked, "Don't you want to know my name?"

"I already know your name, Dave."

He looked up to Jack with a curiosity. "Why does everyone here know my name?"

Jack looked toward him. "You don't have to be here," Jack said. "But you've decided to hang around."

He could have walked out of the car, right now, but where would he go? With this thought in mind, he looked at Jack's attractive features: his perfectly angled eyes, the dark brown color surrounding his pupils, the masculine, lean shape of his body.

Jack then turned his head back to the road and started to drive.

As the car drove through the road, he said, "Since you people know so much, would you mind telling me what the fuck is going on?"

"Oh, now, I can't tell you that," Jack said while looking to the road.

"Am I dreaming?"

"It's not that simple."

"Can you elaborate on that?"

"No."

He sighed. "Of course not, that would be just too easy."

"Exactly."

"What?!"

"You want to know too much. Just experience life as it is."

"So I see," he said while lying back in the seat. "Where are we going?"

"Wherever."

He sighed, again. Once more, the growl shuddered through the sky, echoing into the night.

"Okay, can you tell me what that was?" he asked.

"No."

"Well, then what can you tell me!?"

"Nothing that you don't already know."

A pair of headlights suddenly jumped out in front of them. He could feel his heart leap as Jack swerved out of the way, throwing his body to the left. As they passed each other, he could hear a voice scream, "Die, you worthless piece of shit!"

He pressed his back further into the seat as Jack went back onto the road they were on.

"Who in the hell was that!?"

"Nobody, just someone trying to kill you."

"What!?" he said while quickly turning his head to Jack.

"You're not well liked around here, Dave."

"Well, I pretty much assumed that," he said as he put his head back to the front. "But you're probably not going to tell me why, are you?"

"Of course not."

"Of course not," he mimicked, breathlessly.

He then lay his body back down against the seat while looking out into the road. His mind was reaching a breaking point, but he tried not to let it get to him. He wanted to find some sort of sanity, just something that would make him feel safe or at least accepted. But, he knew those possibilities were far from his reach right now. He felt as if there was nothing he could do but just sit and try to enjoy the ride. But there was still that growing fear inside him, eating through the solid emotions he had left. He tried to breathe deeply a few times, tried to think of something that could calm him. Nothing was helping, though. In fact, trying to end the consuming dread only fed it, and the fire grew.

"You can feel it, can't you?" Jack asked.

He only looked to the road.

Jack continued speaking. "That fear, that feeling of being lost. It's tearing you apart. You could just scream right now. I know."

"Why are you bringing this up? Why can't you just let me be? Why can't anyone here just let me be?" He spoke while still looking at the road. His voice was monotone. It reflected the tiring emotion he felt from this utter redundancy.

"Answers just can't come to you, Dave. You have to go out and find them."

The car stopped. He saw a diner in front of him with a sign on one of the windows saying, "Open all night." The parking lot around the diner was practically barren, only a few cars were dotted throughout it.

"Get out," Jack said.

"What?"

"Get out."

"People are trying to kill me, and you want me to get out?"

"It's not my job to save you." Jack reached out to the door handle. He opened it. "Get out," he said again while sitting back in his original position.

He only sat there for a few moments, looking to Jack for some sort of explanation.

"GET OUT!"

He got out of the car. After he closed the door, Jack sped off.

He turned toward the diner. His feeling of dread had become more emphasized. Everything around him was empty—just incredibly vacant surrounding.

He walked toward the diner, hearing his footsteps extend its sound all throughout the lot. He walked through the front entrance and noticed that there were booth seats on either side of it. The front counter stretched out to both sides of this place. He walked in and sat in the seat to the right of the entrance. A waitress immediately walked up to him.

"Is there anything that you would like?" she asked in an unconcerned voice. She had her pad and pencil out, but she stared at him as if she were annoyed.

"No, not really."

She walked off, not saying anything else to him.

He tapped his fingers on the table. There was no music playing here, just silence. The only people that were here were two men at the front counter, and some high-school students dotted throughout the diner.

He couldn't help but to notice that one of the two men at the front counter was dressed in a business suit and the other in general attire. All of the school kids had a certain familiarity to them.

He sat back as two school students dressed in sports-like attire were looking at a boy sitting in general dress at a booth seat. One jock was sitting in front of the boy, the other, standing. The standing jock then punched the boy, he fell to the floor.

He wanted to get up and do something, but couldn't find the will to do so.

The two other young people walked away from the seat, as the one on the floor stayed on the floor. He could see this boy's hands grasp the ground as if to find some sort of comfort within a discomforted existence. The boy's body began to shiver as he hid his face by turning it away from everyone else. He only lay there, not getting up, looking as if he were afraid to do anything.

"Isn't anyone going to help that kid?" he asked. No one responded, they just continued talking as if he wasn't there.

He sat back in his seat, watching the boy on the floor. He couldn't help but to identify, somehow, with this person. His feelings of entrapment sympathized with his need to stay on the ground, trying not to expose his weakness. He wanted to go help the boy, but he felt as if he couldn't, like he just couldn't reach out to him. For some reason, the boy felt far away.

He looked to the two men talking. It looked as if the man dressed in general attire was curious, and listening to the other man, only interjecting with questions. He watched these two men converse. They were sharing some sort of connection, a connection that didn't look to be favorable to either. Actually, it looked to be like an unwanted conversation, but something that had to be carried out.

He could not hear any of the voices, clearly. All he could make out were sounds that were spoken, like they were quite a distance away. Their words were blurred, just letting enough through to question what was being vocalized. He paid attention to them, though. He felt that there was at least something he could get just by looking at them converse and watching their body movements.

He looked back to the boy on the floor. His body still shivered with a pushed cry. His hands still clasped the ground as if he was looking for some sort of savior hidden beneath the floor.

All he had to do was just walk over to this boy and help him, take him away from these cruel people. It seemed so simple to do, but there was an apprehension inside him, stopping him.

He heard the growl through the sky, again. There was something not right about that sound, something that seemed to be a little too close. It made him feel as if he was being stalked. Paranoia began playing into his consciousness and he could feel it rattle his brain. It lightly shook him.

He exhaled, feeling himself tire from this. He couldn't sit there and watch the boy lay on the floor and cry. There was something that he could do.

He got up and walked toward the two men.

"Excuse me," he said.

The two still talked amongst themselves. Their voices still sounded blurred. He was put off by this. "Excuse me," he said again. He looked for some sort of realization of his existence. But they just continued talking, ignoring him.

He couldn't go to the other school kids for help. They were the ones that put this boy where he was in the first place.

He then turned toward the boy. As he walked to this person on the ground, his cries came closer. The sound was emphasizing itself. He could feel some sort of empathy for this boy, but it was an empathy that felt like an odd connection. He could feel his cries pulling him in further.

He bent down and lightly said, "Excuse me?"

The boy suddenly stopped crying and slowly turned his head toward him. His face gradually uncovered itself. As it did, his eyes became exposed. They were reddened from the tears that bled. The white around the color of his eyes were stained with a heavy red. His eyes looked sore, like he had been crying for hours. He opened his mouth to speak. "What do you know about me?" the boy said in a dilapidated voice. "Why are you even over here? I've just finally realized, today, that the world will never be in my favor. The only friendly intentions I ever experienced have turned to shit. You think you can help me?"

He nodded his head back and forth, trying to speak.

"Well, you can't. You're no better than I am. You're just a lost victim like me, and you won't even try and help yourself."

The sky growled, again.

"It's coming for you, Dave," the boy said. "It's coming for you and if *I* were you, I would just let it get me. Because the way your life is going, you're going to end up just like me."

The boy got up and walked out of the diner. He formed a look of confusion. He wasn't sure what the boy was saying, but it didn't leave him with a good feeling.

He looked back to where the two men were sitting, only to see that they were gone. The rest of the school kids were there, though. He walked backward away from them. There was a certain fear he had about them, almost like an intimidation. He sat back in his seat and only looked at them, hoping that they wouldn't acknowledge his existence.

He didn't know why he wouldn't walk out of the diner, but he felt trapped. He felt as if there was nowhere to go. Everyone that he had met so far was just another person that had intentions to hurt him, somehow. He would encounter the same cold presence, no matter where he went.

He looked away from them, trying to think of something else, something that could take him away from this state of mind. But every pleasant thought he tried to conjure up was rejected by his own mind. He wanted to calm himself, but something inside him wouldn't let that happen. It was as if he was becoming his own victim.

"Who are you?" he heard a voice ask. He looked up and saw one of the young people looking at him, while the others followed his glance.

"I'm, ugh, I'm no one," he answered.

178

"Oh, wait, we know who you are," another said, one of the young girls dressed in a cheerleading outfit. "You're that guy aren't you? Like, the guy that has no life." They all laughed after that remark.

He thought of laughing, himself, but that might only worsen the situation. He tried to look away from them, but their eyes still stared. That made the option of turning away feel like the wrong thing to do. These young people were looking for more of an answer, but he couldn't give it.

"Yeah," one of the male students said. "I know you, now."

He looked up to them and smiled, lightly. He then said, "I'm not sure I know who you're talking about." His face reflected a nervousness he was trying to hide.

One of the cheerleaders walked up to him, slowly. "You're Dave, right?" she asked while tilting her body to the left and pointing to him with a lolly pop in her hand. The other girls swayed their bodies to an immature rhythm. They all looked as if they had something in mind.

"Yeah, we know you," one of the guys said.

"You have no life," one said.

"You're hopeless," another said.

He could feel their eyes burning into him. He had to leave, or at least try to. The situation wasn't going in his favor. He got up and went to the door.

One of the male students walked up to him and said, "Where do you think you're going?" He positioned his body in an attempt to intimidate.

The sky growled with the same noise outside. It spread all throughout the sky and died down in a haunting tone.

"It's coming for you, Dave," the male student said. "It's coming for you and it's going to get you."

The intimidation was beginning to clasp his thoughts. This young person was staring at him, demanding something of him. He wasn't sure what was about to happen, but he couldn't help but to feel an emotion of dread darkening the worries in his mind.

The other students got up and slowly walked toward where the male student was. They walked with a certain power, one that was formed out of conceit and shallow understanding.

"There's no way to run from it, Dave," one of the other students said.

He looked toward the doorway and ran for it. The students only stood, watching him leave. He frantically went for the door and pulled it open. As he ran outside of the diner, one of the students screamed, "You can't stop it! You can't run from it!"

He found himself back inside this empty city. Where the parking lot lay almost completely bare of any cars and all the streets were lonely, only a few automobiles driving through. He could feel this desolation all around him. He began walking and tried to forget the things that had been said to him. He couldn't let this fear get to him.

Another growl then sounded from the sky. Only now, the sound was becoming less grand. It was now coming closer, closer to the ground. He could hear it as a more personalized noise.

He looked behind him, but saw nothing. He looked all around him and only saw barren streets. That stalking feeling was becoming inevitable, like something was, indeed, coming for him. The fear was coming back. He tried to push it down, but it was screaming to be released.

"What are you?" he whispered.

"What are you?" he heard a whisper say back to him. However, it wasn't anything that was around him, it was in his head. He could hear a sound coming from his mind and exiting through his ears, like the pages in the library. It was just a whisper, though, no words clarified it.

"I'm losing my mind," he said as his voice shuddered. The thought of his sanity leaving him was playing into his frightened emotions.

"No, you're not losing your mind," the whisper said.

He grabbed his head with his hands. "Why are you inside my head!?"

"I'm not inside your head, Dave. You're just hearing things as if they were."

"Then you're not real." He spoke while moving his eyes in all directions, listening to the interior of his head.

"On no, I'm real. I'm real because you've brought me to reality."

"What are you? Why are you coming for me?"

"I am just what you think I am. You know why I've come to claim you. You know much more than you think."

"Who are you?!" he screamed.

The whisper was gone. He looked around, trying to look for some sort of formation, a shadow, anything. There was nothing around him or near him. A burning curiosity was growing inside him, teasing him. That lack of knowledge was pushing him into a deeper sense of fear as it lurked over him like a storm cloud. It clung to his insides, weighing them down with a suspended feeling.

All he could do for the moment was walk this lonely surrounding. He felt as if he had no where else to go, and whatever was coming for him he obviously couldn't stop. It was inevitable.

As he walked, he couldn't help but to feel comfortable in this depression, almost as if it were a safe haven. This was what his future held. The embittered presence of a torn heart blanketed him, letting him know that this was the path and nothing was going to divert from it.

Then he heard the sound, the growl. It was a deeper sound, a closer one. The noise progressed, slowly. His fear was returning, and what his ears were allowing him to hear enhanced that emotion. He could feel a slight shudder growing inside him. He was gradually becoming lost within this. The sound was coming closer, preying on his solitary existence, blending his fear and depression together. It put him in a world that was beyond just desolation. It was a complete sense of loss and of incredible loneliness that screamed for some sort of acceptance.

He didn't want to turn around. He didn't want to see what this thing was. He could see its shadow on the ground. Its fingers were moving outward. Their darkened reflections crept through the cement.

He looked up and saw the boy, the boy that was lying on the floor in the diner, crying. The boy stood a few feet away from him. He was under a street light. The luminescence shadowed him in what looked to be a serene existence, a rather holy light around him.

He looked to this young person with despair. He needed something, someone, anything to come and help him. He opened his mouth and nearly shook with his words. "Help me," he said in a weakened whisper.

The boy shook his head back and forth.

That drove the rejection he had carried for so long deeper inside him. His disappointments and sorrows were all gathering in his mind as they laughed at him.

"No," the boy said. "There's no way that I'm going to help you. This is what you chose to happen, and it is going to be like this. No one can help you. Stand there in your own miserable little world and just let it be, just let it happen."

He nodded his head, slightly, back and forth. His face was constructing in a sorrowful manner. "I don't want this."

"Too bad!" the boy screamed. "You're life has come down to this! You have no choice!"

He listened to the boy, letting his words sink in. The powers of those words were thriving from the lost life living inside him.

"No one's going to come and save you because no one really cares. Every friend you've loved obviously has not felt the same way about you. You're just left behind, and dying from this beast is inevitable, it always has been. You're a pathetic fucking loser and you deserve to die! Now turn around!"

He could feel his eyes burning as his throat was choking on the gasps and sudden swallows created from the broken chances and promises he had experienced all throughout his life. Now he knew that he had no choice. So, he began to turn around. While he did, though, he closed his eyes. He didn't want to see this demon that had come to claim him. He didn't want to see his own end.

When he was fully turned around, he opened his eyes, and the demon was gone. He looked around, and was surprised by the surrounding. He saw that he was back in the library. While he was still somewhat shaken, he looked down at the book that he was holding and read the last line in the last story:

"He didn't want to see his own end."

He quietly closed the book and walked back over to the shelf where he found it from. He put it on the top and looked back. Everyone, once again, turned a page, and the sound was emphasized. He rapidly walked up to Nora. He put his hands on the desk and whispered, "Nora."

She looked up. "What do you want?" Her eyes seemed to be insensitive.

"I want to leave."

She arched her left eyebrow, and then said, "You can leave whenever you want, Dave. Just go up those stairs."

He turned around and looked at them and realized that he couldn't walk up those steps again.

"I can't," he said as he turned back.

"Then you'll just have to read."

"But I don't want to read, I want to go."

Everyone turned a page. The sound was cutting into his anger and feeling of entrapment.

"Read what everyone else is reading, Dave."

"What are they all reading?"

"Books, what do you think? Just go in one of the aisles and find a book."

He performed a prolonged sigh as he looked at Nora. She just seemed too indifferent, her face remained careless. He couldn't even tell what she was feeling at the moment since she wore such a concrete face.

She only arched an eyebrow and said, "Dave, just go read. The only reason you're here is because you have no place to go. No one cares about your questions, no one cares about *you*. Just go read a fucking book and stay away from everyone else. You are a disease." She looked down to her book.

Her words ripped into his soul. The meaning of them, how she constructed her face while saying them, like she didn't care about what effect they'd have. He looked around the library and to everyone else. They were all engrossed in their own worlds, away from him. He suddenly felt as if life had cursed him as he walked toward one of the aisles. These people could care less about him, whether he lived or died, whether he was happy or miserable; his emotions, his life was insignificant, even his problems were looked upon as a joke. This brought anguish to his entire sense of being, crushing any chance of contentment he could have. Slowly, he could feel his life being taken away.

He looked into the rows of books and pulled one out. When he brought the book down to his eyes, he saw that there was no title. The hardback cover was embellished in a color of a pinkish red. He touched the material. It felt rough against his skin, an uncomfortable grit. He opened it. The first page had nothing on it. He flipped to the next, again it was blank.

Everyone turned a page, again. He could hear it in his head. He rapidly looked up and wanted to say for everyone to stop, but he knew they wouldn't listen. He looked back down to the book and flipped through the pages, they were all blank, nothing but pink.

He looked to the blank pages as he flipped through them and became fascinated by his own abomination toward their color. It was this detesting emotion that was pulling his strange attraction closer to the pages. The sound of them landing on each other slowed, the slapping of the material extended to a deepening echo, blinding all other thoughts he could have. He became lost in their movement and their shade.

He dropped the book and looked up. He found himself in a different place. He was inside a large-sized room. The room was designed in a Victorian taste and the people were elegantly dressed from a time long passed. They danced next to each other as their fingers were holding up masks covering half their faces. He began to hear an eighteenth-century style of sound played from a piano.

The Kalzon Party

The majority of the room was men dancing with each other. They looked into each other's shrouded faces with entrancement. They were all around him.

As he walked through this room, he saw that there was a mixture of items from long ago and now. Modern-day phones and Victorian curtains, guests wearing Victorian clothing as well as pagers and cell phones.

"Quinton! Quinton!" he heard Nora's voice shout. "Quinton!"

He turned around and saw that Nora was wearing a beige-colored dress that was reminiscent of the Renaissance era. The bottom of it was expanded outward to an extreme limit. The entire dress looked as if it had been made from some kind of curtain material.

"Quinton!" she said, once again, looking toward him.

He looked at her, confused. When she approached him, she said, "Quinton, what in the hell are you doing!?"

His face contorted to a misunderstanding. "*Quinton?*" he asked, as if he had just gotten completely lost.

She smiled at him, "Yes, honey, I assume that is your name," she said kiddingly. She hugged him. His reaction was of a baffled manner. "I'm glad you could make it to the costume party," she said while still hugging him. "I'm so glad you're here. I guess you heard about me and Charley."

She let him go and looked at him with endearment.

"What about you and Charley?" he asked, his voice still trying to find its tone.

"Well, honey, we broke up. We're no longer together. He's a dick, anyway. But, hey, the room is full of men." She laughed. "*Gay* men, so at least one of us will get laid, tonight, huh?"

"Yeah…guess so," he said in a whisper.

"Honey, are you okay? You seem to be kind of…not here."

"Um… no, it's just…I'm a little—"

"Frustrated because of your little dry spell? Well, listen, I'm sure that's going to end tonight. You are going to find a nice attractive man and you are going to have a long, joyous night of mind-blowing sex, I'm sure of it. In fact, I see a few looking," she said. She backed up and laughed in an incredibly trite portrayal.

He was beginning to feel an embarrassment by being around her. He thought that at least Nora had some sort of personality when she was cold-hearted, but this left her devoid from any kind of attraction: platonically and romantically.

"So, what are you going to do now…sexy man?" She animated herself with over zealous action. Her body moved to an absurd rhythm, and she shook her head rapidly while emphasizing the last two words like a person with no intellect. She appeared as if she didn't know how to act in society.

"Yeah, I guess so," he said, nodding his head lightly.

"That's not a real answer, you ninny!" she said while lightly hitting him on the left arm. "Hey, I bet you that you can get a man faster than me!" She laughed, profusely.

"I'm going to go now, Nora."

"Okay, honey, have fun and play safe."

He walked away from her rapidly while looking back a few times in dismayed confusion.

"Quinton!" he heard a man's voice say. He looked to where the voice was coming from. His hair was grayed to white and his flesh was wrinkled. He smiled, mischievously. "Glad you could make it," he said while tapping him on the shoulder. "Where's your mask?"

"I don't know," he said as he looked into the man's harshly colored hazel eyes.

"I brought mine." He pulled up a mask that was half of a pig's face. He held it up to him and said, "Oink! Oink!" He laughed lightly while bringing the mask down. "So, what are you doing later tonight?"

"I don't know," he told the man.

This man was walking closer to him. "I'm sure you do, Quinton. Don't bail out on me," he said this while tapping his fingers on his chest. "No one should ever bail out on Walter Kalgon."

He looked down, his eyes roaming the carpet. When he looked back up, his face had a dismal curiosity painted into it. "And what if I don't accommodate your wishes?"

"We talked about this, Quint." His face grew cold, and his eyes were beginning to burn into him. "You should take this very seriously." Walter then proceeded to caress his cheek with his fingers. He brought his face closer as Walter's breath crawled into his nose. "It would be in your favor if you pulled through on this. You should think about this. Because I don't think you want to be on your own. I'm sure you remember what your life was like before you met me. And I don't believe you want to ruin the good life you have now."

He smiled from an intimidation. His eyes slinked downwards, back at the carpet and tried to find a comfort hidden in its design. "No, I...I guess not," he said, looking back at Walter.

"You're very smart. Have fun."

Walter walked away and kept his eyes on him for a few more moments. There was a putrid reaction he was feeling in his stomach, centering at the pit. He could feel it sicken his thoughts.

He walked around while looking at all the men dancing with each other. Once again, they were all entranced with only each other, and no attention was given toward him.

Each dancing couple was twirling around the room, holding one another. Gradually, each of them removed their masks, revealing faces of masculine beauty, beauty that was attractive and lured sexual attention. Their unmasked faces looked at each other, their lips teasing a kiss. Their hands roamed bodies. Fingers were seducing flesh that lay just beneath cloth.

He could feel the room all around him. It was taunting him with its surrounding. The opportunity for sex was almost palpable, but he strongly felt that rejection. He stood in a solitary existence amongst a seductive hunger.

Then, at the end of the room, through the crowd, he could see Blake standing against a wall. He leaned his head against it as he stood diagonally. He knew that Blake was always attractive, but tonight his features were more captivating than ever. His eyes glowed an emerald green, his flesh was soft against the light, and his hair lay at an exact design on his head, portraying him in a masculine intrigue. At the least, he seemed to derive wanting. Blake's eyes skipped over him, looking through the room.

He wanted some sort of attention from him. There was a burning pressure just from looking at Blake. It was rapid and intense, pulling him to that needed interaction. His heart raced, his skin was dampening from the pressure, and his breath was losing pace. He needed this right now. He could not just stand and watch everyone else. His brain was beginning to flood with a rush of aggressively sexual thoughts, promptly rushing down to his genitalia. It was pumping through him, speaking to his ravenous veins.

Blake then made eye contact with him and for a second, he could feel his heart jump, his skin suddenly becoming cool. There was a relief spreading through him, calming his internal frustration. And the excitement of the next possibility was teasing his mind. But Blake only nodded and gave him a neutral grin with closed lips, then continued to look around the room.

His relief crashed, a fire screamed through his flesh. This disappointment was bleeding through his head, laughing at his solitude. He could feel his eyes becoming heavy, but he would not let this emotion show. He could not falter to this rejection around him. He could only hold it in, letting it devour his secret desires in uncomforting dirt, dirt created from the buried emotions squeezing his life. He could just break at this moment, his skin was begging for it. His only option was to let this hellish infection clasp his insides.

He turned away from Blake, not wanting to see his one-sided love burn through him. He could still feel the hurt cracking his heart and he tried to ignore it.

Through the tormenting haze, he looked up and saw Walter. Walter was staring at him with a hunger. He smiled, showing happiness for his corrupt intentions. He stared at Walter with contempt. Walter only looked back with an exulting stare.

He wanted away from here, away from all of this. But he couldn't find it in himself to run. He was trapped.

He could then hear everyone's conversation slowly come to a silence. It quickly faded into whispered and hushed echoes of which collected into a breathing that was deep and penetrating. The sound burned with a passionate fury. It confused his understanding and he had to see what it was.

As he turned around, he saw that the dancing bodies were naked, completely untouched by any kind of cloth, these men were holding each other, letting their bare flesh touch. Some were in front of each other. Others were facing the back of the other. The masks were strewn on the ground, and they let their faces show. They were all reveling in their own sexual play. The sight was exhaling into his heart and breathing down toward his penis. He could feel himself slowly becoming erect. And like a hand crying of sexuality within its palms, it pressed itself against his pants, needing to break free.

His eyes wildly roamed the room, looking at each body as a different temptation. Each physical build was an immense attraction of external flesh, muscled into sculpted perfection. The bodies were moving with each other as a passionate fire clasped the air heavily. He could only watch as they seduced each other with conflicting motions, coming to a grinding movement.

He lightly touched his heart with his right hand, hoping to calm himself, but his intentions were pulling him inward. He wanted to become apart of this. He spent his life looking, he needed to be touched.

He walked slowly to one of the couples, making his way through the maze made from masculine hungering flesh. Their open eyes observed his motions. Claustrophobia began to haunt his already torn thoughts, ripping mercilessly into the intimate fascinations inside his head. The eyes beckoned him.

When he approached them, he looked, wanting inside their erotic motion. He had to at least touch. And as he extended his hand, he could see one of the men constructing his mouth to speak. From within their constant movement and the moisture coming down their heated skin, the man looked into his eyes and said with a definite emotion, "You're not wanted here." He then smiled with cruel lips as the other mimicked the shape into his mouth of which was caressing the other man's shoulder.

He pulled himself away. As he walked backward, he saw an array of eyes forcing rejection into his broken existence. The claustrophobia was now coming into the form of a monstrous anger, wrapping emotionally tattered threads around his crushed breath. There was a mix of feelings scratching and ripping inside him. It was a collective cry calling him down into a depression. He could feel it in his stomach and its fingers rotted his insides like a plague. It slowly reached into his dreams, overshadowing them in an endless portrayal of nightmares.

The men only need each other. He was the exclusion in this orgasmic surrounding. He suddenly felt immature, like a child in the presence of adults. All his questions and needs were diminished into insignificance, ramming through his mental defenses he had carefully constructed through the years of his abandoned life. Now was the time to let all those defenses wither into the disappointments that had always come to claim him.

He then saw Blake walking through the crowd. Like the rest, he was unclothed. His body was more than tempting. His skin was smooth and begged to be touched. Blake's body aroused seductive thoughts, only to be laughed at in his defenseless fantasies. Blake smiled at him, showing rapture toward his exclusion. His smile was cold, and its lack of emotion tore at his faded confidence.

Blake turned toward the front, still facing him. He then saw another nude gentleman walking toward Blake. This man walked behind Blake and held him. The man smiled, tauntingly. He saw that this man had strangely familiar blue eyes. His hair was of a dark brown that showed through beautifully. His body was just as familiar, every part was somehow identical.

Then, he remembered his own natural hair color was dark brown. This man that he was staring at was himself.

Blake and this other version of himself began to touch, caress, to fornicate. Blake was held from behind, and their faces touched, staring at him. They both started laughing, laughing at his misfortunes, laughing at what he could not have. He could feel his emotions bleed outward, his true feelings were becoming translucent, and he was coming closer to the breaking point. They continued to laugh, it echoed through his brain, shattering the only happiness he had left. Darkening madness was growing inside his disappointed mind, and he could feel a beast inside his heart.

His face began to tremble as he put his fingers overtop his head and began to harshly slide the tips down his hair. "STOP I-I-I-I-I-I-I-I-IT! STOP ALL OF IT!" he screamed as his voice broke through the room.

The bodies rapidly faded away. The only ones left were him and himself. This other version of himself then faced him and put his hand up near his body and away from his face as if he were holding something. With a sudden transformation, a black tuxedo covered his body as a mask came into existence. His hands were clothed in white gloves. The mask had a smooth texture and went over the tip of his nose, extending around the nostrils. The sides were segmented into curved triangular shapes going upward. There were perfectly large circles where the eyes should be. The circles had a sleek look of a pitch black and were pushed outward.

The masked doppelganger then walked through the room and toward the exit.

He couldn't have this person, this other extension of himself, just walk away. He had to see why he was here. He ran toward the shrouded man.

The masked one walked out into the hallway, he followed. There was an elevator far off into the end, and the doors were opening. The masked one walked through them and then faced the hallway.

He ran toward the shrouded double as the doors were coming to a close. The black texture of the mask's eyes entrapped his reflection, endlessly running. The doors closed before he could reach himself. His hands slapped against the elevator's walls.

"No!" he screamed. "No, this can't happen!"

He walked away from the elevator.

He heard a familiar voice say, "Kid."

He looked toward the room where the party had been. The Willfire alleyway was now in its place. It looked like a portal into the alleyway.

"Glenn," he said with the same relief.

Glenn was trapped inside a dense white fog, halfway through the bricked hallway. Glenn's figure was somewhat shadowed. "Follow me," Glenn's voice whispered. "Just follow me and don't get lost."

He walked into the alleyway as he could feel the other surrounding fade away. Glenn walked backward into the fog, physically beckoning him forward. "Just follow me," Glenn whispered.

He followed the shadowed figure as the fog covered his vision.

"Don't get lost, kid, don't get lost."

Glenn's voice almost seemed pleading in its whisper. He motioned his hands through the fog, its hauntingly white shrouding his eyes. He tried to make it through as he could still hear Glenn's voice, "Don't get lost, kid. Don't get lost."

The color of this clouded density became brighter. The strings of smoke began to collect into a more solid shade.

"Don't get lost …" Glenn's voice echoed until it faded.

The smoke rapidly became a burning bright light. He had to cover his eyes with his hands as the light seeped through the crevices of his fingers. He wasn't sure what the light was. However, its presence seemed fatal.

Epilogue

The lights lessened into two glowing balls at the head of a large vehicle. He saw that the vehicle was on a road, and he was standing on that road. An enormous sound yelled from it as a deep, hollow blow horn. It was a truck.

He looked to his left and saw Nora screaming at him. She was standing in front of a field of grass. She was dressed in a heavy gray coat, and he suddenly realized that he was weighed down by heavy attire as well.

He pushed Nora as he jumped out of the road. The truck ran past them, its blaring sound overwhelming their ears.

He got up and looked around as he collected his nerves. He was on a lonely street at night in what seemed to be some sort of city.

Nora got up and he looked toward her. She was bringing herself to tears. "What are you doing!? Why are you here!?" she screamed at him.

He only shook his head slightly as he moved his hands outward in a lost motion. His voice only broke through.

She ran toward him and shoved him. "Why are you doing this?!" She shoved him again. "Why?! Why can't you just let things be?!" She began to cry profusely. "Why couldn't you just let me die?!"

He brought his face to a sudden confusion. "*Die*?! Why do you want to die?"

She looked at him with an annoyance. "I have my reasons. And you should stay out of other people's fucking business!"

"Look, I'm sorry for ruining your plans for suicide, but—"

191

"But nothing. You should have never been here."

"Look," he said with compassion, "Why don't we just walk? Let's just walk and talk. We might be able to make sense of things." He smiled. "Come on, your suicide attempt has already been thwarted, so why don't you try to enjoy the moment and walk with me?"

She still looked to him with an angered curiosity.

He held out his hand. "Come on."

"All right," she said. "But this doesn't mean you're my savior or anything, because you didn't save me from anything."

She moved onto the street and they began to walk through it. He looked around him and saw the surrounding. There were aged factories and decaying buildings built on top of the vibrantly green grass.

"So why would you try to kill yourself?" he asked.

"Like I said, I have my reasons," she said, looking down at the road.

"You might as well tell me, what do you have left to lose?"

She sighed. "True," she said.

A long moment of silence passed as the only sound breaking through was that of their feet walking on the road.

She then began to speak: "Well, it goes like this. I am not a very nice girl. I've said things, done things. I try to make everything right, I really do, but my attempts are never recognized. People that I thought were friends ended up leaving me, one by one. I only tried to help them, and they couldn't see that. They couldn't see that I have a heart, and I want to make them see.

"My life has now become boring and dull. I have nothing left of me to give, it was all taken from unappreciative bastards."

There was silence, again.

"That's it?" he asked.

"That's it," she said as she looked at him. Her eyes were practically emotionless.

He looked to the left and saw a man dressed in ragged clothes shoving something into a garbage bin's fire. As he did so, the flames rose and broke away in an ocean of reddened ashes. They flew through the night, evaporating slowly. The glowing red burned into the winds, rippling the air. It screamed into a faded death as the burnt, decayed ashes slowly fell onto the road. Their charcoal colors were bleak and desolate against the fading gray of the street.

He looked back to Nora. "That's the reason why?" He had to let out a slight laugh. Suicide just seemed to be absurd for something so simple. "Nora, why would you do something so stupid?"

She looked at him with anger, a maddening anger that possessed her entire face. She then exclaimed, "How did you know my name!?"

"What do you mean, Nora?"

He was put off by this. He felt a sudden shock clasp his veins like electricity. "What is your name?! Who are you?!"

He was about to say the word that identified who he was. He searched within his mind as his mouth struggled to form something. His voice sounded in segmented breaks. He narrowed his eyes, trying to remember his own name.

"Who are you?!" she screamed, her voice hitting his mind like a rapid fist.

In a sudden panic, he turned around and started to run away from her. "Who are you?!" she screamed, her voice echoing.

He ran through a night that was decayed from buildings deconstructing from years of existence.

This all rushed by his vision as he ran toward a small shack. The shack was made from metallic materials, and he could see only the shape of it through the darkness of night. He didn't know why he was running toward this, but he felt as if he needed something to run to.

When he got to the door, he opened it. It cried with a squeaking noise. He walked inside and closed it as he became lost in darkness.

He turned around and saw that he was back in the studio apartment. It was now barren, there was no furniture left in it, nor a phone or any appliance. The storm continued to rage outside as he looked to Nora. Her pupils were, once again, filled with lightning.

"What is happening to me!?" he asked Nora in a pleading voice.

She only stared at him and said nothing.

A confusion of thoughts were conflicting in his head. Demons ran inside his heart, treading his insides with a fire screaming into his frustrations. He was running in circles, and he had to know why. "Do I have a name? Do I even have a *fucking* name!?" he screamed as his words were burning in his throat.

She smiled as she curved her body to the right, walked backward and put out her hand as if to present something.

He saw the painting. There was a darkened sky, the clouds held Blake's face within them. He was in the background, falling. His body was small, emphasizing that he was far away. As he was falling to the earth, he reached to the sky.

Nora stood naked, her head was tilted upward and her arms were stretched *over* her head. She was laughing. Her face was contorted into a cold expression, reveling in the depression around her. She laughed as she stood on a garden made of stones. His eyes widened in amazement as he focused in on the sky within the picture. He, once more, became lost in the darkness.

When he pulled himself away from the painted sky, the picture and the easel were gone. All that was left was the shape of the studio apartment. The windows, the doors, everything had vanished. There were no dimensions of any kind, just four flat surfaces embellished in a reflective wood.

He looked all throughout this square shape that had entrapped him. He began to cry. "I want out!" He screamed. "Let me out!" His soul burned to see the outside. His fear grasped him with a strong hold and was strangling him.

The wood faded into reflections of greater clarity. The reflections changed themselves into another formation, of memories, memories that he experienced. He suddenly found himself inside a room built of mirrored remembrances, his own face on each side. Each wall sped through memory after memory, quickly cutting toward different scenes. It was like he was inside a repetitious movie. All he could see were images of himself getting hurt in different ways. These pressing recollections were closing in on him. The walls were coming together. He didn't know where to go, everything became a blur of hurt and pain.

His heart cried as it came through his eyes. His stomach convulsed as it pushed the tears out. His voice was becoming tired. He screamed. He screamed for loss, and for pain, and for misery, and for being unloved, and for rejection, and for everything that brought his life to a redundancy.

The walls then broke, as shards of glass flew through the air. He was falling into blackness. He could feel his body becoming weightless.

The glass was cutting into his skin. He could feel the pointed edges cut into him. As they were cutting through, his body was becoming lighter. The glass was ripping him apart, slowly devouring his entirety. He rapidly dissipated into nothingness as the glass faded into the black.

Then, there was a whisper. This was the only thing that remained. It was a general whisper with an indistinct sound. It was formed from a constant loss, from running away into countless self-induced miseries until it came to the sound that it was now.

Through the shuddering tone spreading throughout the lost darkness, the whisper managed to ask a question: "Who *am* I?"

Printed in the United States
30587LVS00005B/184-228